THE
MAYHEM
WRANGLER

By D.R. Schervish

ISBN: 0615833705
ISBN-13: 9780615833705
Library of Congress Control Number: 2013911212
Lucky Rabbit Publishing
Norwalk, IOWA

ACKNOWLEDGEMENTS

I want to thank my wife, Lori, for her support. You're the only one who believed, and I am forever grateful.

This book is dedicated to Sailor Grace
and Bodhi. Live free little ones.

"Pain is the craft entering into the apprentice."
—A French proverb

"We walk by faith and not by sight."
—St. Paul

"On a journey in a dark place, don't watch where the light dances. Try to perceive the shadows."
—Bobby Doucette

"A friend will help you move; a good friend will help you move a body."
—Jack Mumford

PHONETIC ALPHABET

A	ALPHA	• -	(AL-FAH)
B	BRAVO	- • • •	(BRAH-VOH)
C	CHARLIE	- • - •	(CHAR-LEE)
D	DELTA	- • •	(DEL-TAH)
E	ECHO	•	(ECK-OH)
F	FOXTROT	• • - •	(FOKS-TROT)
G	GOLF	- - •	(GOLF)
H	HOTEL	• • • •	(HOH-TEL)
I	INDIA	• •	(IN-DEE-AH)
J	JULIETT	• - - -	(JEW-LEE-ETT)
K	KILO	- • -	(KEY-LOH)
L	LIMA	• - • •	(LEE-MAH)
M	MIKE	- -	(MIKE)
N	NOVEMBER	- •	(NO-VEM-BER)
O	OSCAR	- - -	(OSS-CAH)
P	PAPA	• - - •	(PAH-PAH)
Q	QUEBEC	- - • -	(KEH-BECK)
R	ROMEO	• - •	(ROW-ME-OH)
S	SIERRA	• • •	(SEE-AIR-RAH)
T	TANGO	-	(TANG-GO)
U	UNIFORM	• • -	(YOU-NEE-FORM)
V	VICTOR	• • • -	(VIK-TAH)
W	WHISKEY	• - -	(WISS-KEY)
X	XRAY	- • • -	(ECKS-RAY)
Y	YANKEE	- • - -	(YANG-KEY)
Z	ZULU	- - • •	(ZOO-LOO)

CHAPTER 1

Goddamn junkie whore. She was gone and time was shifting again. There was some ghostly, unseen Nazi storm trooper's boot grinding down on the top of my heart as I sat there on my couch, groping for the hazard button from the accident of my pathetic life that had me pinned in a crazy, twisted wreckage with salvation just out of reach. I prayed the next petrol lorry rounding the bend of my mind would run me over and explode in a sickeningly beautiful orange and crimson flame. I longed for the release of my own death.

I unloaded and reloaded my .45. I'm not sure what I was thinking. I am too much of a coward to try to kill myself. I just really wanted to see her face once more as I burst into her bedroom and shot the dick off her AIDS-infested, tattooed-musician lover. All I could do was mumble, "Fuck you, Jerry," as I took careful aim on Springer and blew a five-inch hole out of the back of the now smoldering 21-inch RCA.

Gunplay in my building in the wee hours was nothing new, but it would surely bring my old jackbooted comrades around inquiring about the nature of this month's seizures. Another gun-cleaning accident and another TV. I was in hell.

Los Angeles is a miserable place to be alone—a depressing desert suburb with too many broken down, ugly '70s strip malls filled with lying backsliders. Sometimes it simply oozed a bad-smelling puss. L.A. is a town of beautiful sunlight and beautiful people willing to break your heart if they find the tiniest weakness in your armor.

I was torn between wanting to kill her and wanting to tie her to her bed so tightly that only her eyelids moved and make love to her until she came so hard she would stop breathing. Maybe I'll do both. Guns and women are never a good mix, but life without either one seems wrong somehow.

Who am I kidding acting like a tough guy? I wanted to cry and whimper and have her hold me tight. Instead, I just killed my second TV this month.

(ALPHA • -) "Never, and I mean absolutely never, fall in love with a junkie!"

No matter how much rehab, no matter how many times they work the Twelve Steps, they have been so damaged by all the abuse they received as a child and all the bullshit they slung as an adult that they can never be fixed. At least not to the point that when they tell you they love you, they are not telling some shade of lie. They will break your heart in a nanosecond and make you feel like it was your fault in the first place for having dared fall for someone as screwed up as them.

Some psychic I am. I should have run away screaming the first time she leered at me, sizing up my jugular vein, trying to figure out how hard she would have to bite to get the blood out. Maybe it was the vinyl catsuit, or maybe it is because I really can see what others don't. I saw in her the potential to be my perfect mate and best friend. It could have been so sweet. But no—as soon as it started to get too real, a few cracks in the armor, it went sideways. As soon as she realized that I truly loved her for who she was and not the game she was slinging, it was all over. Taillights.

Why do they always wait until it's way too late to stop the madness? Like the dumb ass who kills seven people in a McDonald's before he shoots himself. What do these miserable bastards think? Would the next one of these people please save us all just a little bit of grief and cap yourself first? Sounds great in theory; unfortunately, I would be out of a job. That wouldn't be such a bad thing, I suppose. If I never have to open one more file and get into some screwball's headspace, well, that would be just fine with me. I am weary of this so-called gift. Not that each new nut job is so far beyond the pale of the milk of humankind—that's not it at all. The terrifying fact is that it is just the opposite. It's that they are so damn predictable. The fix is in by the time these people are 7 or 8 years old. By then, if they haven't had their little bones beat until they are black and blue or all their orifices probed lasciviously by some trusted guardian, then they got the opposite: no contact whatsoever. They got the message that they are useless, unloved, and unwanted by anyone. Sadly enough, that is all it takes to grow a monster in this world. Another human time bomb is unleashed to figure out how to best manifest his or her particular brand of craziness. The miserable part about it is that the rest of us are not innocent in the process of the madness. We see it going on and do nothing; we let the weeds take root in the garden. All the time we know so much better and usually tell people at gatherings our fine opinions on such matters. It's a messy thing, being a gardener. So we wait, and the infection festers, until ... until I get another file full of nightmares.

Find the crazy one. Sweet Jesus, if that were the only navigational tool I had we'd all be suspect. Not one of us doesn't have our own brand of kink. Learn how to read people's auras and you will be amazed at the insanity we are all capable of.

"An image of my blue brother's imminent arrival floats up through my mind soup ..."

I unloaded my Colt and put it on my coffee table. I braced myself for the energy. Sometimes, I just can't handle being around cops. Their energy tends to be murky, and their auras are always such dirty, muddy colors. People don't understand why they end up like that. It's not the cops' fault, usually. Sometimes when I walk through the squad bay and the light is just right, I'm startled by someone's bright auric colors. I just don't expect to see it in that place. It's usually a rookie straight out of the academy or some kind of tourist wandering in a place they don't belong. Once, I saw these weird Peter Max colors and shapes radiating from this acidhead who was getting booked. The strange thing was that, as I watched him emanating all his weirdness, it all started to come apart for him. The rush ended and something like fear took over, or maybe the realization of his same old reality flashed in. Either way, he would have been better off not seeing the weirdness that way. Even if the natural way is slow or doesn't work at all, if you are not ready, it's really the only safe way. It's the only way you have some kind of grounding framework and some control. Some way to go out and come back without leaving parts of your mind all over hell's half-astral acre. On the very old maps they had very good reasons to write: THERE BE DRAGONS HERE. There are things that go bump in the night, and they are not all benevolent. That's where the New Agers have it wrong. It's not all light and love; it's light and darkness.

"OK ... he's out in front of the building by the Land Cruiser, time to look pathetic ..."

I was never a cop, but I spent enough time in the military to understand the fraternity of it. They can't really afford to be to open to anything strange or nonstandard. The questions that would arise would put morale into a tailspin. They tolerate me just as you would a barely controllable tool like a chainsaw. You can do really amazing things with it, but you can never take your eyes off it. It's just too dangerous. What we need to understand as a society is that these people get their murky, ugly auras because they are constantly working with and inputting the worst and the most disgusting thought forms our society comes up with. Someday, every two years, cops, teachers, and health care workers will all be given six months to go on a healing retreat to recharge their souls. Until then, everyday cops will become just a little bit more like the perps. The Irish probably do so well because as wacky as it gets, they have that built-in religious framework. But faith is a hard commodity to come by with the really weird stuff. There is just no context to put it in. That's when they send for people like me. It's not so much that they want answers, it's more like they just want to farm out the madness. Spread it around a little, give it to the spookies ... it comes from their world anyway, so let them deal with it. They think it comes from my world. Wouldn't it just be nice for them if that were true. Then they could go back to their 2.5 children, houses with manicured shrubbery, and pretend that devils do not walk among us. Well, I can't pretend—I know where they live and, worst of all, I know what they think. And let me tell you, it gets a little damn lonely. Try finding a date that will do more than just screw you when you tell her you see ghosts.

"Honey, what are you thinking about?"

"Oh, not much," I might mumble. "Just thinking about a gas station attendant in St. Louis who is trying to figure out how to molest and kill a busload of retarded girls that just stopped to fill up."

It doesn't matter that two days later you can show her the headlines that tell all about the burned corpses of the girls they found in the woods an hour from the gas station after the attendant confessed. I've tried to show them that, and then they really become afraid of you.

Kat was different. Maybe because she understood the horror, too. She would just say, "It's OK, baby. Let it go. Make love to me instead." So I would. I would make intense, fierce, passionate love until all the spooky little monsters in my mind left because all that remained was the beauty and honesty of my love for this woman. She liked the ride; she liked it just that way. She had her own monsters that she wanted to forget about. As bizarre and strange as our love making was, there was a grace and a peace that would settle over both of us, and for a short time we could hold each other and look into each other's eyes and know that we actually loved and were loved by another. That love, no matter how terrifying this world could be, that love actually existed.

The problem is that with a junkie, there really are no ex-junkies. A junkie always holds on to a little bit of game, just a little bit of control. Just enough that separates them from everybody else. Without that little bit of control they feel lost, and feeling lost to a junkie means death. So they separate just a little, and if they feel themselves merging with another as you do when you love, they just vanish. No notes, no warnings, no good-bye. Just gone. Empty.

I wonder if she thinks of me at all, or has she somehow managed to compartmentalize her feelings in some little locked box in the attic of her heart? It scares me because I know that if she doesn't treat those feelings with the love and honor they deserve, one day they will find their way out like some mad Houdini and merge with other unfelt things. Then those unfelt feelings will roll right over the ramparts she erected to stop them, and she will have no choice but to die. Choosing not to feel things means after awhile, you can't feel anything and you lose the ability to understand yourself. You become a stranger inside yourself, but it's only a temporary fix, because eventually something will trigger all of those mixed-up, jumbled-up feelings, and you will get both barrels of life right square in the face. By that time it's too late. You've got the cancer, your last lover gave you AIDS, you shot some bad dope. You're so far off your course that you can no longer use your higher powers of intuition and your spirit guides can no longer help you. The white light you're heading for that you think will be your salvation is nothing more than an iceberg that the vessel of your life is steaming straight toward in a cold, black sea.

No, at that point you've failed your test here on this Earth plane. They say it's alright, that you get many chances to try again until you pass your test, but wouldn't you think you would want to get it right in this incarnation? To really hold nothing in your heart but love and to finally be free. To finally pass, move on to the real work of the universe, and be of some use. Easier said than done, I suppose. I mean, look at me: I just killed Jerry Springer.

"Bobby D., you in there? Robert Doucette, are you alright?"

Lieutenant Thomas Quinn, Los Angeles Police Department Bureau of Detectives: my handler and, as much as he can be, my friend. He used to call himself an intuitionist. He even had it on his business card. I think that is why more than anything else he got assigned to the spookies. Not exactly a stellar career move, but hey, life is like that; you tend to end up with your own kind. Tommy told me a story when I first met him about what he called his intuitive journeys. He said he awoke on Sunday morning with a strong desire to drive out to Malibu. After what he determined were directions from a very small voice, he ended up on Encinal Canyon Road on a very dreary winter day. He found a man about three miles up from the Pacific Coast Highway facedown on an abandoned road in the death throes of a diabetic coma. If Thomas hadn't rushed him to the nearest clinic, the man would have been dead in 20 minutes. Tom would never admit in a million years that he's psychic. The truth is you can't openly call yourself a psychic and hold a spot in the Bureau of Detectives. But as much as he allowed himself to travel in the ether, he was one of us.

Most people are psychic to some degree or another. In fact, most highly effective people are. The Henry Fords, the Ted Turners, the Joe Torres, the Gandhis, the Joan of Arcs—these people are downloading information straight from the source. If you follow truly effective businessmen's decision-making processes back to the source, you would be startled to find out that almost all had a system of relying on a still, small intuitive voice inside them. Sure, they may have had a great education. Or not. They may be very gifted. Or not. They may or may not have some special expertise. However, if you ever get a chance to ask them about their actual decision-making process, and if they are honest with you at all, you will learn a very funny truth and a key to living up to your own true potential: What these people have learned to do is to base their whole careers—in fact, their whole lives—on nothing more than a psychic hunch, a gut instinct. The reason they are so successful as opposed to most people is that by training or by accident, they have learned not to edit their intuitional information through a filter or some neurosis: fear, worry, doubt, hate, low self-worth, or, for that matter, love. Any emotion will add a certain flavor or color to the information, and the negative ones tend to block it all together. Listen to Ted Turner speak. Is he smart? You bet he is, but there is something else: He is outrageous in what he says because he does not edit himself. That is what most people do—they edit themselves to fit into some kind of self-deceived, proper place in society. What they really do is cut themselves off from the source of information that has fed all the sages, the mystics, the greatest thinkers the human race has ever known. Not Ted; he understands that to edit himself would take too much time and signal to the mind soup that he really doesn't want the data in the form that it wants to come to him. We know where the brain is, but not one person who has ever lived can tell you where the mind exists. They can't tell you where the edges are.

(*BRAVO* - • • •) "*In the Book of Runes under the rune Raido is a simple prayer for a soul's journey: 'I will to will thy will.'*"

Don't edit the source; take it how it comes. Adapt your will to it, not the other way around. A human understanding will never be able to encompass infinity. Not one person who has ever lived knows enough to be a pessimist. Jung's collective unconscious and synchronicity is close, but it's just a part of it. The model of the Akashic Record is more complete: All things ever known or ever to be known on this plane of existence and others are yours to know if you can just find the right way to listen.

(*CHARLIE* - • - •) "*Do whatever it takes to find the place and the method in this life where you can get still enough to hear your own truth. It's the only path to freedom.*"

(*DELTA* - • •) "*If your motives are not pure, you and no one else will create a hell for yourself that will destroy your chance for redemption.*"

You see, the universal mind options you with a kind of a self-cleaning-oven mechanism. The path is very thin in spots, and the price for stepping off is absolutely lethal. I think that's why most people are content with leading lives of quiet desperation. They think it's better to be lost than to fail, but fear is the real prison. Failure is the final taboo to be overcome.

"Bobby, it's me, TQ. Let me in."

"I'm coming, Thomas. Hold on." I unlocked the door and sheepishly met his gaze as the big, thick industrial fire door swung open.

"Come on in," I mumbled and sat back down on the couch.

"Is the piece unloaded?" he asked very officially as he closed and locked the warehouse door.

"Yep, unloaded, nothing in the chamber. One round fired into the TV, through the wall, and lodged in the doorjamb of the bathroom, though."

"Well, there sure is something to be said for that .45 ACP round," he said, relaxing just a little bit. "Only seven rounds, but if any of them touch your target, it's pretty much over."

"You want a beer or something?" I asked him, playing up the pathetic act.

"No, Bobby, this is official," he said, going through the motions of my verbal spanking. He picked up my .45, checked the chamber, put it back down, and casually picked up the magazine and deposited it on a shelf near a chair where he sat down and faced me. He's a good cop, I thought. It's the details that save you. He let out a slight sigh, and some warmth returned to his pale blue eyes. "When was the last time you heard from Kat?" he asked.

"About three month ago, but I get some hang-ups."

"Is it her?"

"Yeah, she is very ashamed of lying to me and acting like a coward. Knowing that at least keeps me from hating her, but goddamn it, life is fucking short. You need to show a little backbone, don't ya think?"

"She's afraid, Bobby. She never had anyone really care about her. She has no framework to understand this with," he said gently.

"She has no framework. What the fuck about me?" I was disgusted with myself as soon as the words left my mouth, but damn, this hurt, and I just wanted it to stop. There were only two ways for that to happen: to have her in my arms again or to let her go forever. I didn't want to let her go; I searched for too long, I weathered too many storms to let her go now. Damn this lesson, damn this pain. Why did I have to meet her in the first place? What kind of crazy shit are my spirit guides putting me through this time? What did I miss? What detail did I overlook? How did this sapper of love slip under my perimeter wire? I didn't want this. I truly did not need this drama in my life.

"Have you tried calling her?" he said in his best Irish priest impersonation.

"No good. She won't pick up, and I just end up leaving stupid, desperate messages."

"Well," he said slowly, "I don't know what to tell you, Bobby. I'm sorry. Janet really liked her, so did I. Listen, my friend," he said, shifting a little bit back into cop mode. "Brubaker from the FBI left me a message late today saying you're not returning his calls."

"Brubaker," I stammered, "fuck him. That last report he wrote up on me sounded like I was some kind of goddamn national security risk. He's got some fucking big balls."

"Bobby, I know he can be a piece of shit, but there is something you don't know," he said pleadingly.

"Something I don't know," I yelled incredulously. "You fucking tell me what I don't goddamn know Lieutenant Thomas Quinn."

His eyes steeled and all the warmth left. "OK, tough guy, just sit there and wallow in it, but life goes merrily along, and the trail for

Jack Mumford is two days old," his words hanging in the air like an early frost.

Time and space got very confusing, everything sounded hollow. There was something in my stomach that felt both hot and cold at the same time. The refrigerator switched on and sounded huge and menacing. It startled me back to the present moment. This whole scene was starting to take on the stink of a bad nightmare.

"How? When?" I stammered.

"Don't you check your answering machine?" He looked at me like I was the world's biggest moron. "They were transferring him to a separate facility to do some ventilation work..."

"Some what?" I cut him off. "Some ventilation work? Are these people stupid?"

"No, Bobby, no they are not stupid. He killed five heavily armed sheriff's deputies, five very well-trained sheriff's deputies, five deputies who were on high alert with families, loved ones, and friends, and when he was done there wasn't a piece bigger than a sandwich bag. Their hearts and livers are missing, all except for one, which was found in a school cafeteria for blind kids in Tennessee—and two blind girls have been missing for over 24 hours. So you just sit here and feel sorry for yourself ... I hope you have more than one magazine for that pistol because my money is on the story that he is going to come here looking for you, and I don't think seven .45 rounds are gonna stop this guy, Bobby, I really don't."

"Kat!" I almost screamed.

"I've got officers out trying to find her right now, Bobby, but I don't think he'll know about Kat. It was a long time ago that we put him away."

"You don't think? Of course he'll know about her. He'll know about Janet, the kids. He already knows. He will find a way to inflict as much pain as he can. Thomas, you have to get your family to a safe house right goddamn now."

"Easy," he said to me. "Easy, action, they're fine. Settle down, Scarecrow."

A cold fear was settling inside me. Despite all my training and experience to the contrary, a cold, horrible, nameless fear was working its way up into my legs, my stomach, and into my chest, and it was getting hard to breathe. I hadn't noticed that I had gotten off my couch, picked up my Colt, retrieved my magazine, and loaded my weapon. When your mind shuts down, your training takes over.

(ECHO •) "Whatever you do in training is what you will do when shit goes south. So you better train as if your life depends on it. That goes for this and any astral realms."

"Bobby!" Quinn had taken my weapon from my fist and put his hands on my shoulders. "Bobby, are you hearing me in there?"

I looked up into those blue eyes and felt tears welling up in mine.

"Bobby D.," his voice softened, "we'll get through this. I have a car outside, but you have to call Brubaker ASAP."

"OK," I said. "OK, Tom." I pulled away just before the first tear fell.

"You have to stay in close contact now," he said again pleadingly.

"Yeah, OK, sure," I said, turning away so he could not see me wipe my eyes.

"I'm going to talk with Janet. Are you going to be OK?" He looked at me the way he looked at his kids.

"Yeah, I'm OK. I'm fine now," I lied.

"No more flyers, OK, goddamn it," he said, half-kidding.

"No, Lieutenant, no more flyers—every round will be accounted for." I was trying to muster some humor but was pretty unconvincing.

"OK, lock this door after me," he said and snapped back into cop mode as he put my .45 back on the coffee table.

"Thomas," I said to him as he started to walk through my door.

"Yeah, Bobby, what's up?"

"We'll get through this, but it's going to hurt."

"I know, Bobby, I know." I saw a look of fear cross his eyes. "Call Brubaker, take care of yourself, good night."

I stood there alone wondering what kind of madness was brewing. What tear in the veil had happened to wind this up now, at this time? I picked up the auto loader on my way to my desk, and with very shaky hands I loaded the rest of my magazines. As a tear splashed down on the polished copper and brass of a .45-caliber Army Colt pistol round, a whisper escaped my lips. "Kat, I miss you."

CHAPTER 2

The sound of the phone jarred me awake. I rolled over quickly and smashed my face into my .45 lying where Kat should have been. Immediately my nose started bleeding. I was trying to figure out where I was as the blood dripped down on my sheets. I barely heard Agent Brubaker on my answering machine.

"Mr. Doucette, Mr. Robert Doucette, this is Special Agent Brubaker of the Federal Bureau of Investigation. Lieutenant Quinn of the Los Angeles ..."

I grabbed the phone and cut him off, "Hold on, Brubaker, you piece of shit, my nose is bleeding." I threw the phone down on the bed and grabbed a wad of toilet paper from the bathroom and stuffed it up my nose. Glancing quickly at the reflection in the mirror, I did not recognize it as my own. The pathetic excuse of a man staring at me with blood dripping down his face, his nose all distorted by the toilet paper, was definitely not a handsome guy. I walked back in and looked at my bed, the blood reminded me that Mumford was en route my position. I picked up the phone and growled into it with a voice that sounded like I had been chewing on gravel.

"Brubaker."

"Mr. Doucette, I …"

"Brubaker," I snapped again, cutting him off. "It's not the fucking '60s with that dress-wearing J. Edgar, and if I even think that I'm going to so much as get nodded to the next time I try to leave this country, I am going to hold you personally responsible, and I will sue you for every last cent you have. I am not going to end up like Vern Cameron, you hear me?"

"Who?" he asked.

"You know damn well who, you fucking owl. Are we at all clear, you backstabbing cretin?"

Vern Cameron was one of this country's best dowsers and also the inventor of several different dowsing methods and devices, including the Cameron Aura Meter. Dowsing is traditionally a way to find water with a device such as a forked stick or two L rods. In fact, it is really an intuition-interface device to access information on just about anything. Vern, during the height of the Cold War, wrote a letter to the Secretary of the Navy telling him he had a low-cost, foolproof way to locate any Russian submarine at any moment, in real time, with exact latitude and longitude and precise depth. With no more than a small dowsing device, he said, he could do it from a desk in Washington. He was invited to demonstrate his claims and freaked them out. He hung a nautical chart of the world up in front of some Navy brass at the Pentagon and proceeded to target every Russian and American submarine with a method called map dowsing. He pinpointed each real-time location and depth, and the meeting was brought to a quick conclusion. Vern went back home to California and never heard another thing from the Navy. Years later he decided to head to South Africa for a conference on alternative energy and was told he was not allowed to leave the country because he was a national security risk.

Brubaker started to get very stingy with my expense account the last time we worked together. He told me that my costs would be covered to follow up on some leads in southern Florida. An on-scene search is very tedious and time-consuming, especially when the body parts that were buried were cut up a small as these were. I incurred about three grand worth of expenses—and believe me, I was not living it up—and Brubaker welched on paying. He did it just to kiss ass with the then-reigning assistant director. So I kind of went into his financial history with my pendulum dowsing method. I found out he had made a couple of shady business deals while he was a Marine Corps lieutenant colonel attached to the NSA at the Pentagon. I let him know that I knew about his funny bookkeeping methods. He retaliated by making me out to be some kind of marginal freak that needed to be constantly monitored as a possible security risk. The language that he used in his final report was ambiguous enough that I couldn't really pin anything on him, but the damage was already done. As you can imagine, the people in these agencies take a very dim view at best, on good days, of people like me. So sitting there with a bloody nose, a broken heart, and an incoming madman, I felt no warmth for this brown-nosing peckerwood.

"Mr. Doucette, there is a meeting today at the FBI offices at the Wilshire Federal Building in Assistant Director Wolmack's office at 11 a.m. sharp. Can you make it?" It dawned on me that he was being so polite because the conversation was being monitored.

"Will Quinn be there?" I snapped.

"Lieutenant Quinn has been asked to attend, yes."

"OK, Brubaker. I'll be there." And I hung up.

My bed looked like I had killed a small mammal in it, my head hurt, I needed coffee and a lobotomy, and I was already tired of thinking, and the day had just started. I went to the kitchen to warm up the espresso maker, and it started again. I started getting flashes of conversations I had with Kat. I brushed my hand over my butcher block she was fond of sitting on while we made love in the kitchen. She had a funny way of triggering this certain wildness that was insatiable in me. She would ride the wave just like the best surfer alive, getting every ounce out of crest upon crest of our lovemaking. Kat was the only person I ever let in that way, and she'll be the last. I never, ever want to feel this empty inside. It gets in the way of my work; it screws up the receiving equipment. It takes too long to clear myself like this, and I could not afford that now. Not with that crazy-ass Jack Mumford trying to figure out if he would eat my liver while I was still alive or cut me up into more bite-size pieces first.

There was really nothing special about Jack Mumford, except his profound dedication to the bizarre level of violence he could inflict at any given moment. Quinn once said he was just like a garden-variety violent video game that got stuck above expert. When we tried to trace back to his trigger point, we kept coming up blank. Don't get me wrong, his parents died young and he was raised by a creepy uncle in southern Ohio. He did have the right tendencies: cruelty to animals, a loner, not much adult support. But the thing with Mumford is I just think he found something he was good at and he took to it. He was probably always psychic, and I'm the first to tell you that it's not an easy ride as a spooky kid. But there was a moment in Mumford's life that he allowed his gift to help him with his passion. His passion just happened to be demented violence.

Every time I try to remote-view this moment—to try to get a clear clairvoyant vision of it—I feel him aware of me. Then I'm bombarded with such an incredible array of violent, angry emotions and feelings that it's hard to think about it; it is so disturbing.

What I told Quinn and Brubaker, but I didn't put in my report, is that somehow he has help from different realms and from different entities. These things want him very much to succeed at what he does. In fact, one might say they have no other reason to exist except to help him be the best at what he does. It's a symbiotic relationship. The entities, although extremely real in one sense, are thought forms existing because of fear. This all may sound very esoteric to someone who has not seen one of these things or what they are capable of. A sure sign they were there is watching someone they're working with just before death. Once these entities know the jig is up, they abandon the vessel. The funny thing is that it may be days or weeks before the body actually dies when they leave; they know in advance. The host then walks around in a kind of moronic haze, wondering where all the blood came from. Don't get me wrong: The host, sure as the sun will rise in the east tomorrow, has invited these pricks in. It's not a one-way street; hate begets hate and love conquers all. Most people who plead criminal insanity really are crazy, but somehow, somewhere they asked to be that way. As dark and menacing as the world gets, we always have the choice. There is only love—all else is our poor little human thoughts choosing to give in to fear. The etymology of the Greek word "chaos" means "a gap." A gap is a space for things to evolve in a different way. When we wonder why God allows the devil his day, maybe it's a tool he uses to do what we refuse to do. Maybe when we don't evolve the right way, a gap is created to move us back to the plan. Maybe—but the bottom line is that if one taps into these entities, the seeming power they can offer a pathetic little human life can be very tempting. It can be overwhelming. Along your path there will be many temptations, and you will have to run the gauntlet more than once in this life if your soul is to advance. There is no doubt in my mind that Jack Mumford is a very powerful man and that he is being helped by forces unseen. My task is to remember that these forces, these princes and principalities, are only more powerful than me if I allow them to plant the fear in me. Voodoo works because people believe it works. I believe that Jack Mumford is capable of destroying anything I care about if I make a mistake.

There are many ways to mystical knowledge, to your own truth. Confucius said that there are more than a million ways and all of them are valid. One traditional way is the Seven Hundred Volumes. In a typical college education for a bachelor's degree, you end up reading about 244 books. Well, you're supposed to anyway; no one ever really reads all those books, or else Cliffs Notes would not be in business. However, if you had read them, you would have only been 456 books away from a very old occult secret: Sometime on your way to reading 700 books there is a part of your mind that wakes up and starts to tap into knowledge you never dreamed possible. It doesn't matter what books you read—it can be comic books, cookbooks, or romance novels. The only stipulation is that it be a complete thought process written by a single mind. After a while, you will be led to the knowledge you need. One thing leads to another, and you will one day read a paragraph or a sentence and something will just click in gear, and you will start accessing information from an invisible source from the mind soup of the universal. Whatever method you use, it all boils down to what I call the belief point. The metaphysicians are big on this one.

(FOXTROT • •-•) "You are capable of anything you believe you are."

It's that simple—and at the same time that complex—because belief is a component of faith, and faith is a very hard thing to locate in a modern world.

Of all the books I have read about Eastern and Western mystics, philosophers, and sages, my favorite sage still is Daisy. Donald Daizly, Daisy to us, was the crew chief for our helicopters when I was in the service. He was a typical gearhead with his primer-red '72 Camaro with a blower sticking out of the hood. The car only ran about three days a year, but on those days it was a fire-breathing monster that ran like greased lightning. It was the '80s and we had to wear our uniforms off base. Now as anyone who served in the '80s after Nam will tell you, being caught in a uniform guaranteed you two things: one, you never got laid; and two, everyone hated you. So we would roll up into a bar to have a few beers, and no matter where we went it would start. Someone would start trouble, and they would always start it with Daisy because he was so small. His biggest claim to fame was that he crawled inside an inspection cover and got inside a jet engine on an Air Force cargo transport plane that was ferrying us. He was small, and not small the way some men are—small and wiry. He was just small. So naturally they would pick on him to get at the rest of us. They had no idea the world of hurt they were in for.

There is a dance men do when they contemplate violence. It's like a miniature version of two armies sending out probes or scouts to find out the enemy's strengths and weaknesses. In an event with very few participants, this usually amounts to several verbal jabs or maybe some posturing, but very little actual physical contact. The pop-psychological model of fight-or-flight is actually incomplete. There are four possibilities and not only the two. There is fight, flight, posture, or submit in the lexicon of the animal behaviorist. If the aggressor in one of these scouting or probing exercises gets no response, he can assume one of two things: the opponent has nothing in their ditty bag and they are hoping you go away (submit); or the opponent, no matter how it seems, is capable of putting anyone in the hurt locker (a form of posturing). Daisy was not much to look at, but to say a scorpion is small is gravely underestimating the posture. There would be no warning or "telegraphing," as my old marital arts sensei would say. Daisy would just move very quickly to the nearest pool cue or beer bottle—whether it was in someone's hands or not—and unleash a violence that was tremendous. He had no special training to speak of, just an unbeatable will. Within seconds it would be time to leave, and there would be a good deal of blood on the floor.

In a more reflective moment, when he was working on some of the turbine engines he so lovingly cared for, I asked him how he did it, what made him tick. He looked at me with this rather innocent New Hampshire farm-boy look and said simply, "Think bad, you are bad." There it was, as succinct as any 700 volumes. You create your own destiny. "I and the Father are one." "Pick up thy bed and walk, Lazarus." "Think bad, you are bad." Daisy, in his own way, had found one of the occult secrets of the universe: Action follows mind. Occult just means hidden, and the funny part is that from time immemorial, all knowledge that one needs on this Earth realm is hidden in plain sight. Teachers teach in metaphor for a very simple reason: It is a teacher's job to teach, but it's a student's job to learn. If you really want to learn, you must quest with all your heart, as your way is unique and therefore unknowable to anyone but you. It's only a teacher's job to guide until the point where the student learns how to control their own ascent. So teachers throughout the eons have learned to intrigue just enough so students will begin their unique quest for their own personal grail. We tend to make our searches very complicated because we see the evidence of the overwhelming world as such. We must learn to burn this block to our path out of us until we see with something other than the five senses—to search "until our bones stick out," as the Sutras say. It's always much simpler than we want to believe, but that is our test, our mission, our grail.

For instance, have you ever looked at the Mona Lisa and felt a certain sense of intrigue? A thought may have crossed your mind that she has something to teach you. You're not alone; people have been thinking the same thing for over 500 years. The first lesson she teaches, or we might say the great artist DaVinci teaches, is that you should pay very close attention to those feelings that you have and not brush them aside. Those feelings of some kind of vague knowing should be ruthlessly followed to their source until the very fabric of the universe is willing to impart its knowledge to you. The second thing DaVinci gives you is a key to unlock the mysteries of the universe and nothing less. She is here, surviving among us, to teach us how to shift our reality just a little, just enough so we may start to see and feel other realms. The question we would all like to ask Leo while contemplating his coy little biscuit, the question that has been asked all these many centuries, is simply this: Is she smiling or not? The answer, once you know the occult secret, is she is doing both simultaneously. It is incumbent, however, on the viewer to shift their perspective to understand this. You see, if you look at her mouth directly at a comfortable viewing distance, she appears not to be smiling. But if you look at her eyes, and with your peripheral vision see her mouth also, she now appears to be smiling. She is smiling, and learning what this means gives you a key to start on an adventure that will change your life fundamentally, down to a cellular level. The halo painted around older religious figures is real. It represents the human aura. A kind of energy force field that surrounds and permeates every being, and on more subtle levels permeates everything. Science has just started to be able to measure this energy, but occultists have known about it since we made cave drawings. You can see this energy around yourself and others. When you do, you will also be able to interpret and ascribe meanings to the colors and radiations of it. To see this soul-revealing energy, and most importantly to learn how to manipulate it, you look for it the same way you make the Mona Lisa smile. The peripheral is the vision required to see auras. To learn how to see your own aura, try this—in fact, keep trying it until you get it right. Remember, practice makes perfect, and there is a certain learning curve to this stuff. Look at yourself in a mirror, so you see yourself with an evenly lit background. Now look with relaxed eyes and concentrate on your forehead. At this point, let your eyes de-focus and kind of go fuzzy. With your peripheral vision, the same vision that allowed you to see Mona smile, look around your head and shoulders. You will probably see a silvery gray halo, maybe with some color in it. Don't look directly at it or it will disappear. If it does, just start again until you see it. Once you do, things will start to change in your life, and you will be on your way to your special destiny. One sure way not to see it is to say that auras don't exist. The universe lets you keep your prejudices. Just remember they are yours and you decide to have them—no one forced anything on you. Very soon after tuning into this auric energy, you will start to notice other subtle energies. There will be a quickening in your life.

(GOLF - - •) "Don't take yourself too seriously. Remember to laugh."

The quickest way to become an idiot is to think you have some special power. There are levels of this stuff, and any tangent you go off on ends up being a locked box that impedes your growth to even greater things. Be humble and find out how to serve; that is where your ultimate strength and good lie. Refer to (- • •) .

I managed to make it through coffee and was getting ready to clear myself to try to find Mumford. I scrubbed my body with a special skin brush and did a combination of Hatha and Kundalini yoga, with some good old military cranks for good measure. Then, burning some incense and candles, I took a 30-minute salt bath, all the while trying to hold the intention of clearing and relaxing my mind. I dressed in some loose clothes, made a cup of green tea, sat down at my desk, and did a short meditation to bring healing and protective energies into my work space. Something prompted me to look up and see my .45 sitting on a shelf above my desk. A small voice said to remove it for now—too much violent energy—so I put it in the freezer with the hammerless .38 and the soy burgers.

I'm not a vegetarian for political reasons, although the hormones injected into these creatures are certainly no good for us. Truthfully, if an animal is killed with fear in its heart, the meat will retain that energy of fear and transmit it to whoever eats it unless it is blessed and cleared. I don't eat meat for one very practical reason: I'm a better psychic on a vegetarian diet. Believe me, at different times during my training when it got really wacky, I headed right out for a double cheeseburger with fries and a soda. If that won't anchor one to this Earth plane, nothing will. The only problem with it is that it takes about six to seven days to clear it energetically from your aura and tends to block me. This isn't true for everyone, but it works for me, so I try to stay away from those yummy, greasy burgers.

I sat back down in my chair and did some alternate nostril breathing to a six-count. In the left nostril for six, hold for six, out the right nostril for six, hold for six, in the right nostril, hold for six, out the left nostril, hold for six. This is a very good way to bring the body into balance and open the psychic centers. It usually takes me about 10 minutes, but my mind was wandering, so it took about 25. I settled down into rhythmic breathing and went to my safe place …

I usually sail in on a yawl that is an exact copy of Joshua Slocum's famous boat *Spray,* which was the first sailing vessel to circumnavigate the Earth with only one human being on board, old Josh. Sailing up a beautiful spruce-lined fjord, I spend time to smell the sea and hear the boat working as she glides up to my imaginary well-found dock and gently bumps into the protective camel floating in water. I'll take time to make all the lines fast and make sure the fore and aft spring lines have enough slack for my make-believe tide.

"In these visualizations it is critical to pay attention to the details. You are teaching the Earth-bound brain to pay attention to the hidden rooms in your mind. You do not have to force the detail; if you let your mind fill in the detail, it will. Again, all you need to do is to relax. You are trying to get your ego out of the way to achieve a state of mushin, as the Japanese say, or "no mind." In a state of egoless self, in a very real sense, you are creating a real place that exists somewhere. You do not have to concern yourself with where— just know it's somewhere, and that somewhere exists in a very real way."

Making sure all the sails are flaked properly and made fast, I take the halyards off that are bent onto the jib, main, and mizzen, and I make them fast. Then I patrol the deck, looking for any loose lines, called Irish pennants, and take time to coil and sea gasket all hanging lines. Anything left on deck is put in a Flemish coil in true Bristol fashion. I check the bilge one last time and flip the switch for the midship bilge pump to auto. I make sure everything is stowed on the chart table and galley.

"All the time I'm trying to get a sense of the feel and smell of the objects I am interfacing with."

I grab my courier bag, put my trusty old Stanley thermos in it, and climb back out on deck. Screwing down the Charlie Noble galley vent and making sure the main hatch is fast, I take one last look around deck, visually checking the rigging, and upon seeing that everything is safe, I turn my attention to getting my unruly cargo on the pier. My cargo is carefully tied in burlap bundles that are lying on the deckhouse. In these packages I have put all my negative emotions; all my feelings of pain, hate, jealously; all my feelings of low self-worth and fear. Any physical or mental pain—anything that could possibly hold me back from finding out where Jack Mumford is. I put them in a cargo net, take the hoist line from the dock, and bend it to the net. Noticing that the cover is missing from my beautiful brass compass binnacle, I quickly put it on and glance around to see if there is anything else I missed. The devil is in the details, after all. Then double-checking the bowline on the cargo net, I climb the ladder to the pier, my Stanley bumping into me with my bag behind me. Swinging the cargo boom over my nefarious load, I begin cranking it up to deposit it—in what? I quickly visualize a military Humvee with an open top and tailgate on the pier waiting to help. I swing the load over and deposit it in the back of the Hummer. Untying the hoist line and blocking the crane, I make sure my load is made fast for the short ride. Jumping in the vehicle, a joy runs through me as I appreciate the starkness and functionality of the military interior. I hit the starter button and the diesel roars to life. While I wait for the temperature to come up, I check the load one last time. Pulling off the pier, the Hummer climbs up the hill that leads to my beautiful lodge. The smell of a wood fire burning and something like French onion soup wafts in the breeze. The stout truck easily climbs past my wooden sanctuary and bounds up the road that leads to a small airfield. Lining up the Hummer with some painted loading lines on a concert pad, I unleash the cargo and sit the three bags on the tailgate. While moving one bag, something shifts inside and starts to crawl around, making a high hissing sound. Double-checking that all of the openings are well-sealed, I hear the droning of engines start. Off in the distance, the first bit of it is coming into view, with the roaring of the engines bouncing off the two peaks of the mountain saddle it must fly through. My cargo vehicle is part animal and part machine. It is, to be exact, an 80-foot-long great white shark that is fully alive, with engines thrusting out its sides and a gondola hanging below. It's my shark blimp. As it comes into full view, I can see its teeth gnashing slightly as course corrections are made. The cables that hold the gondola to the great fish and the support structures for the three radial engines enter directly into its flesh. A slight amount of blood drips out of the openings, and is atomized in the backdraft of the powerful propeller blades. It is menacing, strange, and is heading straight for me. The cold shark eyes size me up as the head of the motorized beast bobs and twitches, lining up the vehicle for its final descent. The smells of aircraft exhaust and fish hit my nostrils as the mad creature-machine gently bumps the gondola down on the concert pad. Quickly I open a locked box inside the gondola and retrieve a black leather briefcase with my initials engraved on a brass plate affixed to it. Carefully loading my three packages into the container, something shifts inside the last package and struggles to get out. Making sure that the package is holding, I put it into the container, double-locking it, dogging the hatch on the side bulkhead, and I give the all-clear sign to the smart panel on the side of the safety-orange gondola. Immediately, the monster's engines begin revving and the gondola lifts off. Barely 15 feet clear off the ground, the fish begins to swing around to get its return, heading for its homeward-bound course. As the ship gains altitude, there is a taste of atomized shark blood in the air. The crazy bioship finally flies out of sight. I start performing the ritual of the Cabalistic cross and give a short prayer that the negative entities are taken back to be cleansed, healed, rendered harmless and formless back to the universe. Then I imagine the void they leave is replaced with golden healing light. I grab the briefcase, jump in the Humvee, and head back down to the lodge. Inside it is very warm and cozy, and sure enough there is some hot cider and French onion soup waiting for me on a beautiful, thick mahogany table. Eating my soup, I dial in the combination to the lock on the briefcase and it pops open. Inside is the usual cash and a bag of gold, and also today there are some files. One is marked "The final location of Jack Mumford." As I open the file, a screen turns on and a count-down from 10 to one starts like the header of an old movie. As the movie starts, a late-model pickup truck roars past a sign on a desert interstate. The screen pans over to the sign by the side of the road. In highway green and white, the sign says: "Welcome to Nevada."

CHAPTER 3

The Federal Building on Wilshire is always such a pain to get to. Already locked in the glove box of my old Land Cruiser are my .45 and my knife. I just don't want the hassle of dealing with security. Anyone with a shaved head and a goatee is already suspect, no matter how many IDs and permits they can come up with. I park the big cruiser and take the elevators to the first secure level. Passing through the security checkpoint, I retrieve my bag and head for the elevators that will take me to the floor where the Los Angeles branch of the FBI lives. Government types are funny; they start to profile you as soon as they see you. I usually wear a ball cap when I come so they don't get so nervous, but it was a little cool this morning, so I put on a watch cap, a nylon flight jacket, khaki work pants, boots, and a courier bag. I can feel the eyes on me, even though I'm already past security. A chuckle boils up from my belly. Believe me, if I was going to blow this place up, I would dress just like an FBI agent—including the ill-fitting suit and maybe a toupee mock-up of the boring, off-the-shelf government hairstyle.

Approaching some uniformed guards who stand outside a metal detector, I notice that the FBI emblems on the glass partitions behind them seem to be new. The guards say nothing to me as I walk up to the podium.

"Robert Doucette for an 11 o'clock meeting with Assistant Director Wolmack."

"Please wait, sir," the guard says without any emotion. He calls and confirms my meeting while checking my ID. "Please proceed to the counter beyond the glass doors, sir, and await your escort."

"Thanks," I mumble as I walk through the metal detector and retrieve my keys, change, and courier bag and walk past the glass doors. At the counter, I'm met by an agent who is about 10 years younger than me, and she has either put on some weight recently or her outfit is not quite regulation. I'm always a sucker for tight clothes, and the fit looks good on the young agent.

"Mr. Doucette, I'm Agent Amanda Herrill," she says to me as she moves toward me and extends her hand out to greet me.

"Well hi, Amanda," I say, awkwardly grabbing her unusually strong grip. "Are you just my escort or will you be in our meeting today?" Something inside me stirs, and it startles me as I find myself flirting with the attractive young agent.

"Yes, sir," she says, making me feel older. "I have been assigned to the case."

"Good, that's good," I almost mumble as I stand there awkwardly meeting her steady gaze and barely hearing her when she asks me to clip on a visitor's ID and follow her. I tag after her down the hallway, watching her, and I'm vaguely aware of the stares by the other personnel as I pass the open desks.

"Kat," I think, "you see, damn it, absence doesn't make the heart grow fonder. Proximity does. Don't do this, Katrina, it's not meant to be like this. We're not meant to fade away."

We arrive at Assistant Director Wolmack's office, and the young agent opens the door for me. We enter an anteroom, and the secretary motions for us to go in. I notice that although the walls are made of modern office partitioning, the door is made of a carefully matched beech veneer, the only extravagance in this otherwise typical modern office environment. As we enter the room, I feel something invisible and cool brush up against my skin. The hair on my arms starts to prickle and stand up. "Mumford!" I think, almost out loud, and realize that the meeting is already compromised. Before anyone has a chance to speak, I turn to Luna Stewart, a renowned police psychic and occult writer.

"Luna, did you clear the room?" I say, barking at her like a drill instructor.

"Hi, Bobby, its good to see you, too. No, I haven't got around to it yet. Why?"

"It's too late," I say, expelling my breath. "I just felt Mumford here in the room." I detect the young agent Herrill separating herself from me mentally and physically.

"Yeah, yeah," I think to myself. "Too freaky for you. Good luck on the climb up the ladder, sister."

Any illusions I may have had about her and her wardrobe vanish. I glance around the room and lock eyes with Agent Brubaker. He's put on some weight since I saw him last, and even though it's hard to tell with his high-and-tight Marine Corps haircut, it looks like he has lost a little hair on top. Agent Brubaker stands up and starts the introductions.

"Mr. Doucette, this is Assistant Director Wolmack. You've met Agent Herrill. This is Agent Steger, Agent Duke. I think you know Lt. Quinn, Mr. Hank Jacobs, and Luna Stewart. Please have a seat."

I nod to everyone and say an awkward hello. I can already tell I'm not a participant in this meeting; I am the object of it. Hank looks at me and glances back to his paperwork. He's a funny guy, and we have had some dealings. Hank Jacobs is on retainer with

Hughes Aircraft and has been groomed most of his life as an aircraft engineer in that corporate defense contractor structure. Mr. McDonald, of McDonald Douglas Aircraft fame, which eventually was swallowed up by Hughes Aircraft, was secretly responsible for most of the psychic or Psi research labs for almost half a century. Old man McDonald was very much into spooky things. He always left a few clues around, especially when he named two of his aircraft Phantom and Voodoo. Hank was very much a product of McDonald's careful tutelage. He is a very brilliant man but has been in that secret-government-defense-contractor world for too long, and it is beginning to show. Although a very powerful psychic in his own right, his aura is beginning to show signs of some disease. He is probably one of the world's foremost authorities on technical remote viewing, but I think all the spy vs. spy stuff is catching up with him. He's not a well man. I have the utmost respect for him, but our relationship is a little strained. He was in charge of a gold-mining project that a company hired him for to come up with a psychic team that would remote-view ore deposits. He was nice enough to invite me to participate, but I made a stink about payment and the lawyers got involved. I received my contract less than 24 hours before we were slated to begin, and the thing might as well have been in Greek. Basically, it locked me up for years as far as working for anyone else and also limited the skills I could use for other endeavors. Lawyers. I'm always amazed at how much they assume they can get away with from the giddyup. The big print giveth and the small print taketh away. The repercussions of the small print said, in essence, that if I learned of any psychic methods during the job, I was somehow obliged to ask this company's permission if I ever wanted to use the skills again. Well, they had me there; I had never used my skills to find gold. So I would have had to ask their permission if I ever wanted to find gold again. I think not, I says to me, I says. I turned him down, and I think he was a little miffed, but oh well. I don't sign anything in under 24 hours.

Upon sitting down in the last remaining chair, I chuckled to myself, noticing the absence of any payment vouchers that would typically be at my seat if I were to be contracted as a consultant. I'm always punctual, and the fact that everyone else had been here for at least 45 minutes did not go unnoticed.

"Mr. Doucette, the reason you've been asked to come …"

I cut Brubaker off. "So assuming I'm not being retained by the oh-so-benevolent FBI, as I don't see any payment vouchers to sign, I can only assume I'm here at the request of the agency because you imagine that the object of Jack Mumford's wrath is me."

"Bobby, lighten up," said Quinn.

"It's OK, Thomas. It's OK," I said. "Assistant Director Wolmack, if I may, I think I can shed a little bit of light on this and save us all a lot of time."

It was the first time I had focused in on the AD, and the seeming goodness of his heart startled me. This could be a stand-up guy, I thought.

Hank started out slowly, interrupting in a kind of fatherly way. "Bobby, we believe you are in grave danger."

I cut him short, too. "Thanks, Hank. I appreciate the concern, but obviously I'm not the only one in danger here."

"Why don't you just say your peace, Mr. Doucette." My eyes met with Wolmack's. I liked this man, I thought. "Thank you, AD Wolmack," I said, as I broke off the stare and looked at each person in the room. Then I kind of de-focused my eyes and told them most of the information my magic folders told me. "You're not going to catch him, at least not in California. He's going to come here and wreak some havoc in our personal lives, and sure as the sun will rise tomorrow, people will die. But he is not going to be taken here, and he won't be taken by anyone but me."

"Bobby D.," Luna interrupted, "I think you're a little blocked."

"No, Luna, no I'm not blocked at all. In fact, as wacky as this sounds, you're blocked. I know we're not supposed to take this stuff personally, but I don't have that option anymore. Jack Mumford's target of madness in fact is me, and as much as you all think you have a handle on this guy, you don't. There are forces at work that are blinding you all to the true nature of this." I was quite aware that I was starting to sound like the madman Brubaker accused me of being.

"He'll be in and out of California before you can blink. His target is an energy vortex that is forming right now in the high desert in Nevada. If he gets to that before we catch him, he is going to get so strong that we won't be able to stop him before he completes his next cycle of violence. My lowest body count is somewhere around 30 people that he's going to target, and a lot of them are people who are known and loved by people in this room."

Special Agent Duke snickered slightly under his breath.

"Go ahead and laugh, Agent Duke," I snapped, "but he already knows that your son Josh parks his new blue birthday Schwinn behind your garage by the recycle bins."

Agent Duke's hard-core demeanor went ashen, and I saw him stiffen in his chair. I hated to do it this way, with so much drama, but I needed to get through to these people and get through fast. The mood changed, and I hoped I was punching through.

"Bobby," Quinn said slowly, "could you explain what you think this energy vortex is and what you think it will do for Mumford?" I realized immediately that Quinn was running interference for me. By this time I must have sounded like a classic paranoid schizophrenic.

"OK, Lieutenant, you're right, I must sound like I'm one step away from loading all my possessions into a shopping cart and moving to the beach." I'm sure if it weren't for my track record, they would've been calling the good humor boys. AD Wolmack stirred in his chair.

"Mr. Doucette, we are not doubting you. We also know the strain you are under right now."

Oh, well, that's where the friendship with Quinn ends. I forget he's a cop first and he has to cover his ass. They must know everything, even that tight-skirted junior agent Herrill.

"How do you like your coffee, Assistant Director?" I said, locking my eyes onto his.

"Excuse me?" he said in an exasperated tone.

There was a knock at the door, and judging by the reaction of the FBI people, the meeting was scheduled to not be interrupted. AD Wolmack nodded to Agent Herrill, who was closest to the door. She jumped up to open it. There was a government service worker with a catering cart loaded with coffee and Danishes. The woman had on a server's uniform and ID with her security clearance listed in bold black print. Everyone in the room turned and looked at me. Agent Herrill started to apologize.

"Assistant Director," she started nervously, "I left specific instructions we weren't to be interrupted. I'm sorry."

"It's fine, Agent Herrill," I said as I stood up and reached into my courier bag. I pulled out a yellow legal pad. "These are the minutes of the meeting as I saw them about 8:30 this morning, and it says right here: unscheduled catered coffee break at 11:22. It's 11:32 now; I think my timing is off because this meeting is compromised, as we never cleared and protected this room." I paused and passed the legal pad to AD Wolmack then continued. "Boy, I sure could use a cup of coffee and a bathroom." The room was silent. Agent Herrill had been checking the caterer's delivery log. She turned to the AD.

"There is no mistake, sir, she is scheduled to come to Room 205 now." AD Wolmack looked at my itinerary, then at me. A slight smile passed his lips. He paused and spoke.

"Maybe we could take a break and have a cup and a clearing. After all, Mr. Doucette's itinerary specifies that after the coffee arrives there would be a bathroom break." He glanced around the room, then at me. "Ladies and gentlemen, we are way out in Marlboro Country now. Let's take five and catch our breath."

I picked up my bag and headed for the door. As I walked out and looked for the men's head, I glanced at a bulletin board in an alcove and saw a red and green banner hung over it that read "Season's Greetings." As I stood there looking at some tacked-up Christmas cards, it hit me that it was past mid-December and I hadn't given it a thought until now. An incredible sadness started creeping into my heart. A feeling I did not want to think about. A pain and an emotion that I could tell would cripple me if I allowed myself to feel it. A lump started forming in my throat, and I realized that I had to find Kat. She was now in real danger.

"An image floated up in my mind soup of an old tenement hotel near downtown. Then another image came of a windowless bar with a neon sign out front that just said 'BAR.'"

I knew where she was. I'll find her tonight or tomorrow at the latest. "Merry Christmas," I said under my breath. "Merry fucking Christmas."

It's funny how the holidays sneak up on you in Los Angeles. Years like this when there isn't a lot of rain, and you get the jet stream doing a back eddy, blowing the hot desert winds offshore, it seems like mid-July. So unless you have emotionally buttressed yourself with friends, relatives, enough Christmas ornaments, rich candied foods, or gatherings with sweet-souled folks to ward off the impending gloom, you leave yourself wide open to feel the emptiness that comes. The lack of snow and foul weather just makes it all seem worse. At least back in New York, when you're waiting for a bus in 25-degree air with some hideous wind chill and standing in slush, everyone is miserable together. In L.A., the pain seems more solitary somehow. The sunny, hot days add to the surreal depression as you calculate all your past failures, remembering all the things you wish you had said to people while you still had the chance.

Special Agent Jefferson Duke came up behind me and gave a polite cough, pulling me out of my holiday musings. "Umm, Bobby, the bathroom is the other way."

"Thanks, Agent," I said, my heart melting as I saw the fear for his family still in his eyes. "Listen, Jeff," I said, remembering his first name. "It's going to be OK. We'll get to him first." Agent Duke was no slouch, and he could tell I didn't believe my words.

"I don't know about that," he said, his eyes narrowing slightly, "but if whatever you do works, then you better do it."

There was a moment, a slight moment, where we looked into each other's eyes and decided. We decided we would trust each other. We decided we would be on each other's side. Just two guys standing somewhere on the planet, deciding we were safer together if we are going to handle the saber-tooth monster that was lurking outside the cave entrance.

Walking down to the bathroom, I could feel the eyes on me. Even though I know it's L.A. and the celebrity pop-icons believe it doesn't matter if they are saying good things or bad things, as long as they are talking about you, I tend to disagree. There is no way not to be known or seen in the astral realms, so while I'm physically manifesting on this Earth plane, I would just as well be invisible. I think the FBI types might warm up to me better if I wore a purple turban or flowing dresses like Luna. I spook them a little because I'm one of them. I used to be a hardcore like them. I've been in harm's way and pulled my load. So they can't just blow me off as something that almost doesn't exist.

It's funny, but the country kids that hunt a lot always end up on the special teams. I could field-strip 14 different weapons in the dark before I had my first orgasm. So they put you out on a range in the military, and after you've been drilling groundhogs out to 600 yards since you were a kid, well, even on a rainy day it's a piece of cake. After all, the military is always on the lookout for range talent. It's what they do. One thing leads to another, and if you like to volunteer for things, pretty soon you find yourself deep in the kimchi. I found out soon enough that if you volunteered for stuff nobody else wanted to do, pretty soon people started to treat you differently. The last thing my dad told me before I left for boot camp was don't volunteer for anything. Well, it was a little too late for that. Besides, he lied to get in the war in the '40s at age 16. Then he volunteered for Airborne, then the Pathfinders, then he jumped into hell. I guess it's some crazy-ass gene he passed on to me. Some "let's fuck with this shit and see what happens" gene. It sure is a pain in the ass sometimes when your biological makeup overrides your common sense. However, I truly believe evolution is not for the meek, and the universe wants us to play out our part. We need to follow our Tao wherever it takes us, as that is truly our only way out. The only way out is through.

When I was a kid I used to ride my bike way out in the boonies, far from town, to an intersection that was surrounded by cornfields. The only two things at the intersection were a big oak tree and an old wooden phone booth. I would eat my lunch I brought with me, read a book, and watch the world unfold. Every once in a while, a car, a truck, or a farm tractor would roll by. I would watch thunderstorms brewing two counties over across the flatland. Looking out over the cornfields on a still summer's day, I imagined a world of my own construction. Somewhere out there, somewhere beyond the corn. It was a fun, beautiful, strange, colorful world. Filled with adventures and danger and hope and a belief that the good guys always won in the end. I told Kat about my crossroads, so she decided we should take a road trip and try to find it. We searched for three days but never did. We found housing projects and strip malls with graffiti on the dumpsters, but we never found my crossroads. I guess in a funny way I have been looking for the equivalent to that place all these years. I had it a couple of times with Kat, that same feeling. That feeling of peace, that feeling of knowing everything is OK in the world. I know I should be able to have those feelings on board, to be able to carry my crossroads around in my heart. I know, we all know, but we get wound up too tight, and the little things, if neglected, turn into big things and then start to take on a life of their own. So we get tweaked and we spend a good deal of time and money trying to fix ourselves. Even back in the days that you could go to a monastery when you were having a spiritual crisis, most people didn't bother. Now we have therapy based on a bad model of the id and a superego in conflict. Even Jung's process of becoming leaves out what we are just starting to remember after all these eons—that it is body, mind, and soul, not just a brain floating in a jar that's eating and fucking. No one knows where the edges of mind exist; maybe there are no edges, and when that dawns on us, if we are not prepared, that's what makes us crazy. We forget that we are supposed to unplug from the collective thought patterns we were force-fed, climb out of the cocoon we have grown, and fly away with our new wings. If I were smart, I would start building spiritual retreat centers all around the country—buy up all the defunct strip malls that have gone tits up. Then make a database of all the shamans, healers, therapists, psychiatrists, and doctors who believe in the soul and get ready to staff my centers with them when this paradigm goes south. Folks are gonna get whacked with an energy that is so weird and new to them and this planet that they would be standing 1,000 deep with fists full of money, or the equivalent, to get into one of my McSoul centers to work on the madness. Oh well, that has always been my problem with business ventures. To be successful in business, you have to be able to focus 20 minutes into the future, not 20 years.

As I pushed open the door to the bathroom, I saw Brubaker standing at the urinal, fishing around in his pants trying to find his pecker.

"It dawned on me that I'll have to be able to find those old crossroads in my heart if I'm going to survive meeting Mumford out there in the desert."

"You need some tweezers to find that little guy, Brubaker?"

"Jesus, Bobby, you scared the shit out of me," he jumped.

"Careful, Andy, or you'll soil that very fine suit." I had him now, so I pressed just for fun. "As a matter of fact, that is quite the expensive suit for a special agent to be wearing, isn't it?"

"Back off, Scarecrow," Brubaker snarled at me.

"I guess it's just too much for a guy to sound clever standing there with such a tiny prick in his hand, huh Andy?" He sighed and relaxed a little, the fat on his neck rolling over his tight shirt collar just a bit.

"Listen up, Doucette," he started as I sidled up to the urinal next to him. He quickly finished and walked over to the sink and started to wash his hands. "I don't like you and you don't like me, but we happen to be on the same detail. So why don't you lighten up for once in your fucked-up career and just play the game the right way and take your slot on the team like a man," he said, with a kind of fake John Wayne-esque lilt to his voice.

"Well, Andy, you've got one thing right," I released as my piss hit the urinal water. "I don't like you, and I won't until you find out the word 'honorable' means doing what is right even when no one is looking."

"Fuck you, Scarecrow," he almost shouted and headed for the door.

As he swung the door open, I yelled out so anyone in the hall could hear, "Sorry, Andy, I don't do guys." A hand grabbed the door as it started to close and opened it again. In walked AD Wolmack. He showed no emotion, and as I finished whizzing he started. I washed my hands and started to dry them off when he finished at the urinal and turned on the water in the sink next to mine. Without ever looking at me, he said very matter-of-factly, "Do I need to put a muzzle on him?"

I was taken aback at his candor. "No, Assistant Director," I stammered. "Just keep in mind what the anonymous source in the Watergate investigation, Deep Throat, said."

"How's that, Doucette?" he said, puzzled.

"With Andy, you have to follow the money." He didn't say anything, but our eyes met in the mirror. The same thought passed through both our minds. Is this guy on my side or what?

The meeting started back up, and Luna asked that anyone who could not at least be neutral leave the room while we cleared it. No one left, and although Jack doesn't give much credence to powers other than his own, he consented, making a very powerful triad.

(HOTEL • • • •) "Anytime you can get a like-minded person to work with you in the astral realms, your work will be exponentially more powerful. Remember, the Bible is just a coded textbook for learning how to fly without wings. 'When two or more are gathered in My name' is a call to work, not a way to spend a Sunday afternoon. You're meant to do it in the here and now, not in some future hereafter."

I could feel the atmosphere shift in the room, and the air was noticeably fresher. Everyone else noticed it also, even Brubaker, who involuntarily sucked in the now-purified atmosphere. I could tell the FBI folks were a little uncomfortable with the display, as the actual smell of the room changed so dramatically that it was apparent to all. Every time someone new is witness to an energy clearing, I can see the same puzzled look on their faces. Ninety percent of them will convince themselves that nothing actually happened within 24 hours of the event, but the other 10 percent will continue to wonder. If you can clear the air in a room, what else can you clear? How long will it stay clear? What else can I change? Could we repair the ozone layer with only our minds and intentions? Of course, the $10,000 question that everybody thinks but most dare not say is: Can I do it, too? The answer is yes, you can. Anybody who has enough discipline can, because after a certain point, you have to be your own teacher, you have to be your own research-and-development laboratory. You have to be able to learn from your mistakes and become self-scientific. You have to be able to enter your madness, your spiritual madness, and confront the dark side of yourself.

I used to want to do these things in private with no witnesses. As my confidence has grown and my abilities have increased, I've learned not to care so much. In fact, I have come to believe that the more people who experience energy work the better. It has a way of jumping from one open mind to another, and sooner or later, we will hit some kind of critical mass. That is when we will probably start to build pyramids with just our minds again.

When we were finished, AD Wolmack took control of the meeting.

"Mr. Doucette, it must be obvious to you that we have spent a good deal of time this morning kicking this around before you arrived. So if you would, could you pick it right back up again with your theory? I don't think we have much time with Jack Mumford, and I want an OP plan by 3 p.m. today." Again, the AD's candor and directness gave me reason to like him.

"OK," I said, "I will. And I thank you. Folks, I want to take you on a bit of a journey. The Assistant Director was correct when he said we were out in Marlboro Country now. In fact, we are way, way out. If you can keep an open mind until I'm through, I think we can advance our cause of nailing Mumford as quickly as possible. As I've said, I know where he is going and why, so if you can just suspend your prejudices for about 30 minutes, I think I can let one of old J. Edgar's own FBI reports make my case for me.

"I want to tell you a war story, a Cold War story. In 1956, something happened that has been happening on this planet probably before there were humans. Only this time, it happened in front of a crew of 51 sailors aboard the *USS Dediles* near the Sargasso Sea in the Bermuda Triangle. Well, 49 sailors to be exact—two members of the crew were deep cover, which is why we know as much as we do. The reason the event is so significant, what no one except the captain knew, was that two of the crewmembers were CIA operatives. They were posing as Navy weather officers, with two compartments of the most sophisticated electronic gear of the time, with a cover that they were trying to gather anything on Castro they could. The *Dediles* was chosen for the simple reason that no one would even blink while a U.S. Navy research ship cruised the Bermuda Triangle looking for anomalies with two Navy weather-heads. Just another typical boring cruise, so the crew thought. The two spooks were looking for something very special that the United States found out the Russians were looking for desperately since similar events happened during a joint Allied project in World War II. They were looking for a tear in the fabric of our universe, a rent in the atmosphere of what we know as our reality. So if you would indulge me, I'd like to tell you about one of Uncle Sam's weirder secrets, because what happened on that ship, on a little farm in rural Kentucky, and to a group of battle-hardened Nazis during World War II is the same thing that is drawing Jack Mumford like a moth to a flame in the high desert in Nevada."

CHAPTER 4

SS Captain Karl Eckart was chosen by Wilhelm Teudt of the Ahnenerbe Deutsche (the Nazi Ancestral Heritage Organization) not just for his courage and ruthlessness, but as far as the former head of the Nazi Occult Bureau was concerned, he was astrologically perfect. This was not going to be an easy mission. It was hard enough to convince Reichsfüher-SS Heinrich Himmler to divert precious resources away from the Nazi attempt to take Moscow during Operation Barbarossa. Especially to some obscure and strategically irrelevant mountain in the middle of the Caucasus. The small team would be working without any support in a commando fashion with its rather delicate human asset. An asset who had to be deployed at precisely the right moment on the top of a remote mountain peak, completely in the open, in complete secrecy. The talent needed for this mission had to be very specific and well-trained. It didn't matter if the package was recovered or not. Although there were some contingency plans made, they weren't of prime importance. It would be nice to get the old wizard back to Ahnenerbe headquarters, but because of his mixed Gypsy blood, it wasn't considered crucial. What was considered crucial was that the old man do what he was supposed to and psychically secure the power vortex over that peak in the name of the Third Reich.

Captain Eckart volunteered for the Waffen SS for one very practical reason. The SS was the political arm of the Reich, and he knew that when the war was over there would be more need for political appointees than soldiers. He was a well-educated man and imagined himself as a future leader within the party. When he was first approached by Teudt for an assignment, he was unsure of the ramifications for his career. Especially when other officers warned him of delving too deeply in the black arts practiced within the Ahnenerbe. After a short investigation revealed the Nazi Occult Bureau was the fürher's trusted council, Eckart's mind was made up. To perform well in such a small unit that commanded so much attention from the fürher was a godsend for someone like him, who had an eye on a political career within the future Fatherland. So against the advice to the contrary of his most trusted peers, he emphatically told Teudt that it would be his honor to assist his country for the greater good of the German people.

There were some downsides, however, not the least of which was the old Gypsy himself, who was not even sure of his own age. He estimated himself to be somewhere between 55 and 65. An airborne insertion was absurd with a man his age, but he seemed to take to the training very well. Besides, he *was* the mission. The real problem lay in the mountaineers. Eckart had to go outside the SS to find men of suitable talent within the regular infantry. From the start, he did not like the mountain specialists. Although all of them were officers, he thought them rather vain in their obsession and childish in their love of high places. He felt them to be spoiled children of the rich. However, they were recommended to be the best at this kind of small-team mountain operation. Eckart knew from experience that during wartime, no talent was to be wasted, and if their experience helped him complete his mission, then he would learn to use them wisely.

Eckart would have to design many new techniques for this mission, and that alone would be a great legacy. Not the least of which was the maneuver he called the Wagon Wheel. The Gypsy had a very curious need that was stipulated in orders straight from the head of the Ahnenerbe: If the old man gave a certain command, the team was to perform a flanking maneuver that covered the wizard; however, no member of the team was allowed to look at what the Gypsy was doing. In the orders it was specified that if any member of the team violated this no-eyes policy, they were to be immediately arrested and turned over to the Gestapo. This went for the training period as well as the actual mission. The maneuver Eckart devised was a larger version of one he had seen small groups of British commandos use in North Africa—a smaller, circular version of the Roman Phalanx. A squad of commandos would form back-to-back in a small circle and maneuver this way until such a time that they could cover other fields of fire and continue bounding maneuvers. It was known as a Tight 360, and Eckart's Wagon Wheel was the same, only the spokes were elongated so the Gypsy would have room to perform his ceremony or whatever he was going to do. Eckart was confident this was a new maneuver and would surely be attributed to him when the very bizarre mission was completed. He hadn't enough time to train as much as he would have liked, but the large gears of Operation Barbarossa were already engaged, and he would have to adapt his team to that time schedule and not the other way around.

Late that night, when the drills of the day were done and Eckart was alone in his barracks training office, he made sure the shutters and the door were bolted. He opened his safe and took out some envelopes marked for his eyes only that arrived by special courier earlier that day. Out of the envelopes he extracted what, by the date, were very recent aerial photographs of a very remote and forbidden-looking, crag-covered mountain peak. He knew that what he was looking at was his own personal, God-given grail. He was looking at what must consume his whole being if he was to survive, and maybe his life if he wasn't careful enough. On the back of the photographs were simply the mathematical coordinates of the target and the name, Mount Elbrus Caucasus Region.

Hanna Pennrie had been only 30 miles from the place she was born in Louis County near Vanceburg, Kentucky, only twice in her life. The first time was in the early 1900s when she was a young teenager. The influenza epidemics were raging in the rest of the country, but it took awhile to find its way to the back roads and byways of the rural bluegrass country. At age 16, just blossoming into womanhood, Hanna took ill. The Red Cross did not even have the correct maps as they descended on rural Appalachia, chasing the disease and trying to find all the cases that were bad enough to evacuate to a quarantine facility near the Ohio River. Most of the cases that came to the hospice never left alive back then. Hanna was close to death's door many times during her five-month stay, as pneumonia weakened her young lungs so badly that she kept relapsing. During one of the faithful visits that her father would make to see her, Hanna was well enough to be taken outside the ward. It was good to be able to talk to him rather than just wave through the shut wardroom windows from the second floor.

He brought her some books to read and for some odd reason a set of playing cards. They were good Christian folk, and Hanna could never remember her father so much as touching a deck of cards. He told her he wasn't sure why he bought them, but as he was standing in the general store in Vanceburg, he happened to be passing the cards and the same voice that he heard when he prayed told him that she would like a set. He thought that because it was his same prayer voice that it would be alright, but maybe it would be better if she didn't tell Mama about them just now. She asked him if he knew any games, so he taught her solitaire and the little poker he had picked up in the Army during the big war. For some reason she really enjoyed holding the cards and flipping them down during her now-steady games of solitaire. It wasn't long before she had relapsed again, but instead of going down to a kind of plateau and leveling out like she had done in the past, young Hanna's life started to slip away from her. She was in a very, very dark place. Her poor young body was barely able to muster enough strength just to breath when she had her first visit. A beautiful man, whom she would from there on out call her Angel, came to her while she lay so close to death's door. She could hardly keep her eyes open, but it felt so good to look at him that she did in spite of her pain and fatigue. Her Angel said he had a request from God, and that whatever answer she gave would be alright. She tried to sit up and remembered how she must look, and felt ashamed and unworthy to talk to God. Her Angel put his hands on her head and she started to relax. He told her never to feel ashamed, as God would always love her no matter what happened in her life. She started to cry and bravely said she would do her best to answer God's question. Her Angel then told her that God had some very special work for her if she wanted to stay with her family, or she could come home to him if she wanted. It was up to her, the Angel said, and reminded Hanna that no matter what she decided, he and God would always love her. She thought for a moment and suddenly realized there was no more pain and she felt so light, as if she could fly right out the window. She asked her Angel if this is how she would feel if she came home to God's house. Hanna's Angel told her that it would be even more wonderful than she could even imagine. She thought about it for what seemed a very long time, but the expression of love on the Angel's face never changed or wavered. Then Hanna told her Angel that she would like to help God, but she didn't understand how such a weak, silly girl like her could help. Her Angel put his hands on her shoulders and told her she just had to listen to the little voice inside herself and she would be guided as to what to do. He told her once more how much she was loved and would always be cared for. The vision began to fade, and she was slammed back into the darkness and pain of her disease. For two weeks she was in and out of consciousness.

Her father could not afford to take much time off from the family farm, but the last week of her semi-coma, he came to the hospice and camped out down by the river. There was no money to pay for a hotel, and none nearby, so he just set up camp and waited every day on a deathwatch for his beloved daughter. Every night after visiting, he would leave the hospice and go back to his camp where he would lay in his lean-to and read Scripture by the firelight until he fell asleep. It was Sunday morning and he awoke to the sound of far-off church bells somewhere down river. He washed in the river and dressed, then took his Bible to what he thought would be another day of sitting and waiting at the hospice. Hanna's father sat down on one of the benches and pulled his corncob pipe out of his overalls. When he was just about to light up, one of the aid workers came rushing up to him. His heart skipped a beat and his large body almost toppled over, fearing the worst. "Come," is all she said. "Come and see." She took Mr. Pennrie to the day room, and to his amazement, his lovely Hanna was sitting up in a day bed, eating and laughing with a wonderful rosy color back in her cheeks. He hugged his daughter and sat on the bed and held her hands. She could see the look of fear and confusion still in his eyes, wondering if this wasn't the calm before the storm. She held firmly to his hands and looked deeply into his eyes and said, "It's alright, Papa, the Angel said I could come home." The strong farmer and his daughter wept openly for a very long time, thanking their Creator for the miracle.

Hanna's recovery was not instantaneous. The disease had ravaged her lung tissue and she became fatigued very easily. Her father set a small day bed up on the front porch, and Hanna would wave at her father, mother, and brothers as she watched the days unfold into the tapestry of her born-again life. Her younger brother Jonah fashioned a lapboard for her to play her now-constant games of solitaire. One night after a particularly hard day of the seasonal rains that had come and Hanna's breathing was labored, she found herself in a fitful sleep. She was not sure if she was dreaming or awake, but a calm and peace entered her and her breathing returned to normal. Then, as if from somewhere very close, she heard her Angel speak softly and lovingly to her. He said, "It's time, Hanna. Never be afraid or listen to other people's opinions. Just know that the pictures are from God."

The next day her breathing had improved greatly. She was sitting in the front room with her brother Jonah as he studied. As she started to lay the cards down for a fresh game of solitaire, she thought how handsome he was becoming and soon he would find a nice girl. As the thought finished in her mind, something else stirred. A very clear series of images started forming in her mind like at the picture house in Vanceburg, and she saw Jonah being wed to Rebecca Thatcher from down in the hollow. Her lifework had begun. Hanna had become an oracle.

When Hanna left the second time, she was much older. It was early December, and she was sleeping very fitfully again. Finally she awoke and went down to the kitchen. She started a fire in the stove and put some water to boil in the old coffeepot. Ever since her husband, Paul, had died three years before, Hanna had been supporting herself with card readings. Her son, Bo, helped as much as he could, but all the same, this morning she would make a pot of roasted chicory, not coffee. She sat down with one of her knit afghans that she sold and wrapped herself up against the cold. Hanna could tell that her Angels wanted to talk to her this morning, but she would wait until the chicory was ready. The wind was howling outside, and a shiver went through her. She knew it wasn't from the cold; something evil was lurking out in the dark morning. Something ungodly was trying to come into the world. After she got a cup of chicory and sweetened it a little, she sat down with her cards. Just as she started to lay them down, the images started coming. She realized after all these years that something monumental and terrible was about to be revealed. She said a prayer to God and her Angels to send her strength and protection, then relaxed and let the images come.

By first light she was ready and walked the mile and a half to Bo's house. The family hadn't even awoken when Hanna came in and started the potbelly stove. Bo came down the stairs in his sleeping clothes, still groggy from the night. He asked her what was going on and if was she alright. Hanna told Bo that she needed him to hitch up the team and take her to town, and that there was some information she had been given and she needed to talk to Sheriff Walker. Bo knew that look in his mother's eye. She wasn't asking.

As Hanna and Bo pulled into Vanceburg in the late afternoon, they knew they would have to spend the night. The snow had been deep and the old wagon got stuck several times. Sheriff Walker watched them pull up and knew right away something was not right. It was too late for Hanna and Bo to make it back down to the draw by nightfall. He thought he'd better phone home and let his wife, Maggie, know there would be guests. Hanna looked a lot older since he'd seen her at Paul's funeral. He had seen her once since then, when she came to town during the time the Timkins boy went missing. He liked Hanna—everyone did—but it was never a good sign when Hanna just showed up. The sheriff went outside to help her out of the wagon and asked Deputy Lawrence to help Bo put the team up while he took Hanna inside. As soon as Sheriff Walker got her some coffee, Hanna started. He knew enough by now, after 35 years, to trust what she had to say, but this new request was extraordinary. He made a quick decision that he would not try to edit Hanna's request; he would just pass it along up the chain of command and call the FBI in the State Capitol Building. He knew one man from way back in the Army, and if they thought the small-town folk out in the holler had lost their minds, well, that was OK. He was a locally elected official, and he lived here and they didn't. Besides, Hanna was more like community property than an individual, and if people found out he tried to stifle her—well, they just wouldn't, that's all. He was going to let her tell the FBI men what she told him. If Mr. Roosevelt didn't believe that the Japanese were going to attack, that would be just fine by him. His conscience would be clear. The date was December 6, 1941.

It wasn't until December 12 that the team of FBI agents and the men from Army intelligence could make the trip to find Hanna all the way back in the draw. Sheriff Walker assured the men that she was there. He told them quite matter-of-factly that her Angels told her long ago where to build her house, so that she could better hear them. Sheriff Walker was amused by the government men. He knew if it were six days before, if he would have told them what he was telling them now, they would not be taking notes in triplicate. The major from the Army told his lieutenant that the first thing they needed to do was get a telephone in there. The lieutenant said they should improve the road at the same time, and the major thought that was a good idea. It took the men six hours to make the trip. Part of the road had washed out, and their automobiles kept getting stuck.

Hanna didn't have much food to give the men, but she had a lot of canned apples and peaches, so she set about making some of her sought-after pies before they arrived. Her Angels told her she didn't need to worry, that they would bring food, but just the same she wanted to have something ready when the men from her morning vision came. After they arrived and she offered them the pie, she pulled the major aside and asked if the enlisted men could come inside to eat. When the major started to balk, he got a taste of what it was going to be like during Hanna's tour of duty. She simply looked up at him and told him that it was not the United States Army's house, it was God's house, and he wanted those men to be warm when they ate. The major realized he was outranked and invited the sergeants in.

When Hanna came back from her second trip away, things were quite different. She enjoyed her trip to Washington, but it was good to get back home. She wasn't sure where all the men would sleep, but General Ansel had assured her the Army would take good care of the men and they wouldn't be a bother to her. She was getting used to having so much company on the property but felt a little guilty knowing how so many folks were doing without just now. Still, it was good to have coffee, and besides, her Angels told her the coffee would help, so she guessed that it would be alright.

Lieutenant Angelo, a Naval intelligence officer, was just coming from the communications trailer when Hanna stepped out on the porch. She asked if he wouldn't mind going to the smokehouse and bringing in the two hams Bo had put in there yesterday for supper tonight. Lieutenant Angelo was a cheerful man and very fond of Hanna. He was a good Roman Catholic boy from Brooklyn, and to him this was all a grand adventure. He was the first genera-tion of his family to be born in America, and somehow pulling this duty with Hanna way back up in the draw made him feel like a real American. Hanna had let him read the two letters Mrs. Roosevelt sent to her, and he realized then how important this assignment was. Besides himself and his chief radioman, there were three Army sergeants and four corporals. It wasn't lost on the men how much importance the government had placed on this duty station. Hanna was most definitely a national asset, and all took their jobs very seriously. It was an easy place to defend, although Hanna said that would never be necessary. Still, they were ready for any contingence. Lieutenant Angelo had read a good deal about the saints while growing up in Catholic school, and he understood right away that Hanna's house was sacred ground. He looked at his watch and realized he'd better hurry, as it was almost time to receive the transmission from Birdman in England. Even though Chief Ricardo had been checking the gear for the past two hours, he wanted to be ready when the transmission skip started from Devonshire.

Alistair Firth was Hanna's controller in England and had chosen to work with Hanna specifically. He was a civilian now, but had been an officer in British Naval intelligence before the war.

Alistair was a man in his 60s, heading what Mr. Churchill liked to refer to as his cosmic spy detachment. No one at Devonshire was too fond of the fact that 13 of the 17 seers were from the states, but Alistair, or code name Birdman, didn't care. He liked them all very much, especially Piemaker, which was the code name for Hanna Pennrie. He loved talking to her, as her good heart and gentle ways were infectious, and he felt the hand of God every time they communicated. Today, Alistair had a special task for Piemaker, and he was a little unsure how to proceed. He received a message from the Russian. It wasn't until after the war that M-Zed 12, which was the code for Firth's outfit, learned that what they suspected about the Russian was true. The Russian contingent had always said their contact was a singular person, but during the Cold War it was revealed that the Russian was actually a whole conclave of psychics. Their facility was outside Moscow in one of the former czar's smaller summerhouses and employed anywhere from 100 to 150 people. Alistair Firth and his fellows at M-Zed 12 suspected as much, but no one was sure. Piemaker told him that she had seen the Russians' compound, and they were many. So Alistair went by that information, even though the official party line was a single person. He was puzzled as to the nature of the request, and kicked it upstairs to both the British and the Americans. The Russian had asked Piemaker specifically about a singular target. This was not protocol, as the assets were to be determined by the handler, and though he knew the Russian knew the code names of all assets, he had never asked for a specific one before. The message read like this: "Piemaker to 8-ball Target: orange blue alice XZW3929640102." Most of the codes had been standardized by American Naval intelligence and so had their colloquialisms to them. All the assets had the same map and picture books, and the codes were changed weekly by the FARM, which was the American facility in Maryland, and were approved for joint use for all assets by M-Zed 12. The target was a broad area in the southern Caucus region, but what was strange was the 8-ball.

To 8-ball a target was to have multiple assets simultaneously search a target for unknown information, usually with little or no guidance as to what they should be looking for. What was curious to Alistair was why he only wanted Piemaker in on the 8-ball. So he sent a coded confirmation message back, asking if the Russian was sure he wanted only Piemaker in on the 8-ball. The Russian confirmed and sent an even more curious reply, saying only Piemaker would be shown. Alistair had learned quickly that this was not in any way a routine intelligence assignment, and the most prudent course of action was to follow the information wherever it led. So he drafted his message that was skipped to Greenland, then to Fort Lee New Jersey, then to the Pentagon, then to Fort Knox Kentucky, then to Chief Ricardo up in the draw somewhere in Louis County. Lieutenant Angelo decoded the message and pulled the correct map atlas from the safe in the comm trailer. He did not fail to notice the urgent tag on the coded message and decided to approach Hanna before supper. Hanna looked at the proper map book and started to put her cards down on the same lapboard that Jonah had made her all those years before. What she saw was strange and did not make any sense to her. She asked if Lieutenant Angelo would move all the men as far away as possible, and asked them to only think about positive things while she talked to her Angel.

Hanna's Angel explained to her about the power vortex that was beginning to form above Mount Elbrus and showed her the readiness of Captain Eckart's team. Hanna was informed that the German Gypsy must not be allowed to link up with the power vortex, and that this is why Hanna had been given the cards in the first place. This was the special job God had wanted her to do all those years ago.

By the time the information was passed back up from the draw to both American and British intelligence, there were only four days left on Piemaker's timeline to secure the mountain peak. It was obvious that it would have to be a Soviet mission, as there was no time to involve or train any other Allied personnel. When Birdman sent the information to the Russian, he received another curious reply. The Russian's message was: "Have team trained and ready to insert, thank Piemaker."

When the Russian commandos saw the German team land on the flat spot 2,000 feet below the summit, they had already been on the mountain two days, and the vortex had already started to form. Commander Uri Storkaph had orders to not take any prisoners. The atmosphere above the peak was electric, with a strange, rarefied air that made the men of his Black Sea Marines very jumpy. On the second day, he started to get reports from the men of apparitions, and some of the men were afraid to sleep because of the dreams they were having. These were battle-hardened Black Sea Marines, not prone to fear and flights of fancy. He had been told to expect the unexpected and most of Piemaker's data. "Never mind all that," he thought, it was time to execute their OP plan. He moved his men down off the peak to an area just above the saddle between the peak and a false peak. This is the spot he had picked to execute his battle plan. The men of his commando detachment had set up their fields of fire out from their camouflaged hides. Commander Storkaph hoped it would be a simple exercise in aggressive fire and not a pitched battle. He had enough experience not to believe that was how it would turn out, but it never hurt to hope.

The Germans were already past the first rock that the Russian commander had picked as the kill fire zone when the Gypsy stopped. The Gypsy faced east and sat down just as the Russians opened fire. Storkaph had never seen anything like it. It was almost as if the Germans were being prevented from returning fire. They just stood there like lambs at the slaughter, all except the old man, who put his hands up not in surrender, but in a reaching motion up to the eastern sky. From his hidden position Storkaph called for cease-fire, and it was all over in less than one minute. The Gypsy slumped forward just as they heard the sound and looked back up the mountain to see a brownish-red tornado-like cloud forming above the peak. His coded end-of-action message was intercepted by a special American B-25 Mitchell flying over Russian airspace that was trying to get a lock on the operation on Mount Elbrus. The Russian commander made the slight mistake of relaying in his message that the power vortex was forming, and this information was picked up by the radioman aboard the Mitchell.

The race to understand this strange energy source was on. The effects of these energy sources was totally unpredictable, as the men of the *USS Dediles* would one day find out.

Seaman Tulane was on his second rotation of bow watch, and he had two more to go before he could go back to his rack and get some much-needed rest. He was pulling double duty because his buddy Seaman Apprentice Crantz had the flu pretty bad. Even though Tulane was tired, it was a good night to be on deck. The sky was a deep, dark cobalt blue-black, and the sea was smooth and rolling as the *USS Dediles* rocked gently back and forth on the Sargasso Sea, heading on its compass bearing, unaware of what mayhem lay just ahead. Ensign Clemens was the officer of the day, the OOD on the bridge, and had just spoken to Seaman Tulane on his quarter-hour check over the sound-powered phone station located on the bow of the Naval research vessel near Tulane's duty station. Back on the bridge of the *Dediles,* Boatswain's Mate Third Class Willard was steering the ship's large stainless-steel wheel with the ornamental Turk's head knot standing straight up on the wheel, signifying that the rudder was amidships, as the sea was so slight that there was hardly any pressure on the steering system. Radarman Second Class Malmande had the light cover off his machine and the light intensity turned way down, because the visibility on this night was so great. Besides the faint red light from the compass binnacle, the engine room repeater gauges, and the roving scan of the radar, there were no other lights on the bridge. The waxing moon was bathing the ship in a ghostly silver sheen as it rolled its way across the seaweed-mottled deep. It was 01:45 local time when Malmande first noticed the anomaly. He was not constantly watching his screen, as regs dictated; under these conditions he could make five-minute interval checks. At the 01:45 sweep check, Malmande detected what he first believed was a ghost in the upper-right quadrant of his round radar screen. He watched the sweep go around again to try to determine if he had detected a new target 28 miles off the starboard bow, or just some abstract electronic echo bouncing off of a slight atmospheric disturbance. He had been getting strange echoes, or ghosts, all watch long; this was nothing new. It was the highly trained radarman's job to differentiate the information on his scope and plot out any possibilities of intersections with the contacts. He hesitated to tell the OOD after the third sweep because the target was showing the classic sign of being a non-relevant blip. After the fifth revolution of the sweep on his screen, he turned to his OOD to report a possible contact.

"Mr. Clemens, I've got a possible contact bearing 167 degrees true, range 28 miles out. Nothing hard, sir, just a feeling."

Ensign Clemens quickly noted the time and information in the ship's log of the radarman's words before he went to look at the screen for himself. He had already learned an old sailor's axiom well: Cover your ass while you can, as time moves very quickly when things start to change. There was something in the tone of the radarman's call to attention that affected the young ensign in an almost subconscious manner and caused him to make his cautious log entry. Boatswain's Mate Willard watched as the young officer made his entry and moved over to the radarman's shoulder. He saw both of their faces illumined by the sweeping red glow of the radar screen. As Willard looked at their shadowed blank faces staring intently into the screen, he felt a rumbling inside himself, a slight stirring that caused him to automatically check his compass heading. Simultaneously, the ripple of consciousness was felt by Seaman Tulane on the bow. He picked up his 7x50-power binoculars from the strap around his neck and instinctively scanned the horizon the way he had been taught to make best use of his night vision. He scanned in a circular motion around the field of vision, utilizing the rods and cones of his eyes, which would reveal the shape of something in a low-light condition. Although Tulane detected nothing visually, a feeling crept into him that caused him to reflexively turn around as if he had felt someone starting to walk up behind him. All he saw was the faint glow of the red and green running lights framing the darkened windows of the deck-gray bridge, located just abaft amidships behind the derrick and cargo hatches.

Every sailor knows the feeling of something unseen and intangible starting in just this way. A slight raising of the hair on an arm or the back of the neck. A quickening that most often turns into nothing—or at least the mayhem passes by and all one is left with is a feeling down in the deep level of the stomach that somehow something primal and terrifying was averted. This was not one of those nights; the thing that the crew of the *USS Dediles* was destined to face would not be averted. All aboard knew it in one form or another. Chief Engineer McHenery, sleeping in his rack four decks below, turned fitfully in his sleep as the knowing of the subconscious irritant aboard ship entered his dreams.

Clemens went to the chart table, snapped on the red chart light, and extended his dead-reckoning plot to his current position. A faint pencil line on the periphery of his chart designated the outside edge of a cordoned-off area. The feeling that crept upon him caused him to hesitate for just a second longer than he would have normally as he considered the historic ramifications of the *Dediles'* current position within the Bermuda Triangle.

"Sir, I have a hard target range 27.5 miles bearing 167 true," Radarman Malmande reported with certainty. "And, sir, it seems to be a landmass."

"What did you say, Bugs?" the ensign replied in the familiar as he moved to look again over the radarman's shoulder.

"I said, sir, it appears to be a landmass."

"That's impossible," the ensign almost whispered. "There is nothing in between us and the Bahamas except a hundred miles of ocean." As the junior officer softly spoke his last words, he saw the sweep of the radar clearly show a hard line of radar echoes bouncing back to the crew of the *Dediles*. A line of echoes that had formed itself into what was an unmistakable coastline. Willard had alerted another seaman, who was standing by in the ready room over sound-powered phones to report to the bridge. When the OOD looked up and saw the seaman on the bridge, he immediately ordered him to go wake the skipper and escort him to the bridge as he simultaneously put in a call to the sleeping captain.

Malmande switched the radar to a 50-mile scan radius and waited to get a clear signal. What the now-larger area scan revealed shocked both men. There was indeed a circular line across a large portion of the screen, revealing a landmass giving the characteristics of an island 10 miles in diameter.

Captain Louis P. Crane was no stranger to sleepless nights aboard a ship. In the Leyte Gulf during WWII, he was under fire from Japanese warplanes for more than 120 hours as he kept running interference for a resupply effort in his wooden-hull minesweeper. The thought did cross his mind that the young ensign probably didn't need to wake the captain of the *Dediles* for a radar anomaly 27 miles away. He was also seasoned enough to know that if the young officer felt like he needed help, that was enough to justify the captain's presence on the bridge. A man can get into trouble taking on too much responsibility, just assuredly as taking on too little. Besides, he was a maverick officer who didn't go to the academy, and believed that an officer's real training didn't start until he got under way on his first-duty ship, not some academy training vessel. As they ascended the last ladder to the bridge, he thought to himself, "It's lesson time. School is in session."

Crane did not hesitate to give his first commands instantly after viewing the radar screen and hoped the lesson was not lost on the young Ensign Clemens. The captain called for all hands and sent a seaman to retrieve the two science officers temporarily assigned to the *Dediles* and bring them immediately to the bridge.

Commander Taylor and Commander Ascot were up and out of their racks and dressed in less than four minutes. Both men knew already what might be going on. They had discussed the possibility due to timing, atmospheric conditions, and intelligence data that indicated the target they were looking for might start to form within the next 48 hours. They had made sure all their instruments and sensors arrayed in the science package they had brought aboard the *Dediles* were functioning properly before turning in for the night. Although they were under the strictest secrecy about their mission, the accelerated activity around their equipment was not lost on the sailors aboard the *USS Dediles*. The men knew something was up, and they also knew their lives may depend on knowing what was happening and when. The crew of the *Dediles* had been monitoring the two science officers ever since they came on board for this tour. There was something very un-Navy about them. The casualness and superiority with which they conversed with Captain Crane was unwarranted, even for scientists. It was not the first time the men had seen different governmental agency representatives pretending to be Navy, but rarely with this much secrecy and equipment. There were sensors arrayed every two feet around the lifeline stanchions surrounding the perimeter of the main deck. It took two weeks of work with the ship moored in the Norfolk Navy Yard for the science team to wire in all the equipment. The scuttlebutt was that it was for a missile test, but no one was sure. The only thing they were sure of was that security for the tour was the tightest they had ever seen.

As soon as both Central Intelligence Agency specialists got to the bridge and saw the radar output, Commander Taylor went to make sure all sensors were online, while Commander Ascot asked Captain Crane for a private meeting in the pilot's berth right off the bridge. The *Dediles* was a beehive of activity as all hands fulfilled their obligations and reported to their pre-assigned duty stations for the general quarters alarm. Seaman Apprentice Crantz stopped to throw up in the head as he put on his life jacket, and then reported to his duty station on the 01 deck next to the No. 2 ready boat davits. Engineering Chief McHenrey was first of the engineering staff to get to the main power controls in the engine room, except for the engineering watch stander who was already there. Lieutenant Commander Barnes, the XO, told Radioman Second Class Pickrel to send a pre-coded urgent message to Naval headquarters in Washington after conferring with Commander Ascot and Captain Crane. The unidentified target was now 19 miles out, and the *Dediles* was closing at flank speed.

A message was flashed back to Radioman Pickrel from Washington, coded for Commanders Ascot and Taylor's EYES ONLY. Seaman Fountaine, who had delivered the message, was ordered to stand by on the bridge by Captain Crane as the message was read by Commander Taylor and then passed to Commander Ascot. Chief Warrant Officer Williams relieved Petty Officer Willard on the helm. Willard retrieved two .45-caliber sidearms for himself and Fountaine to escort the message back to the radio room and make sure it was destroyed immediately after Taylor and Ascot were through with it.

Radarman Malmande looked up to Ensign Clemens, who was still technically OOD, and reported a strange piece of data.

"Sir, target still bearing 167 degrees, true range 18.5 miles and closing, but, sir, target seems to be increasing in size."

Everyone on the bridge who could gathered around Radarman Second Class Danny "Bugs" Malmande's Raytheon radar repeater screen to see that the strange environmental anomaly that the Naval research ship *USS Dediles* was steaming toward as fast as her engines would propel her had, in fact, grown to more than 14 miles in diameter.

On deck, Chief Boatswain's Mate Silver was overseeing a deck gang preparing two Mark 5 Mod 1 Night-Sun carbon arc lights for both port and starboard of the bow anchor station. Taylor and Ascot had gone out on deck next to the control panel of their science array. The coded message they received had told them that two Navy NC-121K Super Constellations from the secret Project Magnet had been scrambled to rendezvous with the *Dediles* at the anomaly. They were tuning the coded instrument repeaters to calibrated frequencies that would match the data-gathering gear on the aircraft.

At 02:52, Naval Captain Louis P. Crane ordered Chief Warrant Officer Williams to signal Chief McHenrey in engineering to reduce speed to one third, as the anomaly now lay inside the two-mile range marker on Bugs' repeater.

Seaman Tulane was doing his best to shield his eyes from the deck work lights and keep his eyes in his binoculars as he strained to see the target. There was a slight fluctuation in his field of view, and he held his breath to steady the binoculars. He saw it again, a slight movement or imbalance in the atmosphere. He hesitated one more moment before he spoke over his sound-powered phones.

"Bow to Bridge. Over."

"This is Bridge, Bow watch, go ahead. Over."

"Bow to Bridge, I believe I have target sighted, dead-ahead, range-close, but unknown. Over."

"Bridge to Bow, report. Over."

"Bow to Bridge, it seems to be a big, dark, slow-moving tornado. Over."

The *Dediles* had slowed to a crawl as both her Night Sun spotlights snapped on, illuminating a large, cloudlike wall of moving substance that was hovering about one foot off the ocean and seemed to reach straight up into the sky.

The instruments aboard the Connies that were both 75 miles away at 12,000 feet clearly saw the ship, but nothing aboard either plane registered anything about the vortex. The vortex was apparently a local event.

Seaman Apprentice Crantz started to feel sick again and was going to ask the boatswain's mate in charge of detail to be relieved. As he turned his head, he saw all the men of Davit Station No. 2 spontaneously vomit. A convulsive retch went throughout the crew. Captain Crane ordered Medical Corpsman First Class Oxley on deck to see what was happening.

The Constellations were cruising by at 209 knots, 12,000 feet off the deck, and their instruments registered nothing except the familiar signature of the *Dediles*.

Captain Crane ordered the *Dediles* to all-stop, and as she lay dead in the water less than 100 yards from the vortex, the retching of the crew seemed to subside. The National Security Agency's science packages being monitored by the CIA techs were registering nothing. By protocol, Crane ordered the ship ahead slow and closed with the vortex.

Seaman Tulane on the bow was the first to be hit by the energy spike as the bow of the *Dediles* penetrated the cloud. Commanders Ascot and Taylor's instruments jumped once as the energy spike was recorded, then all power and navigational abilities aboard the *USS Dediles* stopped. The ship drifted noiselessly into a rent in the space-time continuum within the Bermuda Triangle.

The Navy Constellations, now flying a circular pattern above the last-known position of the *Dediles*, registered the ship's loss of power just before it vanished off their instruments.

Engineering Chief McHenrey was trying to remain calm as he talked to Captain Crane over the sound-powered phones. All light and power was off in the engine room, and the engineers were in complete darkness 17 feet below the surface of the ocean. Even the battery-powered emergency lanterns didn't work. McHenrey was telling Crane he was going to get off the phones and try to fire up one of the generators when the second spike hit.

It was the last thing Engineer Mumford remembered hearing aboard the *Dediles*.

CHAPTER 5

I could tell as I drove out of the Federal Building's parking lot that on a surface level, the meeting had been a resounding failure. You know when the meeting continues after you are thanked for your presentation that your information has been duly noted and that the decision-making process has been wrenched cleanly out of your hands. At least they asked the other two psychics to leave also. I knew that they were there to monitor me and would be asked later for a report on my sanity. About halfway through my bizarre presentation, it dawned on me that I would be on my own on this one. Maybe it was the breakup with Kat and all that pain. Maybe it was hitting the big 4-0. Maybe it was just because I was tired, but I didn't really care. Somehow I felt like all I had to do was play my part and things would work out the way they were supposed to. I mean, I was sure that it was going to be really crazy, weird, and violent, but somehow it was OK. What else could it be? This thing was going down hard, and there was nothing anybody on this Earth plane could do to stop it. The FBI had its own notions of what to do, and even though they think I'm the crazy one, their plans have nothing to do with the reality of how things are.

I had unlocked my glove box and made sure my .45 was still there and loaded. I was going to go find Kat, and I knew something was wrong. I had not let myself tune in with her for a long time now for two reasons. The first was that it just hurt too much, and it was kind of like an illegal wiretap anyway. The second reason was much too terrifying to me, even now, to contemplate: I was pretty sure the Kat I knew was gone. Sometimes when we embrace the darkness for too long, a gap is created within the body. When you try to find a way out of your body, you basically open yourself up to use by others. You let the monkey boys into the playground, and if you haven't left enough bread crumbs on the trail into the dark forest to find your way back, you kind of give up the right to sole ownership of your body, and some of the squatters are kind of mean. At least they are to us. To them it's just a day in the park, and they want to see as much and do as much as they can before the park police come and shut the gates. When people talk about their mental recovery from addiction, there is an incredible sadness that comes bubbling out. It's usually from guilt of having let the devil have his day when we ultimately know better. I'm not saying it's easy; I'm not saying it's right either. Kat gave up control too many times, and when you do that, you kind of pop up an astral flare out into the cosmos saying, "Come on in and play." If people knew the kind of crazed entities that want to just have one more drink, feel one more needle in their arm, want to have one more boyfriend beat the living shit out of them, feel one more perp make them their bitch in the joint just for fun, they would rather die. You see, to these things, it's all just good fun. It's like going to the movies. It's not their body, it's not their pain, it's not their loneliness, it's not their broken family, it's not their ruined life. To them, in their reality, they are just hitting the play and pause buttons on an astral video game. It just happens that you are the puppet.

(INDIA • •) "Don't assume the barn door is shut because you hope it is. If you think it's open, and you think you hear rustlers, get up quickly, get dressed for the cold, and make sure the rifle is loaded." "The price of safety is eternal vigilance." "Do a mediation for protection, make the sign of the cross, pentagram, or eye of Horus." " Leave the bar, put your pants back on, don't buy the dope." "You're in charge until you give up the right, and then you're just another asshole at baggage claim." "All realms, blah, blah, blah ..."

I drove until it felt right and found myself in the old artist district near 4th and Alameda. I cruised near Al's Bar and didn't see a sign. Al's was famous more for the fact that it didn't have a sign than anything else. I was a little confused; I knew I was right on top of her, so I drove down an alley to get clear and get my bearings. I started to breathe and immediately realized that the images I had seen were not from this time. They were from another time, another place in history. A time when the entity that was possessing Kat was alive and living in the hotel atop the establishment that is now the dive known as Al's.

As I made sure my Colt was loaded and stuffed my hammerless .38 in the top of my boot, I heard a voice say, "JUST LEAVE NOW." If I pretend I don't hear it, then I run the risk of not getting any more data for a while. If I ignore the warning, then I know I'm on my own. I thanked the universe for the tip, stuffed another magazine in my flight jacket, and went in the door of the Tenement Hotel.

Climbing the stairs, time started to shift again and a fear tried to swim into the mix. Why was I so wound up? This is the woman I was supposed to love. I can tell Mumford is nowhere around, and yet it feels like... My hands started to sweat, and I felt hot then cold inside my jacket. Right there on the landing to the third floor, I started to breathe; right there with my adrenaline pumping and enough ammo to take out a squad of riflemen, I started to center and find the light. I had given Mumford an opening without even realizing it. I had left the back gate open. I had let my despair and fear expand enough to leave a gap where hate started to grow. Where there once was love, there was now pain and anger, and it was consuming me. I was on a slippery slope and knew I had to do something fast. I asked for protection and brought down the light. I was screwed up and I knew I needed help. I pulled a small L-rod out of my pocket, a dowsing device that can find water and hopefully people, and asked it to point the way. As I was passing a doorway that was slightly ajar, the rod veered suddenly to my left and centered on what I then knew to be Kat's lair.

I listened, and at first heard nothing. Then I distinctively heard people rummaging around empty bottles looking for something. I heard a man's voice mumble something as if he were very exasperated, then raise his voice and tell someone else to shut up. Then, as if from the grave, I heard my Kat in a very angry voice tell him to fuck off.

My heart jumped up into my throat, and I entered the room. It was like stepping into my worst nightmare. I had stepped into a fully equipped professional domination dungeon. The walls were lined in tufted black vinyl with red velvet curtains over the windows. There was what looked like a metal morgue table, including blood groove, with several ominous medical devices neatly laid out waiting for direction. Several complicated restraint systems were linked to a line of carefully chrome-plated eyebolts securely imbedded into an exposed-brick wall. Kat and the man she was looking for her dope with were both dressed in leather fetish clothing, trying to get stoned before their next appointment. An incredible nausea ran through me, and I started to get a metallic taste in my mouth. I took a deep breath and could smell the sex and the old dope works next to the Bunsen burner on the table they were rummaging around on. I had to clear my throat, and that is when they looked up. A bizarre smile crossed Kat's face as she let her jet-black hair obscure her face while turning quickly away. The man started to get up and was reaching for something when Kat started speaking.

"Johnny, sit the fuck down, he's already figured out 17 ways to snap your neck." She turned back to me, and any trace of emotion that the smile might have represented was gone. She just stared at me with empty eyes that looked like two piss holes in the snow. This was not my Kat. It was the zombie that was now inhabiting her body.

"What do you want, you pathetic shit," she said dryly. "Here to book an appointment with us?"

When the thought crossed my mind to pull out my Colt and put both of these fucks out of their misery, it occurred to me that is exactly what the entity in possession of Kat wanted me to do. They were not my thoughts, and when I realized this, I had a certain detachment that somehow allowed me to deal with this shitstorm I had stepped into.

"I need to tell you something, Kat. It's important, and you're in danger." Johnny Two Bags was again reaching for something under the table, and if Kat had learned anything at all from me, the thing he was reaching for was some kind of gun carefully affixed to the bottom of the table. Kat spoke first.

"What the fuck do you think you're doing, shithead? I told you not to move. Bobby will cut your fucking balls off before you can take your next breath. Just do what the fuck I tell you." She reached under the table and pulled out a Glock 9mm, and put it butt-end first on a counter near her. She never pointed the piece at me, but it was clear the gun was now in play. She is a very smart woman, and the ease with which she now had an exposed gun within her reach was very disquieting.

"OK, big, bad, spooky Bobby Doucette, you tell me what the fuck you think gives you the right to come to hell town—and make it fast, because I want to get high, and I've got a client coming."

Her eyes still had that lifeless look. There was nothing pleading, no sign of weakness, no warmth. Just business. She wanted me to say my piece and leave, and that is exactly what I wanted to do.

"Kat, Jack Mumford escaped from Florida, and I'm pretty sure he is heading here."

"Who?" asked Johnny.

"Shut the fuck up, Johnny. Don't say a goddamn word, you hear me? This is out of your league. Just sit there and shut up until he leaves."

Kat turned back to me and her eyes started to burn.

"You fucking prick, you fucking screwball psychic-wannabe prick. How dare you come here and lay some shit on me like this? That is your fucked-up world, and it doesn't have shit to do with me. And you're a complete asshole for showing up here at all. You're crazy, you know that? That's the only fucking thing wrong here is that you're a goddamn madman. Your stupid little fucked-up world and your pathetic little heart. The only trouble I'm in, the only trouble I have ever been in, has been you stepping into my life. You're just one of those pathetic New Age pricks that owns a gun and can't separate it from his dick. You're a piece of shit, Bobby, just like all these pricks I spank all day and get their nut off in some alley after they leave here. Just some other dude going through some midlife crisis, thinking he can talk to ghosts because he knows he's going to die soon, and can't believe how much he fucked up his life. So you pretend you're some kind of shaman motherfucker. You just like putting pieces from different puzzle boxes together and try to make them fit. There is no boogeyman. There is just a bunch of you stupid people believing in fucking angels and devils and shit like that. You make all this shit up because you just can't believe that the universe is empty. Then you all get together and feel warm and cuddly and hope the fucking aliens come and get you before you rot in some nursing home shitting in a bag every half-hour."

It was too much to hear right then. My attention wavered and I got defensive.

"It doesn't matter what you think, Kat. Mumford is inbound, and you're in danger," I said with a slight pleading tone in my voice.

I had turned toward her as she was talking, and she had strutted a little bit from the table. As my eyes tracked her, Johnny had gotten up, sensing my inattention, and reached for something. From a very primitive part of my mind something screamed out, "GUN!" Reflexively, I ripped up my jacket and pulled my Colt out as I ran toward Johnny, who was trying to swing a shotgun up to meet my oncoming body. My right foot stomped his knee backward at the same time the butt of my father's steel-frame WWII Colt slashed the side of his head as I pistol-whipped him to the ground. He screamed in pain, and again in my mind I heard, "GUN!" I hesitated for a moment instead of looking for another threat; my mind tried to reason with itself that the only threat had been neutralized. I waited one second too long and spun around, aiming my weapon at Kat, who had targeted me with the Glock. We both stood there with our weapons trained on each other as Johnny whimpered pathetically from his injuries. My mind could not fathom the madness I had created by coming here and giving in to the violence. My finger started to squeeze the trigger, and as

I did, the strange smile came back to Kat's face. Time compressed and stood still. This was one of those moments that change the world somehow. No good guys, no bad guys, just a choice of turning toward the light or turning toward the dark side. The smile left her face, and I saw her trigger finger tense.

I dropped my weapon to my side and just stood there, wanting to die. Johnny started to move, and I slowly moved back and kicked the shotgun away from him. I was ashamed and incredibly lonely, and when I looked back to Kat's face, the smile was still there. She was kind of cooing, but the tone was very deep, almost like a man's voice. She started to speak, and as she did her voice started out in a very low octave and raised to her normal pitch, as if someone or something else was speaking through her.

"Time to leave, little boy, or Mommy will have to spank you." I hated her and loved her at the same instant.

"Kat, Mumford is for real." I pleaded, but she just lightly laughed with that same tone that was both hers and someone else's. I walked out of the apartment with her gun tracking me the whole time. I glanced up and our eyes met for an instant. Something flashed through them that looked like the saddest thing I had ever seen. I spoke one last time.

"If you need me, call." She motioned with the Glock for me to leave. As I walked down the hall, a couple of locals monitored my exit and quickly shuffled back in their apartments as I glared at them. I realized I still had my weapon in my hand and stuffed it back into my pants. I heard Kat yell at Johnny Two Bags, calling him a moron. I descended the stairs as fast as I could and ran back to my truck. I had been reduced and needed to get healed. The world was just too big and scary right now.

I drove as fast as I could to my warehouse in Venice. I was a mess and just wanted to hide. The only woman I really loved hated me, and no matter what I thought was going on in her head, I was going to sleep alone again.

(JULIETT ● - - -) "You are going to make mistakes. It's part of the learning curve. Hopefully you'll survive them, and when you do, you must have methods to heal yourself as quickly as possible, as you will not have much time to regroup."

"The battle arcane is fast and furious, and the hits you receive are more like the four barrels of a quad .50 caliber antiaircraft gun than a single-shot musket. Expect the pressure to remain once it starts."

I stopped by The Bookmark Cafe near Main Street and logged on anonymously to the Internet from one of the pay-as-you-go Web portals. In my cover e-mail account that I only use from public Internet portals, I wrote John Red Truck a message telling him I needed a favor and I was coming to do a sweat lodge with him at his sanctuary on Navajo tribal land in northwestern New Mexico. I said I had really stepped in it this time, and my mind was a little squishy right now. I marked it with our code for deadly urgent. Leaving the café, I felt a sensation that I do not feel very often. It's kind of like an internal clock giving you a countdown warning. It is not a good feeling, and I knew it meant that things were ramping up. I wondered if I should leave right now or stay and try to protect Kat. Then another image floated up, and I realized that Kat didn't have long, and it probably had nothing to do with Mumford. I caught my breath and started to get dizzy. Some skate punks looked at me as though I were a clown and started to laugh. I was just standing there kind of vibrating, and I forgot I was in public. I met their gaze, and I'm not sure what I transmitted, but they just kind of wandered off down the street. I went back into The Bookmark and from another e-mail account sent

Lt. Thomas Quinn Kat's address and told him I was heading out of town for a while. Kat and her problems belonged under the jurisdiction of the LAPD now.

By the time I got back to my building in Venice, it was early evening and rush hour was starting to wind down. The wind was out of the west and a damp chill was in air as the marine layer settled down for a prolonged stay on the coast. I opened the gate to my warehouse and pulled the truck inside next to the 27-foot Airstream trailer I lived in and started to get ready for my trip to the desert. I wanted to be on the road in less than 30 minutes.

Inside my warehouse was an open kitchen and a bathroom with several concrete storage rooms with massive steel doors on them. My Airstream had the nylon awning pulled out with a combination of small tiki and trout-fish Christmas lights hanging around it, blinking and awaiting my arrival. I had low benches on some old Oriental carpets, full of futons and pillows. The whole area that the trailer was sitting on was covered by a large lawn-like piece of green Astroturf. There was a vintage '60s TV with bunny ears that was turned on, doing nothing more than lighting the area with a static pattern. I had a fairly good-size hot tub sitting in back near my workbench, with a panel in the roof over it that would slide back on pulleys and expose the sky. I never worried about leaving the power on. At one time I did a favor for a friend of mine, and he repaid me by installing aerospace-quality photoelectric panels on the roof. Between that and the small wind generator I had on the roof, I was off the grid. One of the vaults contained a room full of huge industrial batteries that I got at an auction from an old hospital that went tits up after Congress cut their funding. I turned on some of the industrial lighting that hung down from the roof and bathed everything in a blue magnesium light. Going to one door, I place my thumb on the small panel that was the only thing to be seen on the

er scanned my thumb-

y skin. The unit decided

oor gently clicked open.

g-out bags neatly marked

n some industrial shelving

gs. I grabbed the appropri-

ded it onto a wheeled cart,

vent back through the door,

some more firearms, ammo,

extra pistols, and ammo in a

nd the appropriate mounting

hardwa.. ounted it to the bottom of the

truck. The false bottom is icky to get on. I made it myself, and I'm not the best metal fabricator, but it doesn't look like a gun vault and that's all I need. Taking a quick look around, I decided this was the time to rig the big stuff.

I sent Lt. Quinn another e-mail from one of my home computers and told him I was making my place Mumford-proof and not to let his boys come in here without the plan on how to disarm it. That information would come to him in the mail. I wrote to him that I was sending it to a friend in Brooklyn, New York, and if my friend didn't hear from me, he would mail it to Thomas. I didn't want to let Thomas know what I had if it wasn't necessary. I thought about the repercussions if an innocent person came in here, then realized that if they were in here they weren't innocent, so I decided to rig my place to blow if Mumford made it this far. The claymore mines were already mounted and wired in kill patterns in the roof girders. I took a ladder and armed all the mines and set all the triggers except for the main door. I was getting kind of a rush working and knowing that I had armed mines ready to rip my flesh apart hovering above me. "Easy action," I thought to myself. "Don't get trigger-happy just yet; there are many miles to go before it's O.K. Corral time." I sat down on one of the futons and centered myself. I went to my safe place and started to perform an old protection mediation to camouflage the mines from detection.

The Catholic Church had specialists who would go out to all the old missions in early California and do the same thing. Each mission had its own gold, and as one might imagine, there was really no way to protect it, as these places were in deep wilderness back then. A priest who was a specialist in thought forms would place the gold in an underground hiding place and then work his mojo. The Native Americans, and even some bandits, would be able to dowse the gold reserves, so the priest would put out decoy thought forms that would basically say, "Dig Here." Then he would put a cloak of obscurity on the real gold, and he and the abbot would be the only ones who would know. Most times when psychic treasure hunters come up blank, it's not because there is no treasure; it's because they are finding the decoy treasure thought form. Most people, after they have dug enough holes, just get fed up and go away. So I cloaked my mines with invisibility thought forms and said a prayer that no one innocent would be harmed. I knew I was taking on a little bit of baggage in the way of Karma with this one. But hey, the buck stops here. I felt good about the level of clarity I was having and asked for protection for the trip. I set the last trip for the mines and closed the warehouse door. My rush started to fade as I was getting close to some serious highway time. I pulled out and headed for Lincoln Boulevard. I gassed up the truck, got some munchies for the trip, and dropped the disarming schematic to my friend in Brooklyn in a mailbox. Heading down the boulevard, a wave of sadness washed over me as I thought about how much Kat used to like our trips to the desert. I pulled onto U.S. Route 10 and headed east toward the Navajo Nation.

CHAPTER 6

Coyote had not seen Crow in seven suns, and he wanted to talk. Rabbit was hard to find right now, and he wanted Crow's help. He was getting hungry and was tired of eating Mouse. Mouse was hard to catch, and Coyote needed so many every day to survive. He had been hungry ever since Crow left, and he wanted it to stop. Coyote had talked to some of his others earlier that day, and some last night, and they seemed to be finding Rabbit well enough. They told him to talk to his Crow. So he sent out a dream story to Crow and told him he was hungry and could he please show up. Crow sent a dream story back that he was helping a Ghost Brother, so Coyote would just have to wait. Coyote sent another dream story to Crow and asked if Ghost Brother could help find Rabbit, but he had heard nothing. He knew it was not Ghost Brother's job to find Rabbit, but he was hungry.

It was early morning, just before sunrise, and it was cold. Coyote was skirting the top of a small mesa trying to find Rabbit when he received a dream story from Crow. He knew Crow would be here soon, and he got excited thinking about eating Rabbit. From out of the corner of his eye, Coyote saw a small discoloration in the low light of predawn and started to run as fast as he could toward it. Rodent decided to stay put instead of trying to make for his hole, and it was the last thing he thought of on this Earth plane. Coyote was on him and killed him instantly as his canine teeth tore the throat out of Rodent. Rodent's soul was instantly taken by a Ghost Brother to the new place and was told what the Great Spirit wanted him to do next. Back on the mesa, Coyote hesitated and thanked Great Spirit before he started to eat Rodent's body. Just then Coyote heard Crow. He didn't stop eating to call, as he was too hungry, so Crow would just have to look with his quiet eye to find where he was. He heard Crow call and looked up, seeing him circling above the mesa. He'll be here soon, thought Coyote, and he started to get warm. Rodent tasted good, and Coyote wondered if Crow would want some. He didn't have long to wait as Crow landed close to him and was laughing.

"Look at you," laughed Crow. "You're all skinny and look like Ghost Brother wants you to come home." That made Coyote mad, and he stopped eating to tell Crow what he thought.

"Ghost Brother doesn't want me yet, and if you would do your job and help me find Rabbit, I wouldn't look like this." Crow just laughed, and Coyote went back to eating Rodent. Before the next bite, Coyote asked Crow if he was hungry, and Crow just kept laughing. So Coyote just kept eating. He knew that Crow had filled himself with Lizard and Bug when he started acting like this. Coyote was almost through and he started to feel better, so he turned his attention back to Crow and asked him what Ghost Brother wanted.

"I told you three moons ago what this was about," said Crow. "But you never listen, do you?"

"I listen good," replied Coyote. "You just think too much after you see Ghost Brother and forget about Rabbit."

"I don't forget about Rabbit. I never forget about Rabbit, but you don't listen. Do you know what Ghost Brother told me about you and Rabbit?" Coyote just kept eating but looked up. "He told me that you ate Rabbit too much, and you knew about it in before time. Is that true, Coyote? Did you know about eating Rabbit in before time?"

"Sometimes Ghost Brother is not right. I heard you say that once, Crow," Coyote mumbled as he crunched down on a small bone of Rodent's hind leg.

"You did know about eating Rabbit in before time, didn't you, Coyote? Coyote, you can't eat Rabbit when you're not supposed to, or Ghost Brother will have to have council on you." Coyote let out a low growl as he finished eating Rodent's liver. "Don't growl at me, Coyote. I don't need trouble from you. There is enough trouble coming to this desert when the Empty Man comes."

"Who?" asked Coyote. "Who is the Empty Man?"

"See, you don't listen, do you?" squawked Crow. "Empty Man is why Rabbit won't come right now. Empty Man is coming to meet the dark wind, and Ghost Brother doesn't want Rabbit here when he comes."

"What does that have to do with me?" chewed Coyote.

"Coyote, you don't listen. I told you every moon for three moons when I got the stories in dream time," said Crow. "Empty Man is coming now, and Ghost Brother says it's time to make sacred this part of Earth Mother." Coyote just kept chewing, but Crow had his attention now; this was important. He hadn't known Earth Mother wanted sacred time in Coyote's home. The hunger was starting to fade. Coyote hadn't seen sacred time since he was a pup, and he was trying to remember what to do.

Crow spoke again. "Empty Man is coming for the dark wind, and the dark wind is coming to Coyote's mesa. It … means … "

Crow said slowly, as he could tell Coyote did not know what to do. "It means Ghost Brother will walk with Coyote while the Empty Man is here so he can see with Coyote eyes."

"What does he want to see?" asked Coyote, smacking a small bone out of his jaw.

"He wants to see if Medicine Brother can see with heart."

"Why does Ghost Brother want my eyes?" asked Coyote. "Why not your eyes?"

Crow was tired of talking to Coyote already; sometimes he just didn't listen. So he flapped his wings and took off, snagging Coyote's ear with a glancing blow of his talon as he flew over him. Coyote yelped and snapped reflexively as Crow flew by.

"Why, Crow, why hurt Coyote?"

"You don't listen, Coyote, and Ghost Brother won't give you much time."

"Did Ghost Brother say something about Coyote?" Coyote had stopped eating all together and was standing now, watching Crow fly low around the mesa. "Crow, you're supposed to tell me what I need to know … it's your job, Crow. … what did Ghost Brother say? Did he say I can't have more Rabbit?"

"I have to go now and talk to my others, Coyote," Crow squawked. "Crow will come back at sundown to help Coyote Brother."

"Crow, come back, Coyote is hungry," yelped Coyote. Coyote watched as Crow covered the distance in a few minutes that would take him a day. "Crow will come back," thought Coyote. "He will come back at sundown and help find Rabbit." Coyote went down the north side of the mesa that was still in deep shadows and started hunting for Rabbit. After all, Ghost Brother never told him not to eat Rabbit; he only told Crow. Sometimes Crow is not right; sometimes he is wrong. Coyote sniffed the air and smelled Mouse. He descended the mesa to the high Nevada desert floor.

Jack Mumford was getting ice in Las Vegas before he headed north into the high Nevada desert. One of the coolers that he had in the back of the truck wasn't holding up too well in the heat, and he didn't want his cargo to spoil before he could get to where the vortex was going to form. He was going to use the meat he had been putting in the coolers for several days now to help him get strong enough to be able to withstand the energy from the spikes he would receive inside the vortex. The last time he had received a spike, the effect laid him up for almost a year before he could function halfway normally again. He could not afford that now. He had to be able to get the energy he needed from the vortex and be strong enough to get on the road within several hours. The time factor was critical, and he didn't want to take any chances. The fact that a worldwide manhunt for him was in progress gave him the ability to focus clearly on the details of the tasks ahead of him. There was a lot of work to do, and he needed to start purifying himself soon. He had spent a lifetime researching esoteric religions, most thoroughly those from Egypt. He always found it funny when listing to so-called Egyptologists, especially those on TV, how they missed entirely the point of the information they would so eagerly wrench from the ruins. The message was so great from those silent hieroglyphics that their puny little minds just could not handle it. To them, it was all just so much legend and science fiction, but to Jack it was his life. In his early 20s it became harder and harder to relate to others with the knowledge that he was carrying around, so he just stopped trying. When his psychic abilities started to manifest themselves, he spent years honing them in the vast anonymous cities of America. He spent time in Chicago, Los Angeles, New York, Dallas, Miami, and lots of little places in between. The cities always afforded him the opportunity to find dislocated people with no history and no one looking for them to perform his rituals on. He found that he could get away with about a year to two in most places before he would have to alter his pattern. Most people Jack noticed had no idea what was going on three feet from them, let alone in the next apartment. As long as you considered smell, sound, and how to control it, most things were possible.

Jack officially left the Navy two years after the incident aboard the *Dediles*. Most members of the crew were wounded or killed as the ammunition magazines caught fire when an energy spike arced in an electrical junction box. The amount of ammo was small but enough that the ship began to burn. The crew for the most part was incapacitated from the way the energy spikes affected the human nervous system. So the ship burned, and most of the crew was helpless to stop the fires. Mumford managed to crawl out of the engine room and made it to one of the lifeboats. He had the opportunity to save several sailors along the way but chose not to. In the debrief by Naval intelligence, that piece of information was why he was eventually selected for the intelligence community's Pentalpha Program. The crewmen who survived the sinking of the *USS Dediles* were quarantined in a locked-down facility near Langley, Virginia. Most of the crewmen went insane in a matter of weeks. Mumford seemed to have the ability to ride the emotional wave of dealing with this new energy. After several years of still being attached to the Navy, he was the only one left of the crew who was still cognizant enough to think in a relatively sane way. The crew-members had a good deal of experimentation done to them in the name of national security and science, and cover stories were supplied to deal with the aftermath of the ordeal on the minds of the sailors. It wasn't very hard; the vortex and the later testing by Defense Department psychiatrists all added to most of the sailors' loss on the tenuous grip they had on reality. All except Jack. He seemed to thrive in the environment that he found himself in. In the '60s, the United States Government was testing the Phoenix Program in Guatemala, which would later be used as the model for the rural pacification program in the Vietnam War. The idea was pretty simple, taken straight from "The Prince" by Machiavelli. You target the leaders of your opponents underground by killing them, and the rest of the cadre would fold. At the time, some pretty nefarious characters were in charge in Guatemala, and they used the program to target their enemies. A good deal of people were killed who were really just innocent labor organizers, teachers, and religious workers. Jack Mumford, as part of the black op known as Pentalpha, had been sent to Guatemala to see if an asset such as himself could be effectively used to target insurgents. A colonel from the Guatemalan Defense Department who was attached to the psychic spies from America understood Mumford like no one in his life ever had. In Jack, he had found a willing tool that he could corrupt and use very effectively against his enemies. When a prostitute employed by the Guatemalan Colonel Adolfo was sent to find out Jack's particular weakness, she wound up almost dead and badly mutilated. She was a skilled woman and took Jack for a several-week period on a sexual roller coaster. When she started to challenge his performance and ego after exposing him to all manners of sexual perversity, Jack retaliated. This experimentation was done to Jack without his or anyone else's knowledge, and when there were no consequences for his actions, Jack put the pieces together quickly. Colonel Adolfo basically gave Jack the power of a demigod as long as Jack would help him with the agenda that the members of the Guatemalan military had tasked for him. They put him up in a small villa outside Guatemala City and ran interference with the American handlers in the Pentalpha program. Jack's taste in the perverse and the bizarre soon grew as he was allowed to indulge his every fantasy. When he finally understood the level of violence that the Guatemalan Defense Department employed on its own citizens, Jack wanted to experience it firsthand. This, probably more than anything else, led to Jack Mumford's taste for human flesh. He was left alone with the victims of the government's experiments one too many times, and something just snapped. When the officers in charge of the Guatemalan Defense Force Building, where the torture chambers were, came back in and saw the blood dripping from Mumford's mouth, he was taken away and was not heard from again. He had been sanctioned by the U.S. government; he had been turned into a ghost. Jack had entered a twilight world that operates among us that only a privileged few will ever know. It's a world where law and civilization as we know it do not exist—only ideas and concepts on how best to put certain agendas into action. A place devoid of human emotion and humane empathy. It is organized to perpetuate itself and that is all. If you can help, then you are an asset; if you cannot, then you are a liability. The punishment for being a liability is almost beyond the scope of human imagination and understanding. It is a tool of ultimate violence and depravity. It is the embodiment of evil. Jack Mumford had become a tool for darkness and was in the process of becoming something that his handlers could not control. He went on to some rather famous assignments, and if there were a record of his accomplishments that one was able to peruse, it would lead you to believe that he was actually a national asset. However, just a list of assignments would not divulge the missing children, mutilated corpses, and extreme violence he left in his wake. Jack was on the inside, and certain liberties were granted. Teddy Roosevelt once said of a president of El Salvador, "He may be a son of a bitch, but he's our son of a bitch." The same graduated device was used to evaluate Mumford's performance. He was ours, we made him, and we would deploy him.

Eventually Jack realized that he would one day be too much of a liability to the people he worked for, and so developed a strategy to survive. He started to secretly document the missions he was tasked for and collected data on everyone and everything. He was a natural psychic from the time he was young, and when he felt the specter of death hunting him, he played his hand.

After a series of gruesome murders began in Florida, certain members of secret cadres within and outside of the U.S. government started to get very incriminating pieces of information and photographs delivered to them. Mumford was blackmailing for his freedom. He was getting ready to go public and take his chances in prison. It was strongly inferred to his enemies that if he would not be allowed to live, then he had certain mechanisms in place that would leak the information he had to every news organization and governmental oversight committee that existed. His game was hamstrung by a rather tenacious psychic on the FBI payroll named Robert Doucette. When the jig was up for Jack in Florida, he realized it was OK. Prison was a good cover until the time of the next event.

Nothing mattered to him except melding with the power in the vortex. He had tapped the secrets of the universe and learned its ways. Pyramids were just poor copies of the naturally occurring anomalies. The Pi Ray, discovered by several scientists and dowsers and studied in-depth by Dr. Christopher Hills, existed within the negative green energy generated by the pyramids, and was a poor substitute, at best, for the power that could be captured by someone tuned in to the correct frequencies of this natural force. Mumford found that solitary confinement in a federal prison was the perfect place to discipline himself. He didn't need a computer or books or even paper or pen. The exercises he performed on a daily basis were mental in nature, and no one ever suspected what he was doing. He was as safe as he could be and working diligently to perfect his mental capacities. What better way to hide than to emulate his beloved ancient Egyptian teachers and hide in plain sight? It took Mumford two weeks to figure out how to escape from the maximum-security prison where he was incarcerated. He had several methods and would update his data on his escape routes weekly and sometimes daily. The facility was designed to contain a certain level of violence and cunning that was as much as its designers could comprehend. It was not designed to deal with the extremes of intellect and violence that Mumford was capable of. Mumford stayed for five years of his life sentence, all the while getting stronger and tuning in to the universe for the knowledge of when to leave his forced abode. True genius has the ability of dropping any preconceived belief systems or data in favor of something better when the information shows up. Mumford decided it was time to leave as he remote-viewed the time and the place of the next vortex, and he knew it was time to put his timetable into action.

When he finally escaped, it was with none of his carefully-thought-out plans and contingencies. He was simply being transferred and saw a lapse in security that happened to fit his schedule and escaped. Most of his plans depended on an ability to execute extreme violence beyond the scope of his keepers' ability to respond to it. Although well-trained, his guards just could not fathom the cunning and depth to which Mumford had studied the ways to kill a human being. He liked to employ many methods of mind control, including the ability to implant thoughts quickly into the minds of his victims. The way he killed most of the six law officers who were escorting him was by making them shoot each other, thinking it was him. All Jack had to do was duck, and the mayhem he created took care of the rest.

He knew through clairvoyance that there would be a place he would be safe in Nevada near where the vortex would appear. It was here where he would start remotely controlling entities that would wreak havoc in his name. When the Hawaiian Kahuna death prayers that he would invoke would start to have effect in California, it would seem as if he would be there instead of safely tucked 350 miles away at the bottom of a small mesa.

It took Mumford three and a half hours to drive into the remote wilderness north of Las Vegas. During his short stay, as he cruised several grocery stores stocking up for his stay in his trailer, he noticed several adult dancers buying things, obviously just getting off their shifts and preparing to go home. Jack had to check himself several times as he started to send thoughts of attraction to these women, as the temptation of their flesh was almost too much for him to resist. One woman was particularly susceptible and followed him out to the parking lot. Mumford was particularly bothered by her very revealing outfit and almost succumbed to his lust. He quickly recovered himself and wiped her mind clean of ever having seen him at all. As he watched her walk back to her car in a rather confused state, he became extremely aroused and started violently twisting his nipples under his stolen shirt.

When he arrived at the proper turnout, it was just before dawn, and he waited so that it would be light enough that he would not have to use his lights but his dust trail would not be visible. As Jack started to drive down the old mining road, he got the distinct impression that he was being monitored and his danger receptors redlined. Quickly shutting off the stolen truck, he tuned in to the being or entity that was monitoring him. He was confused, and somehow he felt an intelligence that did not make sense. Just then, on a ridge that was exposed to the creeping dawn, he saw movement. He instinctively reached for the pistol that was lying on the seat next to him and quickly got out of the truck. He covered the distance slower than he thought he could, because his body was still not working well from the confinement and the driving. When he crossed a small wash, he again saw movement and raised his pistol. In the sights of the issue Smith and Wesson he had taken from the corpse of an Ohio state trooper, Mumford tracked the movement and started to take up the slack in the trigger mechanism. About 40 yards away, a coyote appeared from behind some sagebrush and turned to face Mumford in the early desert light. Jack Mumford relaxed for the first time in a long time and started to laugh. He took his finger off the trigger and returned his weapon to safe. This scrawny little coyote was the source of his scrutiny, and Mumford could tell he was now safe. He got back in the truck and continued up the dirt road. Several times he thought the truck would get stuck, but the hard pack was enough, and he made it across several dry washes.

He was far from anything now, out in the American wasteland, a place that is too inhospitable for anyone to make a go at it for long. A land filled with abandoned things. Abandoned mines, abandoned towns, abandoned trailers, abandoned people. It's a very harsh place, and things remain in a tenuous balance with each other, knowing that the slightest tilt in either direction would be enough to start a slide onto treacherous ground. It's a place where people don't ask many questions or make much eye contact. It's too open and remote a place, where weird things tend to happen. Help is usually very far away, so people don't look too long or too hard, and things tend to get lost. They just get swallowed up by the land and are never heard from again. Folks just don't want to know too much or get too close. In a land where everyone is a hunter, people tend give each other space.

Jack arrived at the trailer, and it was just as he had seen it in his mind's eye while he was in prison. There was a corrugated-steel shed next to the trailer with the door ajar. Mumford put the truck in there and shut it off as quickly as possible. He wanted the engine to cool down so no satellite thermal imaging could see his vehicle's heat pattern. He unloaded the truck and started placing the weapons he had accumulated in strategic positions inside and outside the trailer. The trailer had been abandoned about 10 years before, and because of its remoteness, it was not on any vandals' hit list. Mumford unloaded all the food and water he needed for a two-month stay, three if he had to. He found where he was going to sleep and covered the walls with aluminum foil, so as not to be detected thermally by satellite, aircraft, or patrol. Jack had seven alarm clocks set to different times; these were the times that he would be visible to the different orbits of spy satellites. The alarms gave a five-minute warning to get undercover. He went back into the shed and pulled down some siding that was in back next to a small escarpment. He wanted this place to be as ventilated as possible while still being able to hide his vehicle. This is where Jack would perform his rituals and meditations, and take control of unsuspecting beings and have them wreak havoc in the lives of people who would have him dead or punished. He began clearing the area and preparing it for his ritual incantations.

Jack was preparing to practice the blackest of magic, and he was fully committed to the harm he was about to inflict. He knew Bobby Doucette was hunting him and was the only one capable of finding him. For some reason, Mumford could not get a lock on

Bobby, and he found it slightly disconcerting. He knew Doucette was much weaker than he, but somehow he was not able to locate him or get a reading on him just now. It didn't matter; Mumford was sure that Doucette hadn't learned that much. It might just be an environmental anomaly. Still, Mumford was planning on hurting him the most efficient way possible. He would kill the woman Doucette loved. Mumford was sure this strategy would cause Doucette to make enough mistakes that he would pose no threat. He could tell this was Doucette's weakness and would hit him as hard as possible there.

Later that day, Mumford had settled in and was starting to perform the first of his rituals. He would remotely use discarnate entities to visit his victims and influence them through any weaknesses and guilt that they had in their subconscious and were unaware of. His first victim would be Doucette's black-haired lover. Mumford had remotely viewed her many times in prison and sent very debauched and horrible thoughts to her as he imagined killing her in a slow, ritualistic fashion and torturing her by degrees. He had gathered up his *papa,* or forbidden objects, and prepared to give his *ana-ana,* or death prayer. He started to concentrate his lascivious and insane thoughts and directed them at Kat. Jack began his rhythmic breathing and started contacting his discarnate entities he had enslaved to use as his messengers for his dark prayers.

He began, *"Oh lauano, listen to my voice. This is my desire, rush upon the black-haired one of Doucette and enter her world. Enter a weak vessel near her, get inside her, expand and contract, expand and contract. Tear at her flesh, cause her skin to become foreign to her. Cause destruction to her body. Cause destruction to the bodies near her. Cause great destruction and pain. Use any vessels near her who are weak. Use them to destroy and bring misery. GO NOW, IT IS DONE!"*

Hundreds of miles away in her vinyl dungeon, Kat felt her skin twitch and instantly wanted to get high. Outside of the shed that Mumford was in, a coyote watched in the burning heat of the day as a crow circled above.

CHAPTER 7

Somewhere on the reservation, the money from the gambling consortium that the Bureau of Indian Affairs had delegated to improving living conditions was evident. That money was nowhere near the unimproved dirt road that I was now bouncing down in four-wheel drive, heading toward John Red Truck's house and sweat lodge. John is three-quarters Navajo and spent most of his life here on the reservation in northwestern New Mexico. The first time he left was to join the Army at 18 years old in 1966. His father had been a code talker for the Army in the South Pacific during WWII, and John wanted to follow in the warrior tradition of his people. His father had been subject to intense bigotry during his experience in the war, but he was extremely patriotic anyway. He had told John at a young age that some evils in the world are more terrible than petty differences between people, and the Axis Powers were among these dark forces. Part of John's family from his mother's side had been medicine people, and she had told him that a tribal elder had seen the nature of the evil that the Germans and the Japanese people represented at the time, and so his father went to war. When John was 18, he was on a vision quest and it was revealed to him that he too should follow the warrior's path. Despite the protest of the antiwar movement that had invaded some of the reservation in the guise of mostly draft-evaders seeking refuge, John decided to enlist. He ended up in a Ranger battalion and was one of the first members of an LRP, or long-range patrol team, designed to fight a more guerrilla-style combat and bring the war to the enemy. John was an enlisted man and quickly rose to staff sergeant. He had almost completed one tour in Vietnam and was contemplating a second when a bullet from a Russian-made AK-47 entered his lung and continued out his back, killing a radio telephone operator behind him by entering his eye socket then lodging in his brain somewhere near the Laotian border. By the time he made it out of the hospital in Hawaii, his tour was up, and the Army was kind enough to let him go as unfit for duty. And so on a medical discharge, under honorable conditions, he landed in San Francisco, walking with a cane and wearing his summer dress greens and his black Ranger beret. A woman came up to him outside of the TWA terminal and threw a bag of dog shit on him as she started screaming, calling him a baby killer. John went into the airport restroom and took off his uniform top, washed it out, and put it in a paper bag. He boarded a Greyhound bus and headed back to the reservation.

In many Native American traditions, any warrior who comes back to the tribe after a major conflict is not allowed to be part of the community again until the warrior has had a cleansing of the mind, body, and soul. To the ancient North Americans, this only made practical sense. The human mind and body is not equipped to sustain massive amounts of violent energies for a prolonged amount of time without consequences. The one-year tour was implemented during the Vietnam War because it was found that after a year of being in harm's way, the average solider efficiency and mental capabilities dropped significantly. If the solider was forced to endure the violence of modern warfare for much longer, the phenomenon named in World War I as shell shock would start to set in. The effects of this prolonged state of mind and body lead us to the understanding of post-traumatic stress syndrome, a condition not dissimilar from sexually and violently abused children.

When John Red Truck finally made it back to the reservation, things had changed and so had he. Most of the old ways were not practiced anymore, and John was on his own. The small towns surrounding the reservation were always trouble spots for the Navajo, and it was there where John finally broke down and used the violence he had learned in war to settle a score with some local white boys. As anyone could have predicted, it did not end well, and John served seven years of a 25-year sentence for second-degree murder. An Army buddy from Chicago who had become a lawyer learned of John's case from another Ranger and did some investigation. It turned out that the evidence used against him was false, and he got John's sentence commuted. John went to live with a great uncle, who was a medicine man and showed him how, with the Great Spirit's help, he could heal himself. To come back after going so far into the darkness is no small feat; to learn how to help others down the same rocky trail is the true test of the warrior's path. John had set up a rehab center of sorts for misfits who got lost on the road of life. It was not an easy school, but it was one that got results. I know because I graduated top of my class.

The road to John's place goes from bad to worse and ends up just a Jeep trail in the high desert. It is a natural fortress, with a small gap heading up to a mesa where people trained to look for safety in terrain features feel very comfortable. This is land that was used for healing work before a time anyone can remember. It is sacred land, and has been used by healers and medicine people since perhaps before there were any Navajo.

The first time I saw this piece of dog-patch mesa was after my life had fallen apart the last time. I had lost my wife and everything I cared about, and all I wanted to do was vanish. The first truth that I had learned on the mesa was that I was the only one to blame, and I was the first one I needed to forgive. It's not an easy thing to forgive yourself. No, not easy at all. All the pain and bitterness that one may have harbored for many years has many strange ways of hiding in behaviors that would take more than one lifetime to figure out. Modern therapy isn't enough most of the time. In fact, as Albert Einstein once said, you cannot solve problems with the same mind that created them in the first place. You can't dream them away, you can't lay on a couch and talk them away, you cannot scream at them and transfer all your anger and pain into a stuffed animal. You cannot massage them away, you cannot drug them away, you cannot stick needles in just the right places or move your spine a little to the left or right. You cannot hold an unnatural pose for hours, nor not eat for days to get rid of them. You cannot understand them by the sexual obsessions you may have, and you won't know them by certain fears that manifest inside of you. You cannot just heal the disease they have caused and expect the sickness to not come back in another form. You cannot wish, you cannot just recite platitudes or new thought affirmations. You cannot chant a mantra of an ancient religion and expect it to do the work that you and only you can do. No, you must enter the darkness. You must go to the one place you are most afraid to go and meet your doppelganger. You must meet your dark self. You must walk with faith into the valley of shadow, naked without any weapons or support, except your belief that there is a power in the universe that is perfect and you are a part of that perfection. Your pain and your horror are part of the perfection. Your fears and your hope are part of the perfection, and you must trust. You must trust when there is nothing at all that would signal anything you could ever imagine that is trustworthy. You must have faith—by will, not by knowing—and you must go forward into the abyss unsure and unworthy. You must walk into a very dark place alone and under your own power, and you must be willing to be destroyed or reborn anew and not care which outcome fate decides to choose. You must be ready to be decimated or exalted, and be ready to except either fate with grace.

That is what you learn on John Red Truck's mesa. It is a school for the soul, and there are no diplomas or credits. It is a place to take a broken life and fix it, not to its past or future glory, but to a place of grace and acceptance of the beauty and sadness of just how things are.

The house is not very far from the sweat lodge kiva, and it is the first thing you see as you bump over a small hummock and go down into a bowl that contains John's house and his pathetic looking dogs. There is nothing much to the property; the house is a rather ramshackle but cozy unit with a great front porch in need of a paint job. There is another small building that is a bunkhouse toolshed-type of outbuilding. Two parachutes are attached on top of old telephone center-poles and guyed out for shade and soul work. The two circular tent-like spaces are next to each other and about 20 feet away from the entrance of the round sweat kiva. One has crude but effective cooking spaces and tables under it, and the other is dedicated to a meeting space of a less sacred variety. You're expected to bring your own food and enough for your host, and maybe just a little bit more, as John's place has a way of attracting more than a few lost souls. On the surface it is certainly not much to look at, but that is kind of the point of the exercise. Nothing that is dealt with at Mr. Red Truck's camp is about the surface. It is most emphatically about what lies beneath. The main activity of the encampment seems to happen under the outstretched parachutes where the group cooking and meeting areas are. The olive-drab nylon material has a way of making veterans feel safe and lends itself to very intense rap sessions. Anytime, day or night, you may find very serious-looking men leaning into each other and talking soul talk as if they are drowning men and this is their last best hope of making it out alive. No violence is tolerated here, and if you have already violated tribal law and brought weapons with you, there is a very stern warning to deposit them in an underground cache that only the caretaker of this land of the misfit toys knows about.

I pulled my truck up into the yard and saw a couple of ex-military types with a little too much weight around their stomachs and necks eye me suspiciously. I got out and started to unstrap my gun case from the bottom of my truck when Patton and Stubbs, John's two smelly mutt dogs, came bounding over and started to give me a tongue bath. I don't know who was more excited to see each other, me or them. I could see the vets under the chutes relax a little bit when the dogs recognized me. I had spent eight months here, and we had become fast friends. John is a small, muscular man with a long, graying ponytail who always seems to have on the same thing. He wears blue jeans, cowboy boots, and an olive-drab Vietnam-era military fatigue top with the sleeves cut off, showing all the world his Ranger and Airborne tattoos. On his left bicep is a tattoo of the country of Vietnam with these words in it: "When I die I know I'm going to Heaven 'cause I've done my time in Hell." After getting the dogs off me long enough to remove my weapons from under the truck, I deposited my pistol and extra magazines that I had in the cab in the case and stood up facing the house. As was his custom, John was standing on his porch with the biggest of shit-eating grins, waiting for me to acknowledge the proper protocol of a man entering a sacred space carrying weapons.

The men under the tents had stood up, and I could see their eyes fixed on me as the bottom of the chutes ended just about eye level. I looked at John, and he just stood there waiting, arms akimbo.

"I have weapons," I yelled over the hot breeze that was blowing and listened to the silence and the ticking of my slowly cooling engine.

"Take them out by the big rock by the gate and wait with the others in the meeting tent."

I knew what he was going to say before he said it, but this was John's world and we all played by his rules. They are sacred rules and they are very old, and you learn fast that respect starts and is maintained in very small ways. In fact, respecting the small things is exactly what this holy piece of the world is all about. I picked up my weapons case and carried it out past the gate, where there was a boulder about the size of a VW Bug just over a rise, and left them there. By the time I made it back to the tent, John was in his pickup and drove by me, waving to signal he would be right back. I went under the chutes, and immediately the temperature dropped 15 degrees; it's amazing what a little bit of shade will do in the desert. I nodded to the other two men but did not introduce myself, as this was not allowed just yet. The men nodded back and returned to their discussion about airmobile tactics and their use in the Vietnam conflict. I poured myself a cup of coffee and sat down, realizing that this was one of those few places in the world that felt like home to a wandering soul like myself. The men had arranged themselves so that they could monitor me in case I tried to follow John and see where the weapons were hidden. They knew I would not follow and I knew I would not follow, but that was their job and I would have done the same. At this point in the process, I was kind of in a quarantine mode and so was not to direct my energy toward anyone. I needed to purify myself and deal with all the energy that I was carrying around before anything else happened. The other men looked like they had been there about two to three weeks and were in a very vulnerable spot energetically, so at this time we would not mix. The rock by the gate was a sacred rock with a high quartz content that was programmed to deal with any negative energies someone might bring with them, known or unknown. Still, if a person was not careful, they could breach that astral sentinel and bring some nasty things in here. Believe me, the negative energy that gets released here is like a beacon in other realms, and if it weren't for the big medicine protecting this place, dark things would rush in quicker than a New York cab ride.

I sat and started to take stock of myself and my predicament. Everything that I seemed to care about was in flux, and the worst outcome that I could ever imagine seemed inevitable. I kept telling myself that it was alright, that this is how it was supposed to go down and not to worry, but it was all a sham. I was a mess inside and I knew it. On the ride here I kept playing a mental game that everything was a lock and somehow I would be protected, but the reality is I didn't believe that at all. I was terrified and headed to the only place that made any sense in a world that seemed completely insane. All my tricks, all my meditations, all my successes, and all my beliefs seemed to vanish as soon as I hit the reservation. I had kidded myself that I was alright and capable of handling Mumford my own way, but here, now, in this place, looking at the cup of coffee in front of me and listening to the two strangers tell war stories, I felt terror. My hands started to shake, and I realized that if I picked up the cup of coffee it would probably spill. I was adrift and nothing worked, and I seemed to use my last ounce of steam getting here and was now coming unglued. It's a strange thing when your body overrides your mind's directions. You tell yourself that you are fine, that you can handle what you have to handle, but then your body decides it has its own agenda. All of a sudden sitting there I started to get tired, as the adrenaline of the trip was rapidly wearing off. My eyelids started to droop, and there seemed to be nothing I could do about it. I put my head down on the table just for a minute. I told myself I would close my eyes just for a minute, and proceeded to fall asleep.

I was awakened by John gently tapping on my shoulder and speaking to me.

"Get up, brother. Get up now, Scarecrow. Let's move it into the bunk room, huh?"

My head snapped up, and the first thing I saw was Patton and Stubbs just sitting there, looking at me as if they were very worried about me. My eyes focused on John next, and the two vets that were standing next to him.

"Ben and Sully put your gear into the bunkhouse. Bobby, I think it's time to get a little shuteye."

"Yeah, ah, yeah … John, that seems to be a right … err, I mean good idea … yeah, sleep, that sounds good. Thanks, I won't take too long. I mean, I want to do a sweat tonight if you are doing one. I'll just take a nap."

"Bobby, this isn't a race, you have plenty of time. Just get some sleep, and we'll take it from there." I paused, not sure exactly what to do. "Go on now, Scarecrow, time for Spirit Land."

"OK … OK, I'm up, I'm movin'." I picked up my untouched coffee, not sure what to do with it, and Sully just took it from me. I looked up into his face and met his eyes. They had a sad and lonely quality to them. I think all people who have seen a little too much in life get that quality to their eyes. Kind of like they have seen too much and just want to know if you are an enemy or a friend. Sully put his hand on my shoulder and guided me in the direction of the bunkhouse, and I started walking. I walked the 20 yards to the bunkhouse and looked in the open door. The sun was casting deep yellow and orange shadows of late-afternoon desert light through the windows of the bunkhouse. I climbed the steps up to a small covered porch with some chairs and a table on it and entered the open door. There were five double bunks crammed into the tiny space, and my gear and my sleeping bag were on the bottom bunk farthest from the other two men's gear. The bunkhouse was plain pine on the inside with no paint, and it lent itself to a very cozy feeling from the golden light dancing off the bright, unfinished wood. I knew that in my current state, if I did not take my boots off before I sat down on the bunk, I would have them on until I woke up wondering why my feet were so uncomfortable. Sometimes you have to sleep with your boots on, but thankfully this was not one of those times. I pulled off my boots and flight jacket, took my pants off, and sat down. That was the last thing I remembered; my body just gave out, and I surrendered to the sweet feeling of sleep of the weary. I was out like a light and was about to enter dreamtime on the reservation.

Sometimes it's not until we get to the end of the line and we give up pretending we know what to do that grace occurs. I was lost and managed to get myself to the only place in the world where I knew it was alright to say so and melt down. Everyone needs a place like that; everyone needs somewhere and someone who they can be real with. A place that nothing matters except the next thing, and all that thing might be is taking your clothes off and getting into bed. Sometimes just falling asleep in a safe place is the most important thing in the world. Everyone needs a safe place, and as my eyes were closing the thought crossed my mind that I could also have a place like this someday. A sanctuary for the misguided and lost. A place where someone could just sleep and know that tomorrow might not be better, but at least they would not be alone and they would be safe. I shut my eyes and fell asleep in the land of the Navajo and started to dream.

I was walking up a beach that reminded me of the East Coast of the United States, somewhere like New England, maybe Nantucket or Cape Cod. It seemed like a winter day, the way the cold, bright light was glowing off the rolling surf, but I felt no chill. I had a faint realization that I was dreaming, and I wanted to try to continue the dream as a lucid dream. A lucid dream is one in which you become aware that you are sleeping in dreamtime and you will yourself to continue with an awareness of participating in another dimension rather than just allowing it to happen to you as random events. Lucid dreaming is usually the precursor to astral projection, and the information that you can glean while in this state is quite profound. Modern dream interpretations try to make sense out of archetypal symbolism of the subconscious as if we are only observers but not participants. If you can get your mind around the concept that in a lucid dream you have as much control or maybe more than you do in your waking life, things start to get very interesting. The realm of dreamtime seems to be a place where things are more liquid, and the opacity of dealing with problems and obstacles is very thin. You can fix things in dreamtime that you cannot seem to change in waking moments. It's not a very hard skill to learn, but it does take dedication and training. You must crawl before you can walk in the astral realms. This dedication is why most people never find this way of knowing. They read a book or hear a concept and try it once or twice, and because it doesn't work immediately they give up, believing that it's all just a pile of baby caca.

(KILO - • -) "There is no free lunch. Any of these concepts takes about a year-plus to learn, and it means a daily effort. You may learn in less time or it may take you longer, but you are required to dedicate yourself in order for it to work. Once a week, three days in a row, and skipping a week won't do it. You will be given glimpses if you dedicate yourself, usually in less than three months, and most of the time within a month. The truth is if you give a half-hearted effort, you get little to no results. If you want to know the secrets of the Universe, you must make yourself worthy."

I was walking very heavily in the sand, and I decided to try to alter my perception in a small way. I stopped and concentrated on having my steps be lighter, maybe even float over the sand. I picked up my foot and had a slight ripple in my reality that felt like a lack of faith, and immediately I could not move. Everything felt thick, and I realized I was equating my life on my Earth plane to where I was now. I forced myself to relax and breathe, as the inability to move while life was going on around me was very disconcerting. I realized I could not move because in normal life, I could not float on top of the sand … I could not fly. I was somewhere different now and the rules were different, so I decided to give myself permission. I decided to play.

Immediately my foot floated about a half-inch above the sand, and I pulled the other one out also. I took a few faltering steps and started to float on the sand in the direction I wanted to go. The thought crossed my mind that if I could float, maybe I could fly, and then the doubt crept in and I found myself stuck in the sand again. I centered, grounded, and started with my baby floating steps again. It seemed a little easier this time to get up and going, so I just stopped concentrating on improving anything and relaxed into the moment. Off in the distance I saw what appeared to be a flock of seabirds rapidly approaching my idyllic romp. As they grew closer, I realized that these were no seabirds I had ever seen, and they looked very menacing. They were red-feathered, pterodactyl-looking things heading straight for me. I felt a small warning wave of nervousness, and immediately the air and my movement became thick again. I realized that after so much practice in these places, my emotions were the thing I needed to control to have a beneficial experience, and the mad flying creatures coming at me full-tilt boogie were a warning to not go negative. Energy follows thought, and I did not want a bad trip. I started to breathe and concentrate on being calm, but as they approached, small waves of fear started to well up inside me. Every seeming foot they got nearer, some other menacing detail would pop up into my consciousness. My steps were getting thick again, and even though my conscious mind knew that giving in to the fear was silly, especially here in dreamville, I just could not shake it.

The birds circled once and landed in a circle around me. Immediately they started to morph into more jackal-looking creatures with a kind of hyena grin on their now-salivating mouths. These were beasts from an astral hell, and they meant no good. I was immobile and wondering what to do. The beasts started to close the circle, and the gnashing of their toothed beaks and the horrible noises emanating from them were terrifying. I started to get a little mad at myself, realizing that, although these crazy things were real enough where I was at the moment, the cure for what they represented was also inside me. An ancient truism flashed through my mind.

(LIMA • - • •) "No matter where you are, no matter if it is in the Earth realm or astral, whatever predicament you're in, whether lost in the woods with poison ivy, in a bad part of town with a flat tire and a crack gang looking at your Lexus, or about to be devoured by red-feathered pterodactyls, your survival and everything you need to survive is within 300 feet. Get calm and think, but all the tools will be there. Sea, desert, woods, glacier, or dreamtime, it doesn't matter. You just have to get calm enough to know that everything for your survival will be provided if you can just listen and see."

I looked around and saw that the little bastards were starting to close their circle on me. I then noticed something quite peculiar as they walked toward me. They kind of wobbled and looked pretty goofy doing it. They had not quite made up their minds if they were birds or mammals yet, and the indication of their half-evolution, although ugly and menacing, was at the same time kind of comical. Bang—it hit me in a flash! Of course, when anything bad happens to you energy-wise or in one of these astral planes, or in just plain old vanilla life, to laugh at it is one of the strongest of medicines. I was taking this all too seriously. It's just life, and if I really am a divine being, then nothing can destroy me.

They had almost closed in on me when I started to laugh. I did not feel like laughing, so I just started faking it. "HA HA HA HA HA HA HA HA HA HA," I yelled out. "HA HA HA, you little ugly bastards. HA HA HA." As soon as I started pretending, a strange thing started to happen—I actually did begin to get a tickle in my funny bone, and the red devils seemed to get even more silly and awkward. I started again with more of a belly laugh that felt more convincing, and bang-o, the stupid things started to shrink even more. At this point their wings were too big for their bodies and were getting in the way of their locomotion. Simultaneously my feet seemed as if they wanted to move, and sure enough, my feet started to lift out of the sand again as the floating feeling started coming back. At this point the bird beasts were very small and having the hardest of times lugging their now-too-large wings through the sand. Then something wonderful happened. The hunted became the hunter. As I was laughing at them, I saw fear in their beady little eyes, and they started to move away from me. I kept laughing and started to float again up the beach, and the shits ran away like fiddler crabs detected after a passing wave. I imagined a large ball of purple fire floating about 10 feet away, the pure violet fire of St. Germain, and when my little red friends saw it they did everything they could to get away—except their wings were too large for their frames, and their attempts to fly were very stoogelike. I released the purple flame, and they were consumed in the violet fireball that rendered their energy harmless and formless back to the universe. I was again alone on the beach, floating an inch above the ground and quietly chuckling to myself.

The light had started to change but there was no light source visible; it seemed to come from everywhere at once. The light now represented a beautiful sunset with a magnificent orange, blue, and purple sky, with the light dancing and playing off incredible cloud formations. I was transfixed, looking at the splendor and floating up the beach and splashing through the surf. Again, there was no feeling of cold, just a warm and tingling sensation as the water receded and splashed over my floating dogs. I was just enjoying myself when it hit me that I was walking on water, and I started to laugh again. I started humming a little song to myself to the tune of the old song "I'm a Girl Watcher." *"I'm a water walker, I'm a water walker, watching water go by, my my my."* OK, it was corn-dog silly, but I hadn't felt this good in years, and I was damned if I wasn't going follow this joy to its source.

I looked back up the beach, and off in the distance I saw a fire glowing just a little bit up from the surf line. I immediately got an impression of warmth and safety, so I continued my heading and enjoyed the evening. As I looked around, the terrain seemed to be only endless dunes and dune grass heading back as far as I could see. Every once in a while there was a salt marsh with things that looked like egrets and one of my favorite birds, the great blue heron, but they were all very peaceful and benign, unlike the little red menaces that plagued me before. I could see the fire now and realized there were people sitting around it. I still detected only peaceful feelings and probably would have continued on if I hadn't. I was curious about what things I had to learn here in this place. As I approached, I could see there were 12 people floating about a foot off the sand in different sitting postures. They were dressed in all manner of clothing that seemed to span the gamut of human history. One was dressed as a Tibetan monk, one seemed to be dressed in garb of the Middle East with crude sandals and in the kind of clothing we would equate with the time of Christ. One looked like a Zen Buddhist, another like an ancient Greek. One was dressed in the clothes of a homemaker sometime in the 1940s, and still another wore some kind of uniform that seemed somehow futuristic, but I could not place the markings on his chest. One was obviously Native American and the only one who showed any natural aging; all the rest seemed to be in their mid-30s. As I got closer I could see the fire that was burning was floating above the sand also and did not seem to have any source of fuel. It was just a burning ball of yellow and orange fire hovering over the sand, and it had a slight blue tinge on the periphery of the flames. All the people were sitting with their eyes closed as I walked up. I wanted to sit with them but felt it was not my place to enter the circle. As soon as this thought ran through my mind, one of the sitters, who was dressed in the garb of an ancient Egyptian, opened her eyes and looked at me. She had the most serene and beautiful gaze I had ever known and I felt very much at peace. The circle began to open into a U shape as the sitters started to float outward, opening the circle. When a spot up the beach facing the ocean opened, she motioned for me to sit and join them. I took my assigned seat, and as I got comfortable on the sand, I started to levitate also. I did not float as high as the others, but I could definitely feel the weight of my body being suspended, and it was extremely comfortable. It was like sitting on a giant water bed that offered no resistance to my weight. I was marveling at my antics when I noticed the circle had closed slightly and all the beings had their eyes open, looking at me. The man dressed as a Native American of some rank, his horned bonnet very feathered, started speaking in an unintelligible tongue and spoke a few sentences. As he finished, he looked away from me and started to chuckle. The Egyptian woman began to translate for him.

"Black Crow says that you should think about your questions and only ask what is truly burning in you heart to know."

"Truly in my heart … OK … ahhhh … well … first, who are you people?" I stammered.

"We are Watchers. My name is Waters," said the man in the futuristic clothes. As he spoke, I noticed that his face wasn't very animated, as if his skin was too tight. I realized his small mouth did not move when he talked.

"You are correct, some of us have different ways to communicate. Mine is more telepathic in nature. We seem to retain certain characteristics of our time. Our healing abilities link us to certain times of power in our Earth lives. It is more convenient for us to remain with those particular time links for different types of contact; it is safer for you and us."

"So what do you watch?" I asked, wondering how silly I must sound.

Black Crow laughed again. He spoke quickly and motioned at me with a feathered stick, then laughed some more.

"He said we watch you," spoke the Egyptian. "My name is Osiris, and welcome, Bobby. We are all very excited about this meeting. We have been working a very long time to form the link with you in your Earth time."

"What do you mean you watch me? Do you mean you all, I mean, all of you watch me or monitor me specifically? I mean, is that your job?"

"Bobby, my name is Hanna," said the woman in the 1940s garb. "Yes, we chose you and that is what we do now. It is a great honor for us, and we are very, very thankful that we could meet like this. It is rare that this kind of meeting can happen, and you are welcomed and loved here."

"My name is Philip," said the man in the ancient Sumerian garb. "I am an Essene from a time that you would call about 80 years A.D. and was one of the students of the teacher you call the Christ."

"You mean Jesus Christ? You knew Jesus? I mean, how if he was dead? I get it, you were his student 80 years after he died or whatever happened, holy shit … oops, sorry, it's just a leap, that's all. I think this is the most amazing dream I have ever had."

"It's not exactly a dream as you know it, Robert," spoke Philip again. "But we may not have very much of what you know as time right now, so if you can concentrate as Black Crow suggests, then maybe we can be of some service to you."

"I am Dysosines," said the ancient Greek. "It is a great pleasure to meet you, and if you would allow me, I think I can help. I have had a few first meetings like this, and it seems to work more effectively if you would limit your questions to one or two, concentrating on large questions of the macrocosm, more in the line of fundamental truths rather than specifics. This is what Black Crow was saying. We are not allowed to help you as much as we would like just now, but we can tell you that you are in a battle arcane, and there is certain information that can help you."

"Can you help me find Jack Mumford?" I said quickly.

Black Crow looked deeply into my eyes, said two words, and pointed his medicine stick at me.

"He says think bigger," said Osiris.

I looked deep into the medicine man's eyes and saw a kindness and a warning at the same time. As I stared transfixed, he seemed to plant a thought into me that took a lot of energy for him.

"What is the nature of evil?" I blurted out.

Black Crow sighed and laughed a more subdued laugh and seemed a bit drained. He looked down and sighed, then looked up into my eyes and spoke in perfect English.

"The nature of evil is error. It is a perversion of the one original thing. It is a limiting of the infinite life force that is always creative and forcing it to be competitive."

"What?" I stammered, trying to understand and sounding like an idiot. "I mean, are you saying that bad things happen just because people can't see God in a garbage dump? I mean … " My words trailed off as I realized that the moment I stopped listening and started rationalizing, the information and images started to disappear.

"OK, OK, I'm listening," I said emphatically, but it was too late. The images started to get fuzzy, and I could not hear what the members of the circle were trying to tell me. The atmosphere was becoming very thick, and my movement through it was increasingly harder. I could see and feel that there was more the gathered had to tell me, and that a few of them were trying to get through to me. I looked at Black Crow and he smiled at me, and he started to laugh at me as if he knew exactly what I was feeling. I could hear his laugh now as if it were right next to my ear. Then everything faded to black.

It felt like late morning. I could feel the air starting to heat up in the sun that was streaming through the windows of the bunkhouse. I lifted my head off the pillow and noticed there was more gear on another bunk; there were now four bunks taken, including mine. I lifted my head off the pillow as if I were actually going to get up, but it just dropped back down and I went into my best catlike stretch. As if on cue, Patton and Stubbs came running in and started licking my face. I heard John's voice coming up to the building, calling my name.

"Rise and shine, Scarecrow, that's enough sleep for you."

I saw a shadow come across the light that was falling through the doorway. As John Red Truck entered the bunkhouse, he walked over and plopped down on the bunk next to me. I blinked my eyes and rolled over again, facing him with my head still on the pillow.

"What time is it, Red Truck?" I yawned.

"It's 1 o'clock in the afternoon, tough guy, and it's time to get up. We saved you some chow, but if you don't hurry, I'm going to give it to the dogs."

"One, are you kidding? I thought it was about 10 in the morning."

"Ten, that was a while ago, sunshine. Rains On Grass said you were given a vision last night. Do you remember it?"

"Rains On Grass, what is he doing here?"

"He said he started traveling many days ago because of the visions you will see now. He said he was told to come here and help you understand your visions. He said it's your time to step up to your destiny."

I knew that Rains On Grass only traveled by foot and he lived very far away, although I wasn't sure where—I don't think many people knew. Some secrets stayed on the reservation.

"Yeah, I saw a lot last night. I feel like I kind of blew it though. Like I wasn't quick enough on the draw to figure out what was going on or something."

"That happens. It's good that you're here, Scarecrow. You're playing with some big medicine now; you need some friends."

"Tell me about it. I feel like a fish that forgot how to swim."

"Well, get up now. Chow's just lying around, and the only ones eating are the flies."

"Yep, yep, I'll be there shortly."

John got up and started to walk out, and Patton and Stubbs ran out ahead of him. He turned and stopped in the doorway and looked back at me. He started to say something to me but stopped short. Something like a dark cloud passed across his eyes. He was not the kind of man who would avert his eyes, but he did this time, and I involuntarily shivered and pulled the blanket up over my chest.

I dressed, and as I walked out into the brilliant cool light of the mesa, I saw the four men gathered around a table underneath the chow tent. They all seemed to be listening intently to a broadcast coming from a hand-crank survival radio. As I walked up I could hear that the news was grim as usual. In the past few years, terrorists had managed to somehow get the technology right on how to build a homeland horror. Ever since the terrorists leveled the World Trade Center, everyone had been worried that they would find a way to deliver a mass-scale weapon. Then they did. As I walked up I just stood there, listening to the newscaster tell of the Homeland Security forces monitoring the radiation levels in Madison, Wisconsin, after some idiot managed to light off a dirty nuke. It didn't quite go the way it was supposed to, and most of the radiation had been contained to the campus of the university. Mass hysteria had broken out, and everyone had left the city as the Homeland defense forces moved in and declared martial law. There had been a complete news blackout in the whole state of Wisconsin since the event happened six months earlier, and now Homeland Security was giving out briefings letting people know what areas of Madison were safe to move back to. A refugee camp had been growing about 70 miles outside of town on some abandoned farmland that was too toxic from chemical fertilizer to grow crops anymore, and protests were happening daily in the camps. The people didn't trust that the government was telling the truth about the safety of Madison, and meanwhile children and the elderly were getting sick from the toxic land in the camps. We still hadn't gotten used to being in a free-fire zone here in America. We still thought that kind of thing happened in someone else's country, that somehow we're above all the violence and mayhem, and that the now almost-tri-yearly attacks would magically stop. Then we could all go back to talking about new Plymouths and baseball and know that our lives will never be touched by a madman's deviousness. It would be nice if we could just get to the year Zero, like a Sesame Street version of the Khmer Rouge's new deal. We could just stop and forget that there was slavery, bigotry, torture, corporate greed, corrupt secret governments, blacks hating whites, whites hating yellows, yellows planning raids upon their unsuspecting countrymen just trying to bring in the rice harvest. We could concentrate on building a society that wanted to teach each child to bring their own personal gifts into the world and channel each person's creative energies toward something magnificent. But alas, we have voted for the mediocre, we have allowed our bid to go to the lowest, we opted for strip malls instead of parks and gardens. And now we are reaping a bitter harvest: the land is toxic, the water foul, and the humans sad and afraid.

Patton and Stubbs were sitting patiently, waiting for someone to notice that all the food had not been eaten. I grabbed a plate and loaded it up with some plain but hearty food, and the dogs seemed to become almost as sad as the humans near them. I went over to the other shelter, as I just wasn't in the mood for mayhem right at that moment, and never while I'm eating. You can become very vulnerable while you are eating because you are ingesting a product that will soon be used by your system to create your body and your thoughts. Having any kind of distress will become part of the eating process, and you literally start eating fear. Fast food is usually made by unhappy people who could give a shit about you or your needs, and that attitude energetically becomes part of the building blocks of your mind. The understanding about praying over your food has become lost over the years; even most rabbis don't know what they actually do when they make food kosher. Modern Reiki schools teach a way to raise the energy of food by basically finding the energy aura of the food and then bringing in more energy and increasing it. This is the original meaning of praying over your food. It's a fairly easy procedure—you put your hands out about three feet over the food you want to change and concentrate on it. Then you simply bring your hands down until you feel a slight pressure, and that is the energy level of the food's aura. With any processed food the level will be quite low or even nonexistent. At this point you visualize white light entering the food and raising the level of it, or just pray and ask whomever you conceive you are praying to, to raise the energy level of the food. Then raise your hands again and bring them in, concentrating on the food and trying to feel the energy level of the food. With not much work you will notice the level is considerably higher and the food even looks and smells better. Needless to say, it is much better for your body, and you will notice a difference right away. This is also the way ancient people released any fear in meat that had accumulated by the violent killing of it, and it still works today. All you have to do is ask that the fear be taken away and it will be. The most important part of the whole equation is not letting your mind go to disbelief. The little voices will start immediately if you let them, and they will get louder and louder until you absolutely believe that you can't trust anyone or anything, and then that becomes true.

(MIKE - -) "You are allowed to keep your prejudices and your fear, just as you are allowed to keep your hopes and dreams. What you must always remember is that the power is with you always. If it exists in a Tibetan monastery, then it exists in a drive-through at McDonald's. There are, however, better places than others to do your praying, and your task is to find them. There is usually a reason people pray in a monastery and not in Mickey D's."

I finished my chow and went back to get another cup of coffee. Everyone had left me alone while I ate, and I was thankful for the respect. The situation was pretty much the same in Madison, except there were now reports that Homeland Security was offering reduced mortgage rates for government-confiscated land that was now deemed livable. It seemed whoever built the bomb got the calculations wrong, and the nuclear material did not spread as the lunatics had planned. A small section of the campus had been leveled by the blast, and Homeland was now saying that radiation levels were low and the decon crews were doing a fast job of cleaning up most of the leaks. Funny how they just got rid of a huge center of learning so fast. The mechanics of making a bomb are pretty simple, as far as engineering one goes. The hard part is getting the ingredients right. It's kind of like making sourdough bread for the first time. You can go by a recipe that your ancestors on the California gold rush used more than 150 years ago to keep them alive every day—just a little bit of flour, water, and yeast, really—but get the measurements or the temperature wrong and sequence out of order, and basically you have mush. It's the assembly and caring for a bomb that makes the difference between a hit or miss. Thank the Father, Mother, God that the mooks in Madison got something wrong in their calculations. Most of the radioactive material that the explosive part of the bomb was supposed to disperse and render Madison unlivable for 10,000 or 20,000 years was disintegrated by the initial blast and only left a small part of the city, the University of Wisconsin campus, which was ground zero, radioactive and easily containable. The problem was that when the teams from the Department of Homeland Security showed up, life became a police state, like it or not. There was some kind of notification as I was stopped at four different roadblocks on my way here from California. I still hadn't gotten used to the fact the we now have random road checks here in America, just like any other Third World country. There were some reports of bandits dressed like law enforcement staging roadblocks and performing robberies on a fairly large scale. Thankfully, most of them were not using lethal force, and only a few murders had happened. It is almost impossible for a law-abiding citizen to get a weapon these days, but with all the illegal firearms coming in from Canada and Mexico, the level of violence during petty crimes has skyrocketed.

The average price for a small caliber pistol had dropped almost 800 percent from 10 years ago. Anybody can be a gunslinger, and Homeland Security can't do anything to stop it. Arizona is the only state that still has a right-to-carry law, and like it or not, they are the only state that has a low crime rate. I try not to let my mind go to these dark places, so I just stop listening to news. Mostly, they are trying to sell me something anyway, so what's the point of the exercise? They can't sell me what I won't buy. Still, I wondered about Madison and how many universities would need to be destroyed until our populace was rendered ignorant and easily controlled by a shadow corporate government.

As I was trying to remember that I was safe and that for the time being I did not need to worry about the hoards coming in over the ramparts, Rains On Grass came over to me and sat down. I didn't say anything, but when I looked up from my coffee he was looking right into my eyes.

"So you think you are safe." As he spoke those words, he started to laugh in a soft chuckle. "You will never be safe again, Scarecrow." He paused, and as he did the hair on my neck stood up. He was calling the shots, and I knew truth was being spoken. I didn't want to hear what he had to say; it was going to be painful and ugly, and it was exactly why I had come here, but to be face-to-face with the reality of what was coming next made me just want to crawl out of my skin.

He continued, "You will never be safe again in this world until you face the lesson the Grandfathers are trying to teach you. You have wasted too much time and let the horses out of the barn once too many. Your path is very narrow now and it is hard to see. It had been left alone for too long, and the grass and sage make it hard to see with even Eagle eyes. You need to prepare yourself in a sacred manner. You need to do a sweat tonight, Scarecrow. I have seen the two outcomes you now carry within you. One is bad, the other worse. You need to be stronger than you think you can be, and when the pain is too great you must be even stronger. This is the place you have been training for all these years. Do not blame others for this; you have designed this test even before you came to this Earth Mother. You have been working on it in your dreams. Your sleep was merely a veil to get you to this point in time. You can leave if you want, but you will be a haunted man. You will be one lost to time."

I felt a calm enter me, a kind of stillness, as if warm glue was poured down inside me from my head to my feet. I realized I just wanted to stop. That all those years of trying to get in front of something, trying to get there just a little bit ahead of the next guy, was such a silly way to be for someone who said that was the behavior they hated in others. I was giving up and surrendering to a process that was beyond me. It was the end of the world as I knew it, and I felt fine. Finally, I was at a point where it really didn't matter what happened next. All I had to do was chop wood and carry water, and the play of it would work itself out in its own special, maniacal way. I still felt fear, but somehow it was just a room inside me that I could visit if I wanted to and I didn't have to stay there. It hit me in a flash that my thoughts were just that. They were random things floating in my consciousness, but they weren't the me that I thought they were. I was the chooser of the thoughts and not the thoughts themselves, so I was free. I could choose whatever I wanted to think, so I could choose what I wanted to feel, so I could choose what reality I wanted to happen. At least that was the theory of it—the practice was a little hard to fly; I still had those rooms inside my head and my heart. Those fucking rooms full of fear and terror and self-loathing ... every once in a while they demanded attention. However, not today. Today all those little bastards were on a busman's holiday to Coney Island, and I felt at peace. Sometimes when you're at the end of the line, everything becomes clear and you know exactly what you have to do. You know what foot you have to put down next, and you start to have grace. The kind of grace that is very humbling as you are hyperaware of the shit you have stirred up before and how far you have fallen. So then every step becomes a step of ascension, even if you are ascending to your own inevitable demise. In the Vedic scripture there is mention of the Place of the Five Rivers. There you are standing at this kind of watery crossroads, and you have to choose the one river out of five to go down. Clinging to the side and trying to get out only smashes you into the rocks and certain death. You have to choose a river and boldly swim to the middle to take the fate of whatever your chosen river takes you to. The trick is to know that eventually all rivers lead to the same place. Most people spend their lives being unable to choose what river they think they should go down. They weigh this option and that, and like Immanuel Kant's tree of life, they spend their lives trying to decide what piece of fruit they really want to eat while the fruit withers and drops from the branches, leaving them with nothing but the vague notion that they could have been a contender. No, you have to jump in and swim for your life, and you have to learn to have grace, and you have to learn to laugh out loud at the absurdity of your situation. You must learn to embrace the river, to dive and swim underwater and avert the rocks at the last second by anticipating the pressure of their mass, dogging their wrath like a salmon driven to spawn. You must let go of theory and embrace the now, and the now, and the now, and the now. You must let yourself be guided by an unseen light that is known only to you and follow it blindly as if it were your only chance at life. For in the reality of the now, it is your only salvation.

I took a deep breath and looked at Rains On Grass for what seemed like several minutes. The chiseled features of his weather-worn face were shaped in a kind of semipermanent smile. As I met his gaze again, his eyes twinkled and his lips turned up slightly into the begging of a grin, and I started to laugh.

CHAPTER 8

Bill Weaver had owned his own software company since the early '90s and made bank within the first two years. He married a woman who looked good on his arm and gave him two physically beautiful children, and there really wasn't much more to the family than that. They were rich and perfect-looking and never talked about anything that would seem untoward or seedy, in public or out. In fact, so much was about the exterior that it was hard to see if any of them had a personality at all, at least on the surface.

Underneath was a different story, at least for Bill. When Bill was a young teen in summer camp, he had a sexual maniac for a bunkmate named Roger. Roger had been molested, the first time when he was only 8 years old, by his parish priest, at least nine times. The problem with sexual molestation to a young person is that it is incredibly hard for the one being molested to make sense out of the very adult feelings of pleasure, especially when it is surrounded with secrecy and guilt. Immediately the sexual preferences are surrounded by something bad and wrong, and yet the gratification and pleasure cannot be denied. The most tragic thing that is passed on is the secret need to seduce another into the dark world of pleasure and guilt. It didn't take Roger long to get Bill to masturbate with him, and then finally submit to ass play. They were close friends, and boys of that age like to have secrets anyway. By the time Bill left camp, he had developed a voracious appetite for anal sex. He spent his whole adult life dating women, and on the rare occasion that he would find one who was more adventurous, he would try to get her to indulge his secret desires. After much humiliation and rejection, he learned that his needs just did not fit into the picture he saw of himself in society. More importantly, he knew the reputation he was building as the athlete and businessman would not tolerate any sexual perverseness of his variety. Bill just shut off a part of himself that would only be controlled but not denied. During his junior year on a road trip for the UCLA Bruins to an Eastern school, he chanced upon a prostitute late one night in downtown Boston. The woman was well-schooled in the sexual arts, and as they climbed the five flights of stairs to her Chinatown apartment, she realized she could prob-ably take all this young athlete's money by finding his particular brand of kink that was well-hidden but obvious to a person of her talents. She laid him down on her soiled sheets and rubbed him with wonderful-smelling oil, knowing that to open his coffers wide she must not let on to the experimental nature of her work. While she was going down on him, she played with his balls and gently let her long ruby fingernail caress his anus. Immediately she felt him pulse and arch his lower back, and she knew she'd hit pay dirt. She started by massaging him with a very small vibrator, and by the end of the third day, after he had wired home twice for more money, she had advanced him quickly to a rather large strap-on dildo. Bill had found his kink. He was quite happy with the secret aspect of visiting hookers for his weekly bouts of ass-reaming that was kept completely secret from his wife, his children, and the life he had made for himself in his expensive gated Southern California community.

Bill was not aware of the deviousness of the women he was dealing with, until he met one who almost took him to the cleaners and exposed him to his family and friends. By this time Bill was a pillar in his community, and as his business grew, so did his public stature. An astute hooker in a seedy Hollywood flat that Bill started to frequent had seen his picture in the *L.A. Times* at a groundbreaking ceremony with the mayor and realized she had a meal ticket when he asked for ass play. As the blackmail grew in size and proportion, the spending habits of the hooker did not go unnoticed by the Hollyweird underworld. Bill Weaver was approached by a man who said he could take care of the problem for a fixed amount and it would never be spoken of again; there would be no repercussions. The strange man was connected and had outstanding references for his work. It struck Bill simply as a business decision that was fairly foolproof and made sense. Besides, the problem needed to be handled, and the woman had crossed the line and put him and his small empire at risk. Bill surprised himself by quickly agreeing to the proposal, and within hours the problem had been permanently taken care of. At first he thought he had feelings of guilt and remorse about hiring a contract killer, but he soon realized the only way it really did affect him was the stress that he might be caught and charged as an accomplice to murder. After a few months passed and he realized there would never be any repercussions, the bad feelings quickly disappeared and were replaced by a sense of well-being. He felt he was truly a man in charge of his destiny.

After Bill was sure he was safe and more in control of his world again, the old feelings started to creep back. He wanted to find another arrangement but realized it would have to be more sophisticated. He needed someone with more discretion. Bill's company had developed some software that was quickly becoming the rage for all the computer-animation houses in Hollywood, and so he found himself invited to some of the most well-to-do gatherings the filmmaking elite had to offer. On one of these occasions he found himself wandering alone at a party while his wife and children were home asleep. As he walked up to the bar near the softly lit swimming pool just off of Mulholland Drive, he noticed a woman who seemed to be eyeing him in a manner he had become familiar with ever since that time in Boston all those years ago in college. The woman was very careful not to seem too open and forthright as she sauntered over to him and made it obvious he could engage anytime he wanted, but she would not force the issue. When he started to make small talk with her, the woman got right to the point, saying that she was here at the request of a client and that she would be willing to talk later if he needed to. She handed him her business card with her phone number on it that simply stated, "For discreet dominant service, Kat."

When Kat left the bizarre but comfortable world of Bobby Doucette, she struggled to make a go of it back at her old profession as a set makeup artist for TV shows and the occasional movie. She had gotten lax about taking jobs, and Bobby never asked her to work when she didn't want to. In the new Hollywood, with all the production jobs going to Canada, Mexico, and other states, not returning calls is almost the death-blow for a career. It takes a long time to be a producer's first call and when you have dropped to the fifth or sixth call on a job-category list it's time to start looking for a waitress job, fast. Kat started working the graveyard shift at the Goldmine Diner on Santa Monica Boulevard. It was frequented by the transsexual, gay, and after-hours crowd, which would come there after the bars closed and before the late-night street business started. Kat hadn't seen her friend Missy since they did a reality TV show together years before, so when she walked in surrounded by some very high-rolling new Hollywood types, it was obvious to everyone that Missy was very much in control of her world and her finances. Her outfit was an exquisite design that must have cost well over $2,000. When Missy saw Kat, she insisted that Kat sit down right then and there and have dinner with them all. When Kat hesitated and said she really couldn't until her shift was over, Missy got up and pulled Kat aside. She told Kat that she could give her a job starting the next day making $1,200 tax-free a week for about 10 hours of work spanking businessmen and never having sex with them. Kat asked her how, and Missy told her the story of how she was now the owner of a very high-priced dominatrix house in Beverly Hills and was looking for some new girls. The ones she had weren't holding up too well in the very discreet business and didn't get that no sex meant no sex. It seems the girls were freelancing on the side, and that was intolerable to Missy and her legal requirements under California's state law. It took Kat about 30 seconds to be convinced, and she went to her manager and turned in her apron, sat down, and had a Bloody Mary with her new boss. Kat was working for Missy about six months before she started getting her own clientele. The money that was available for freelancing was too much of a temptation, and Kat started working on the side. She realized that sooner or later, Missy would find out and that would be that. But Kat had a plan. She would go to another part of town and open up her own dungeon that specialized in kinkier aspects of sexual needs that weren't covered under the standard kinky types that Missy's dungeon covered. Not the kinky boys who needed to be spanked and kiss feet; she was going for the freakier clients—the ones who needed to be urinated on and tied up and abused with various strap-on accoutrements. Sure, there was a risk, as this behavior got directly into what the law would consider sexual favors. But Kat had noticed that the men who need this kind of training and sexual gratification were very secretive and wouldn't for the most part want to spoil a place where their secret desires could be realized. So she rented a small flat and did most of the work herself on the decorations and appliances, and she told Missy she was moving on. Because Kat was honest with Missy and didn't put her at risk, Missy returned the favor to Kat by sending her clients who couldn't be serviced by Missy's more tame establishment. In no time, Kat was making a large amount of money and had a new musician boyfriend, but something wasn't quite right, and it started to work on Kat's psyche. She was, for all the world to see, a sophisticated, intelligent woman in charge of her world. But she, like everyone else, had a weakness.

There are a certain amount of feelings that must be put aside when taking something as sacred as sex is to human beings and using it as merely a biological function for entertainment. Almost immediately, all involved become out of balance and depleted somehow. In the ancient religions, it was well known that to have a deep emotional experience as one does in the sex act somehow binds you to that person on an energetic level and links you with every other person they have been with in a sexual manner. There are simple ways to clear yourself, but after you have, you end up not wanting to be put in that particular vulnerable spot again. In the Buddhist tradition, there is an understanding that as you become more aware, the Kundalini starts to rise. This is the ancient way of understanding that energy blockages in the chakras, or energy centers, throughout your body begin expanding and are capable of downloading new and greater sources of subtle energy. Kat had been sober with Bobby and around his highly developed energy for some time, and she had even started learning about her own spiritual awakening. There is a false point in the process where one tends to think they are powerful and in control, and the energy released throughout the body can be very dangerous. The ancients knew this and had a very specific way of dealing with it, as it was natural for anyone who was on a spiritual path to enlightenment. A young monk would be carefully monitored, as he was expected to start having sexual feelings when the energy centers started to wake up. There is nothing at all wrong with this; it is quite natural and was planned for in the old monastic life. This new energy, if properly guided and harnessed, was the thing that gave so many of these early monks their seemingly special powers.

One of the tests typical of young Tibetan Buddhists was to take the rising of the Kundalini energy and perform a simple exercise to demonstrate that they were able to control the energy and were ready to move to the next level. The young monk would strip naked except for a small loincloth and sit in a fresh snowbank over some rocky ground. With concentration techniques he had learned and the ability to channel his Kundalini energy, he would be able to melt the snow in a circle around him down to the bedrock. Depending on how big the circle was, his teachers could efficiently monitor his progress. Seventeen feet was considered mastery. The meditation techniques are very simple. What it means to chop wood and carry water can turn anything into meditation if done with a singular relaxed-yet-controlled focus.

(NOVEMBER - •) " Get a hobby! Learn to garden, build a model of an old sailing ship, learn how to paddle a sea kayak, find something that you can sink your mind into with no distractions. Not for the sake of producing anything, although everything should be done to your best expectation, but for the sake of having a quiet, focused time where your mind learns to apply itself. There is no perfection, so don't make it an exercise in self-hatred, but

you must try to better yourself every time. You must learn to link what you are doing with your mind and body to what you are feeling and thinking so there are no blockages. At that point you will be ready, and as the old saying goes, when the student is ready the teacher appears ..."

Johnny Two Bags had been off and on heroin so many times that he probably held some kind of record. He called himself a musician but had not really accomplished much as far as writing goes for about a decade. There is a false sense that drugs create in a person, where they feel that they cannot create without their particular brand of poison. With heroin specifically, there is about a two-week period after you start taking the drug that's most seductive. If you are an artist already and you start with the smack, you are able for a brief period to tap into a part of your psyche that remains hidden most of the time. You can create amazing works if you have trained yourself already to be able to produce. But the ride is pitifully short, and after about a week and a half you start to lose the connection and the panic sets in. You realize too late that the only thing to do is to hang on and try to stay stoned because now you're a junkie and must feed the beast. Sometimes it's enough to fool an artist for a long time into thinking that if they can just get back to that magic place again, greatness would be assured. It's a false game, and anyone who finally gets straight starts to realize there are other ways to tap into the muse without destroying yourself and everything you care about to get there. One of the hardest things for someone who is unbalanced is to realize that maybe the reality of their own life has nothing to do with the myth they have created about themselves. This is who Johnny Two Bags had become. He was a shell of himself, a little rock-and-roll boy who never grew up, and in never growing up, never had to realize that the small amount of talent he had and wasted was never going to be found again as long as he was a junkie. He blew it and had become a caricature of himself. He still had the skinny, junkie rock-and-roll look with impossibly tight pants, but the bottom line was he was a man in his mid-30s with one hit record over a decade ago, and the pants were starting to look silly on a man of his age.

Kat had been in the other room with her new client for over an hour and had told Johnny to just chill out until she was done. Johnny had felt the itch a little earlier and knew he wanted to get high, and it was all he could do not to cook up the last of the dope they had. Kat had Bill Weaver tied over a leather-padded wooden horse and was teasing him. Bill had hinted that he was ready to try something more risqué, or as he had put it, he wanted to give up more control in their now biweekly sessions. Early on Kat had asked Bill if he wanted a man to pleasure him, and by Bill's angry response she knew immediately that special sessions with Johnny and her would be out of the question. Johnny somehow decided it would be OK for him to shoot up the last of the dope after the pressure in his mind had become almost unbearable. He started cooking the dope and preparing himself for his fix. Kat was in the other room and had just put a ball gag in Bill Weaver's mouth when she smelled the dope works cooking. She told Bill that he was going to have to wait while she took care of some phone calls in the other room. She turned the music up and marched into the hidden alcove just in time to see Johnny Two Bags shoot most of their remaining dope into his arm.

Kat was furious, but she knew there was nothing she could do to the idiot who was already starting to nod. An incredible wave of fear and loathing passed through her as she stood watching the scene and all she could hear were voices telling her to get high. All she wanted to do was turn off the feelings and make the whole world she was living in go away. She thought of a time years before when she was sitting in Big Sur, California, and felt completely at peace. That is where she wanted to be right now. She momentarily thought about the bound client she had in other room and the money he represented and did a quick junkie calculation that everything would be fine. She heated up the rest of the heroin and injected it in her arm. Seconds later, she nodded out on the couch next to Johnny Two Bags, and as she did a trickle of saliva seeped out of her mouth.

Johnny Two Bags was clean and sober for eight years before this round of becoming a dope fiend. He had gone to rehab and been in several recovery houses and attended Narcotics and Alcoholics Anonymous meetings as if they were the source of life itself. To say that Johnny was in a cult was not quite getting to the point of his dementia. AA and NA save the lives of people who would never be saved anyway else. The problem is that when someone gets sober, it's just the start of an exercise that can take more than one lifetime to sort out. In Johnny's case, he got sober and started to rise to points of leadership within the organization and became a mentor for others before healing himself. His problem was that he had never dealt with the reason that made him use in the first place. After several ruined relationships and job opportunities, and probably permanently screwing up the people's lives he was a sponsor for in the program, the reality of the deep, unhealed sickness within him started to boil to the surface again. As if another entity were controlling him, he mysteriously started to get cravings after almost a decade of not using. The voice inside his head that told him that everything would be fine, that he could handle his high this time, started to make more and more sense. He had started to hang around Kat, and they were both drawn to each other as the sickness inside them was driving them to find release. Almost as if by magic, they simultaneously started to use even though there was close to 20 years of sobriety between the two of them. These were not stupid people. In fact, they were highly intelligent and prided themselves on not being part of the cowed masses who could not see through the mist of modern culture down to what they both took to be the real thing. They would collectively make fun of a society of sheep that marched in lockstep to whatever political and economic whims the prevailing societal winds were blowing that year. This separation, pride, and elitism were what eventually became their downfall, as finally the clique they had invented for themselves became a support group of only two hipsters in a city used to finding people's defects and pressing on nerves until the walls that protected that particular weakness just melted away. Johnny had come unglued, and Kat had fallen with him. They were making money and seemed to be in control of their lives, but it was only an illusion that would be quickly blown away by an evil wind blowing in from the High Desert in Nevada.

Johnny stumbled out of the room that he and Kat were in to take a piss and started the chain of events that would lead to his and Kat's deaths. For several months now he had been helping Kat with some of the clientele in different ways, depending on their kink, and was making good money for his time. Many of the clients were men with severe power issues who could find no release because of their inherent fear, except in a domination scenario. Usually these were powerful men who had made their way in the world by being bullies and never found a place where their softer, more feminine side could come out. Because of their unwholesome lifestyle, they became out of balance and would look for some kind of ritualized, sadomasochistic scenario where they could meet the needs of the other side of their split personalities. Most of these men harbored deep feelings of worthlessness and wanted to be punished for their self-loathing. Johnny would take the position as Kat's assistant for the ones who needed extra humiliation from both a woman and a man. So when Johnny saw Bill tied across the padded-leather horse with a ball gag in his mouth, unable to talk, he assumed in his narcotic haze that the man before him needed to be worked on. As Johnny Two Bags applied some pain and humiliation to the man spread out before him with all the bizarre sexual devices at his disposal, he could not hear that the man was screaming out his safe word that was supposed to put an end to the agony. For over 45 minutes, Johnny Two Bags tortured Bill Weaver until Kat finally heard the muffled screams and became cognizant enough to put a stop to the madness that was being inflicted on her client whose main concern was privacy and secrecy.

By the time Kat had untied Bill, he had already made his decision. A block down the street from Kat's dungeon was a pay phone where Bill Weaver called a number he had memorized and had never written down anywhere. After a quick meeting with his mystery contact, Kat and Johnny Two Bags were clearly identified, and Bill gladly—for the second time—paid the fee and did not ever think about them again. The strange man watched the couple for two days before deciding on the method he would use for his black work. When both of his targets had left the dungeon, he merely slipped inside and placed some super pure heroin in several locations around the apartment. When Kat and Johnny returned, their junkie logic of finding all this free dope led to the reasoning that the good dope fairy had left them something they both deserved. They did a quick taste test and everything seemed fine. Johnny was the first to shoot up, and everything seemed OK to Kat as she watched while wanting desperately to get high. As she loaded the syringe with the dope that was much too powerful for her and started to inject it into her vein, a nameless, horrible fear shot through her consciousness for the last time. She had a feeling of extreme danger, and she started to understand that something terrible was going down. She hesitated and tried to get a lock on what was happening when she was overcome by a strange, terrible feeling of something inside expanding and contracting. It felt as though she wanted to rip her flesh off and eviscerate the thing that was tormenting her. She found her remaining good vein, and with shaky hands shot up the super smack. Johnny stopped respiration at approximately 4:05 p.m. that day, and Kat's obsidian head dropped forward for the last time 8 minutes and 42 seconds later as she retched a thin stream of vomit from her mouth.

Venice Beach, California, is a place where people who are searching for their own personal grail end up when they have run out of other places to look. It doesn't mean they even know they are looking, but they do know they have given up pretending they can exist in normal society. It's a place of artists, losers, lunatics, and prophets who are working at finding a key to the secrets, at minimum wage. The very air is rarefied there, and as it creeps into your bones, you start to get used to a world that in any other town would be called a circus. The boardwalk in Venice is nothing more than a concrete street with small shops and arcades that line the oceanfront. It is filled with every kind of human-powered conveyance ever known: surfboards, rollerblades, any kind of bicycle you could think of and some you couldn't. It is a moving menagerie incessantly looking at itself to see what it should do next. One of the icons of Venice Beach is nothing more than an old piece of plywood with some wheels attached. Skateboards were invented here, and the people who ride them seem to have a tenacity not found in many athletes except of Olympic quality. Any given day and well into the night, there are hoards of parentless children and young adults testing their skills in the city's only skate park, about a stone's throw from the Pacific Ocean's famous Venice surf break. It's on the other side of Windward Avenue away from Muscle Beach, and to the uneducated it looks like nothing more than part of a sculptured and manicured ocean park full of palm trees and people with staples in their noses. But to someone with a skateboard and a pair of sneakers, it is a world full of danger, challenge, and tests, and a hierarchy that would rival a medieval fiefdom. These are very serious young people who will mangle and maim their bodies in the quest to find a way to perfect some arcane flip, twist, spin, or spiral that allows them to defy gravity for a fleeting second, and to soar like an albatross over the concrete sea, suspended in time and for a moment free of the earthly gravitational laws. For a young person to step up in front of his or her peers and take a turn at riding the concrete berm, they must have already practiced enough hours to become proficient enough to enter the Julliard School of Music on an accordion scholarship. This is a sport that invented itself out of a need to have nothing at all to do with something other than being one with the energy of the human body. Unfortunately, as with all human endeavors, somehow the corruption set in and the dark side of human ego placed itself squarely within the mad world of Venice skate punks. Like their elder brother surfers, somewhere between 1966 and now, skateboarding has become less about self-expression and more about competition. It has become very serious, with corporate sponsorships and the pressure that comes with representing a product in a capitalist society. So skate kids, like fans of any other sport, tend to emulate their heroes and try to look like they do, as they bend and contort their bodies flying into the netherworld of momentary zero gravity.

Joshua Duke didn't mind so much that his father made him wear a skateboard helmet. After all, most of the professional skaters wore them, and kids didn't make fun of you like they used to only a year before. What bothered him was that his dad insisted that, on the weekends down at Venice Beach while Josh was skating, he hang around. It wasn't that Josh minded that his dad was the only one of the kids' parents who would hang around; in fact, he kind of liked it. The problem with his dad was that, on duty or off duty, he always looked like a cop, and it made the other kids nervous and they kind of kept clear of him. Josh was a good kid with a good head on his shoulders, and he didn't feel the need to fit in with the kids who got high and smoked. It wasn't that he was a straight razor as much as he was focused on a goal he had as small boy to become a doctor. It was near Easter when he was 5 years old that his mother gathered him and took him to the hospital, where his father was being treated for a gunshot wound to the chest, that Josh first took notice of the gravity and powers of the medical profession. He had seen his mother worry before, but not like this. He could tell that if something happened to his father, his mother might not be strong enough to take it. His father was in surgery for nearly six hours, and his aunt had come to take him home, but Josh demanded that he be able to wait with his mother. When the ER surgeon came out and pulled his mother aside, Josh held his breath. The doctor looked like the most important person he had ever seen, the absolute ideal of what is profound and important in the world. He calmly told his mother that his father, FBI Special Agent Jefferson Duke, would pull through. Surrounded by the men from his father's agency when the drug sting they were working on for nine months went bad, his mother's legs gave out and the men guided her to a nearby couch in the waiting room. Josh could see that his mother was going to be alright and kept his attention on the doctor. The doctor came over to him and knelt down, with his green surgical scrubs still on, and started talking to Josh. He couldn't remember anything the doctor said, but he just kept looking in the most kind and compassionate eyes he had ever seen. From that moment on, Josh knew what he wanted to do, and he was going to let nothing stand in his way. So it wasn't that he cared what the other kids thought about him; it was in fact that at the tender age of 13, Josh Duke didn't want the other kids to feel so uncomfortable that he and his dad were at the skate park that they would leave.

Tim Ashley, at 15 years of age, spent more time on a skateboard than he did off it. He was an incredible athlete, capable of the most intricate of skate tricks. So much so that he was being courted by the big skate companies to see if he had the stuff of a competitor. He had been featured several times in different national skate magazines, but besides some new sneakers and a couple of T-shirts had never gotten any of the big endorsements that could make a star out of a local Venice kid. Tim's father had left the family when he was 3, and his mother had not done a very good job of raising him and his younger brother and sister. Tim's mother had been in and out of rehab several times, and the kids had been in several foster homes. She was back from a new program the state of California had implemented trying to use different modalities of rehabilitation for single mothers. The program included yoga, meditation, and organic food intake, and it seemed to be working miracles in many women's lives. The problem with Tim Ashley was that although his mother might be doing better, a certain kind of fear had been instilled in him that was waiting for its chance to wreak havoc in the boy's life.

There was a new board trick that Tim was trying to master on the low berm before he went on to anything higher. It was sort of a barrel roll when you came off the berm. The rider would skate to the top of the berm and ride it about a third of the way round, and then come off as the board started to roll about one to two times. The rider would then get back on the board and ride it back down or jump onto the flat concrete. From 20 feet away, to the uninitiated, it looked like nothing. But up close, to the trained eye, it was a complicated, gravity-defying move. Tim had been working on it for a good part of the day before Josh and his dad had shown up. This was enough time for some of the other kids to start copying the move. One of the skate kids who copied everything he saw was a 17-year-old boy named Eddie Jinks, who was on the semi-pro circuit. Eddie had a couple of endorsements and was trying to get picked up for sponsorship in the Gravity Games. He had been running a little dry in the tricks department, and so was slumming down at the beach trying to see if anything new was happening. Eddie had been watching Tim all day. Anyone who cared knew that Tim was prone to coming up with something new more often than not. Eddie was hanging out with some girls who knew of his local hero fame and pretended to not pay attention to Tim. Tim was aware of what Eddie was up to, and it made him furious. Eddie had stolen his tricks before, and Tim had even seen him on cable TV talking about how he had invented Tim's own tricks. Eddie got up from the circle of admirers around him just as Josh arrived and started to copy the trick that Tim had been working on all day. Tim stopped and watched as Eddie's showmanship made him look heroic while trying out Tim's newest trick for his fans. Tim just watched. Inside the anger turned to hatred, and he started to have violent, adolescent thoughts about what should happen to Eddie. Somewhere, from a very dark place, something was shaken loose from where it should have stayed and made its way to the Venice skate berm. Tim could see the mileage Eddie was getting with his trick and decided he would do him one better and roll his board not once or twice, but three times—a trick he only practiced by himself in an abandoned pool near where he lived with his mom. Eddie had just come off the berm with a near-perfect version of Tim's trick roll and pointed his fingers at him in a taunting way. The switch tripped inside Tim's 15-year-old brain and something dark attached itself to the will of the young skater. Tim saw a younger skater setting himself up for a run on the berm. Skate protocol, like its elder surfing rules, dictates that the person who lines up first is the one who gets the wave—or, in this instance, the one who gets to perform a trick on the berm. Tim's pain and humiliation got the best of him as he disregarded everything except wanting to win, to get the best of Eddie, and to have everyone look at him and give him the recognition he so craved. Because of his anger, Tim came into the berm a little too fast, and his board arced off in the lethal direction of the young skater now committed to his run on the berm. Joshua had his helmet on but had not buckled it like his father told him a hundred times. The careening board hit Joshua at a velocity of around 65 miles an hour as it ripped his helmet off and hit him between the nose and the eye socket. As Joshua tumbled backward, his head hit the steel reinforcement of the berm, and he was unconscious a split second after his head hit the concrete. Blood was starting to trickle out of his left ear by the time his father, Special Agent Jefferson Duke, picked him up and started running for the Venice Beach police station.

Jedidiah Wolmack was riding bicycles literally before he could walk. As a small boy, he had a slight palsy in his legs and could not walk, but somehow he managed to teach himself to ride the red cruiser bicycle his father had bought for him in hopes that someday he could ride the suburban Connecticut streets. When Jedidiah was at Stanford as a young undergrad, he got a tryout for the Olympic bicycle team and nearly got the site, except for the fact that it interfered with his goal of selection for the FBI. His decision on a warm New England fall day was that nothing would stand in his way of getting into the FBI, but he never gave up his passion for long-distance bike riding. Part of the reason he took the placement in Los Angeles from Washington was that he could ride year-round. He contacted several riding clubs and found one that seemed pretty serious as soon as he found out he got the appointment to the Los Angeles office. After moving his family into their new Santa Monica home and checking in with his new office, he went to the most upscale bike shop he could find and bought himself a brand new carbon fiber and titanium road machine. He even had a custom red paint job put on the bicycle. By the time he got his spandex matching club uniform and paid his yearly dues, he was close to six grand into the equipment. His wife just laughed when he pulled out of their driveway for the first time. She could still see that 6-year-old boy posing as an FBI assistant director. The Frequent Flyers bicycle club met every Sunday at 6 a.m. to start their 50-mile ride. This weekend, one of the members—a Los Angeles city councilwoman named Felts— had designed a course e-mailed to all 253 members that included a loop of downtown LA's infamous Skid Row. The Frequent Flyers was a very influential group, and her intention was to shed some light on the problem of the homeless population getting out of control in downtown LA. The Frequent Flyers' weekly rides were legendary for their eclectic nature, and one of the main draws was that a different member, based on a lottery, was required to come up with a new course every weekend. Sometimes the rides were politically motivated and sometimes just bizarre, but never boring. And it seemed to work, as they never had any shortage of members to ride with. Jed Wolmack had paced himself about a third of the way back in the pack; he was a little sore and just wanted to pace off the miles and not try for any legendary run through Skid Row. As they started into Skid Row, about 10 miles from their safe parking area, the Frequent Flyers entered a bizarre and sickening world full of hundreds of human beings camped out on the streets and sidewalks of downtown Los Angeles. All the sidewalks were crammed with boxes and tents and makeshift shelters where human beings by the droves were just starting to rouse and shake off the cold of the night spent outside in the open in their own little piece of hell. A small, deformed midget named Clive with an Afro hairstyle had just taken a dump in the street near a storm drain when he saw some of the local crackheads heading for him. He knew they were going to take all the money he had begged the day before if he couldn't get away. He would be glad to give it to them so they would see him as a source of revenue and not kill him, but just as he was preparing to give the mob his earnings, a truck pulled between him and his pursuers. Clive decided to make a break for it. He started running as fast as his three-and-a-half-foot frame would take him and darted out into the street. A man named Thomas Fong who was going to his import-export business swerved to miss Clive and lost control of his Lexus. He was on his way to try to get rid of some illegal food products he had brought into the country. Fong, tipped off by a crooked Customs official that he was going to be raided later that day, was doing 70 miles per hour trying to arrive in time to get rid of the illegal shipment.

Out of nowhere, AD Wolmack heard Bobby Doucette's voice screaming at him to stop immediately. The Lexus crashed through the throng of blue, green, and orange spandex-uniformed bicyclists, killing three of them instantly, including an investigator in the local district attorney's office whom Wolmack had just been riding abreast off. Wolmack had stopped just two feet short of the mayhem for no other reason than a voice in his head.

Lt. Quinn was ushered into the FBI office situation room, and right away he could tell the whole floor of the Los Angeles division of the FBI was a bit spooked. The level of security was up a notch, and everyone was a bit jumpy. When he entered the room, he saw what remained intact of the Mumford task force. AD Wolmack was leaning over a table that was very busy with people on computers and phone lines and papers and maps, and there was a grim sense of urgency gripping the room. Agent Herrill looked a mess, and she didn't have her makeup on. It was no wonder. She had narrowly escaped a serial rapist who had been haunting the west side. If it weren't for a .38 snub-nose strapped to her ankle, there was no telling what would have happened. As it was, her face was still black-and-blue, and she was moving very slowly from her two broken ribs. Wolmack looked up at Quinn and held his gaze. Quinn could tell the AD was glad to have him attached from LAPD, because he was probably the only person who could figure out where the hell Bobby Doucette was. Quinn looked around and saw Agent John Steger, who was on a phone and computer simultaneously. Steger's eyes looked up momentarily; he nodded and quickly looked away. Steger and Quinn were the only ones untouched so far by what was starting to be known in LA law enforcement circles as the Mumford curse. Quinn could tell that everyone in the room looked at him as if he had some kind of disease, wondering when the other shoe was going to drop on him. He snickered to himself as he realized this is how Bobby must feel around here. AD Wolmack came over to Quinn and grabbed his hand in a very warm way.

"How are you holding up, LT?" Wolmack asked as if they just come from a wake.

"Not too bad, Jed. How is Andy doing?"

AD Wolmack grimaced as he thought about Agent Brubaker.

"No too good, Thomas. It seems the stroke paralyzed not only his right side, but his bladder and bowl functions seem to be non-functioning. They're trying to keep him pumped out, and he is on dialysis, but it doesn't look good. It's touch-and-go."

"I'm really sorry. Brubaker was a standup guy," Quinn said in a low tone.

"No he wasn't, Thomas. In fact, I think Bobby was right; he was as dirty as they come, and I'm going to find out how dirty. Still, he's in a bad way, and all this is just plain weird. Speaking of weird, have you gotten a lock on Bobby?"

"Yes, that's why I called you. It dawned on me today that he told me a dozen times the only place in the whole world he thinks is safe. It's out in Navajo country on a reservation."

"In Arizona?"

"No, the northwestern corner of New Mexico. It seems there is this Nam vet medicine man that has some kind of clinic for lost puppies that seems to get results."

"Sounds like we need to take this whole crew there when this thing is over," AD Wolmack said in the solemn tones of a new believer.

"Maybe you're right on that, but I'm going to go out there tomorrow and try to find him."

"Is your wife OK with the safe house?"

"Yes, and I just want to officially thank you and the bureau for that," Quinn said.

"No problem, Thomas. Unfortunately, I didn't have to fudge anything to get it approved. Listen, Quinn, I'd like to give you a man because the LAPD is doing us a favor on this one, but the only guy I can really let go is John, and I know the how that must sit."

"I was hoping for some backup," Quinn said. "Steger is fine, he'll be just fine; he's a good man."

Both men paused and looked at each other as unsaid things darted across their eyes. They turned and looked at Agent Steger as he simultaneously looked up at them. A cold chill ran down John Steger's spine, and he felt a rush of air as if an invisible wing had just flapped past his face.

CHAPTER 9

Crow was looking for Coyote again after he did not show up when he was supposed to. Crow sent out a dream story to Coyote some time ago but had not heard back. So Crow just relaxed and let a guide wind from a sky spirit take him to where Coyote was now. He saw a small light fly by him and drop into a draw near some scrub pine and disappear. Crow circled lazily around the draw, following the path of the light, and dropped down onto a sand flat next to Coyote.

Coyote was busily chewing on the remaining carcass of a prairie dog when Crow landed in front of him.

"Crow!" Coyote yelped. "Look what Coyote hunted down! Look, Crow, Coyote has Rat," Coyote said as he tore off the meat of the prairie dog's right hindquarter.

"Coyote, did you not see Ghost Brother's dream story that we were looking for you?" Crow said in an exasperated way.

Coyote knew that Crow would know if he lied, but he thought he would try it anyway.

"No, Crow, Coyote saw nothing. I was hunting Rat because you were not here to help Coyote find Rabbit, so I had to hunt Rat. I think Crow might not be doing his job helping Coyote, and I will tell Ghost Brother when he comes," Coyote said, pulling off some more meat.

"Coyote," Crow said sternly, "it doesn't matter what you think; you cannot get away with not doing your job now!"

Coyote continued to eat and pretended as if he could not hear what Crow was saying. Crow continued, "Ghost Brother knows what you are up to, Coyote, and you had better be back to Empty Man's hideout or it will not be good for you." Coyote just kept eating, tearing out part of the prairie dog's liver and intestinal tract. The meat snapped back as it pulled free of the carcass and hit Coyote in his eye, and he dropped the meat in the sand. Crow started to laugh and squawk at Coyote, and as was his nature, Coyote started to get mad. Coyote pretended not to be upset, and while standing up slowly made his way over to Crow as if he had forgotten something. Crow was four feet into the air by the time Coyote lunged at him. Crow landed on a branch in a nearby scrub pine and waited for Coyote to notice that a Ghost Brother had arrived from the shadow world. Crow stopped laughing and stood on the branch, blinking in the sun and listening as Coyote growled and paced back and forth in front of him.

"Coyote," Crow said in a warning tone that was disguised a bit to try to alert Coyote to the visitor.

"Coyote, there is someone here …" Crow was cut off.

"Crow, you make me so mad. I will eat you if I can catch you, and I don't care what you or Ghost Brother think! You are supposed to help me find Rabbit, Crow, and I haven't had any Rabbit for a moon. I think you are not doing your job, and I will tell Ghost Brother about this. I don't think Ghost Brother is doing his job either, because he is supposed to bring Rabbit to me. I do what I'm supposed to do and find Rabbit and Snake and Rat, and what do you do? Fly into the tree and squawk." Crow thought about trying to stop Coyote from ranting but decided he would just wait and see what would happen next.

What happened next was a rent in the time-space continuum, an opening of the thin veil that separates one world from another. It is something usually seen out of the corner of one's eye. A movement, a shadow, something that we tell ourselves is not there. But the hair that is standing straight up on our arms and the sinking feeling in our stomachs let us know that our rational mind is a liar. From a place that we only visit in our dreams, a place of wind and lightning and force of unimaginable strength, something came to visit our world and appeared next to a small, ragged coyote and a black obsidian crow.

(OSCAR - - -) "When you become sensitive to forces outside and inside yourself, you become sort of a light to others in this world and beyond. It is at this stage that you become very vulnerable to your own vices and weaknesses. The thing that lives under the bed is real—it always has been and it always will be. Walls can't stop it. Concrete can't stop it, steel can't stop it; it slips past a lead, titanium, or garlic buffer like a hot knife through butter. The one and only force that can stop it is you. You never have to take delivery on any package in this realm or others if you remember that they always need your signature. You have the power to stop all of this if you choose, and you should always do so until you find out the entities' purpose and motives. You are the sentry of your own mind and body, so challenge whomever or whatever wants to come to visit. If it's beneficial and loving, it will wait or recede until you are ready. If it's not at all friendly, you and only you have the power to send it back to where it came from, until you give up the right. The strong will eat the weak. What the weak have to remember is that power is a choice given to all. Die on your feet or die on your knees, you decide … death will come to all."

Coyote looked at Crow and stopped his ranting. He could tell Crow was looking at something, but it wasn't Coyote. Coyote turned his head and saw a black shape in the outline of a human that was vibrating, as if it was trying to tune in to this moment and the frequency was not quite right. Coyote could feel the awareness now and knew the entity next to him needed his help. Coyote had known about these beings for as long as he could remember and knew their work was important. He sensed what the being wanted rather than heard and immediately gave his permission for the request. From Crow's point of view, Coyote looked as if he had been struck by lightning as he contorted and yelped, and the dark shadow shape of a Ghost Brother slipped into the now-motionless body of a very small and ragged coyote. For about 15 minutes, the body of Coyote did not move. Then he got up and stood there as a shaft of light known as electric purple seemed to come out of nowhere and animate the body. The coyote looked at the crow and flashed bright green and yellow eyes. Then it took off across the sand wash, heading in the direction of Jack Mumford.

Chief Black Crow was standing on a grass-filled prairie watching me as I tried to understand what was going on. The last thing I was aware of was the box canyon that my team A-392 was in near the Pakistani border when we were hit by rocket and mortar fire. I remember looking at a small depression in the ground that was no more than two or three inches deep and trying to become part of it as the dry terra-cotta-color silt of the canyon bottom groaned when a second RPG round hit. The last thing I remember was meat and bone from the eviscerated torso of 1st Lt. Asker hitting me in the face, and I was momentarily blind. The grenades and ammunition started cooking off his body, and as the shrapnel started hitting me, I went down to a very dark place. The next thing I knew I was in a beautiful plain full of American wild grass that was blowing gently in a warm midsummer breeze. I was dressed in the desert camouflage, clothing that my unit had decided would best blend in and make us look like some of the Pakistani and Afghan herdsmen of the Hindu Kush at a distance. I couldn't get oriented and was hoping the old Indian medicine man could help me figure out what was happening. I was about 200 feet away, so I slowly started walking toward him. I realized as soon as I started moving that I was still carrying my equipment and it felt incredibly heavy.

We had been loaded for a long patrol because we did not want to give away our position by resupply. The team was going to paint bunkers near the Pakistani border that were being resupplied for Al Qaida by targeting them with lasers. Air support would then fire laser-guided munitions at the targets. That was the theory anyway. Our only contact was an Afghan guide who was given to us against our will, as we did not know for sure whom we could trust. He left after the first three days, saying he could not keep up because his health was failing. He started breathing heavy and said his chest hurt. We sent a coded message asking to abort the mission and extract us and the guide. Apparently, someone somewhere thought it would be a good idea to let him return to his village by himself, unescorted, and for us to continue the mission. My team's specialty was stealth and subterfuge, and we had just lost our most important tool of survival. Team A-392 sent one more request to abort the mission and received an urgent reply to continue. We all knew from that moment on what the stakes were. We were naked babies and someone wanted to pitch-fork us into the cleanup chute. Politically we knew there were elements that wanted to start a skirmish near the Pakistani border to bring the war back up to full boil and involve the full support of the Pakistani people against us. We had multiple briefings about the exact location of the border, and we knew it was as porous as the Titanic. We had accounted and trained for every contingency except being sold out by someone in the allied coalition. We thought about it, and then were told to take it as another risk in the game.

I don't know what happened after I got wounded, so all I can go on is what the survivors of that day tell me. Lt. Asker had made the decision to go through the box canyon the day before. Team A-392 was more of a democracy than most of the places I have ever been, and there was a general consensus that we should take the extra two days necessary and skirt the canyon as it just reeked of an ambush. For some reason that day, in the middle of a planning session, Lt. Asker pulled rank and called out our order of march. Team A-392 was an extremely disciplined group of soldiers, so not a word was ever spoken, though we all knew what each man was thinking.

When the firefight started, Master Sgt. Arenas was the next man closest to me, and he had a small rock to hide behind. What he told me of those moments seven months later when I was still in rehab went like this: The rocket-propelled grenade rounds found us right away; whoever it was knew we were coming and had set up very effective kill fire. Apparently the second round that killed the lieutenant and wounded me was the last round to touch any member of Special Forces Team A-392. I had started to get up and everyone was yelling for me to stay down when they started to return aggressive fire. At that point I stood up and kind of spun around and faced a position where the enemy fire had come from. My arms were outstretched and I was bloody from my head to my boots. Al Qaida or the Pakistanis or Afghans or whoever had targeted team A-392 opened up with everything they had.

For 27 minutes before the F-16s and the helicopter evac showed up, I stood there with my head bowed and my arms outstretched as the mayhem of modern warfare came at us in an angry rain of fire and metal. What Master Sgt. Burroughs relayed in the debriefing got him a trip to the division shrink. He said simply that there was a kind of bubble that surrounded team A-392 on that February day that ended in a circle about 20 feet away from the perimeter of the team, and as long as I was standing with my arms outstretched like a scarecrow in a field, that nothing, not even a scorpion, could get through.

I decided I would put my pack down before I went to talk to Black Crow as I perceived no threat at the moment. I knelt down and put my rifle on the grass to remove my pack. When I looked back down from a quick, reflexive scan of my area, my rifle morphed into a prairie dog and scurried away. I realized then that I was in dreamtime. As I got up, Black Crow was about 10 feet away from me, softly chuckling to himself and shaking his head. Then he spoke in his native tongue and laughed out loud. I was still a bit bewildered and tried to orient myself to my surroundings when I heard a voice and turned my head to see a very powerful wolf talking to me.

"How many times will you keep going back there before you just accept the fact that you didn't die that day?" Wolf said.

"Who the fuck are you?" I asked rather puzzled

"I am a wolf spirit, and I am Black Crow's voice for this place in your time structure."

As soon as he spoke, I started to vaguely remember that I was still on the reservation with Red Truck and I had been in the kiva sweat lodge for about three hours with Rains On Grass, Red Truck, Ben, Sully, and few tribal elders. I realized that I must be in the middle of one of the visions that Rains On Grass said I needed to have. It was taking me awhile to let go of the madness I was just in reliving my war story. I turned back to inventory my pack as it morphed into a giant turtle that was slowly moving off in what appeared to be an easterly direction, according to the sun that was low on the horizon in the opposite direction. I heard Black Crow say something, then start to laugh. I turned to the wolf and spoke.

"What did he say?"

"He says that the turtle spirit is a very good sign; he didn't think you would be so lucky." For a moment I started to ponder the novelty that my interpreter in my alerted state was some kind of talking Walt Disney Wolf, but as I did there was a slight fluctuation in my vision field, and I backed off immediately and just flowed with what was happening. When I did, the colors and my surroundings started to solidify in some way. I heard Black Crow speak again and there was no more laughter in his voice. I looked at the wolf and waited.

"He says you need to head off to the north and travel hard until sundown." I looked around then at Black Crow. A cold breeze started out of the north, and there was no humor in Black Crow's eyes. I bowed slightly to them both and started a quick march off in a northerly direction. A feeling of being observed passed through my consciousness and I turned around to scan my surroundings, but I was alone. Both my new spirit guides had vanished. I traveled for what seemed to be two hours and saw an object about a half a klick off to the north. As I got closer, it was obvious that what I saw was an old rusted Buick that looked as if it had been sitting in the same spot for at least 50 years. By the time I got close to the car, the sun had started to set and the wind that was blowing in from the north started to increase and get colder. I looked in the car, and the only thing I saw was an old sleeping bag neatly rolled up in the cavernous backseat. Immediately I started to get incredibly tired. I tried the door but it was stuck. So I put both hands on the old pitted, chromed push-button door handle and gave it a good tug. The door popped open with a groan and a creak as the cold air rushed in. I climbed into the backseat of the old piece of Detroit iron and pulled the door shut behind me. A smell of ozone from old rotting electronic equipment and the musty odor of an old car interior invaded my nostrils as I unrolled the cotton sleeping bag with a flannel interior that included scenes of duck hunters and dogs and wrapped it around me. As soon as I lay down on the couch-like rear seat of the Buick, I started to dream inside a dream.

My dream was an actual event that had happened some years before. I had been invited to a workshop and lecture series on psychic phenomena that was going to take place at the Esalen Institute in Big Sur, California. Big Sur is perhaps one of the most beautiful stretches of coastline anywhere in the world. Its majestic mountains rush down to the Pacific Ocean in daredevil drops as the Pacific Coast Highway clings to its side like a great serpent that is terrified of being flung onto the foaming rocks below. The fogs that cover the aquamarine and slate blue lagoons seem to roll up off the ocean and back to the green-forested mountains, blowing away only to reveal a beauty that is at once terrible and mighty and almost too much for a human mind to grasp. The dramatically treacherous land lends itself to a magical interpretation that can only be talked about in terms of oil and canvas, kiln-fired clay, smoky campfires, and states of consciousness.

Kat wasn't sure she wanted to go and be around so many "new-age hacks," as she put it, but she couldn't turn down an expenses-paid week living on the edge of the sea in Big Sur. The final salient point for her was that free massages and saunas would be provided for all lecturers and one guest. We had checked in early on a Monday and walked down the steep steps to a platform that jutted out over the Pacific where the massages were being given. After about four hours of massages, saunas, cold showers, and warm sunshine, I don't think we had any tension left in our bodies at all. We were wide open, and the majesty of the Earth surrounded us. I found us a couple of cups of very sweet chai tea, and we sequestered ourselves in one of the many areas with different benches and carved-wood seats that were strategically placed for meditation, soul talk, or just wondering when the aliens were coming and if they were Republicans with leanings toward the NRA. I could tell Kat was getting a kick out of the people and asked her what she was thinking.

"They seem so much like lost kids, like they would believe anything at all just so they had something to cling to," she said in a jaded, snickering way.

"Well," I said defensively, "at least these people have the courage to ask the big questions of life."

"What do you mean the big questions?" she said in a more playful tone. "You mean like did Elvis make the crop circles or did Bigfoot do it?" She laughed that sarcastic, crazy laugh that used to make me wilt.

"No, no seriously, Kat, these people ask questions that just 300 years ago would have gotten them tortured and burned."

"Umm, now you're talking big, fella," she purred coyly.

"Back in the old monastic life, a young monk would train for perhaps 15 or 25 years just to be able to ask the abbot one question.

The questions that these people ask on a routine basis are the big questions of life, like 'Why am I here?' 'What is the meaning of existence?' 'What is my purpose?' would never even have been allowed to be asked until some significant training of the mind and body had taken place. They knew that once you asked those questions, your whole life would change, so they structured their lives and trained themselves for the spiritual madness that would ensue after they basically opened themselves up to great forces of transformation. Once you ask the question, 'What am I here for?' you get answers whether you're ready for them or not. Most people aren't ready, and that is where their pain and confusion come from."

"What was the point of the training for anyway?" Kat asked sincerely.

"The point of the exercise is that you would train for 20 years to get the opportunity to ask the abbot of the monastery one question. The abbot was God's representative, so you would train and ask questions that you thought were important, testing them on lesser monks. This is where the Zen koan comes from. You would ask a question that you thought was so important, and it would be answered with a riddle that pertained to just where your teacher thought you were at. You would have some imposing large question like, 'What is the meaning of existence?' and your teacher would say that the meaning of existence would be to do the dishes. He wasn't blowing you steam, he was just trying to get you to realize that if the meaning of existence could be found in an auspicious meeting with the abbot, then that same knowledge could be found doing the thing you were doing right now. He was trying to get you to understand that the truth you needed to know, that anybody needed to know, was waiting to be found right where they were anytime they wanted."

"Jesus, Bobby, you sure can blow some hot wind when you want," Kat said, jabbing me with her foot. "So, Mr. Buddha, what all-important question would you ask God if he was so kind as to grant you an audience?" she asked, snuggling up against me.

I thought for a moment and said with all the solemn self-importance I could muster in a very deep and serious voice, "Dear omnipotent Heavenly Host, oh, my sweet and terrible and just Lord, wouldst thou please grantith me this one small trinket of thou's great wisdom?" I spread my arms out wide and bowed to the now-orange fireball of a sun sinking off the northern California coast. I continued as Kat giggled. "Why, oh, just and mighty Heavenly Father, does your feathered creation the magnificent avian, the common black crow, come in threes?"

Kat cracked up and so did I. Unknown to us, some of the participants had gathered behind us and were listing as if they were going to glean some secret knowledge they were all craving so much. When Kat and I noticed, we both cracked up and the people walked off rather sheepishly. I kind of felt bad, but we did stick out a little like the bad seeds in that place of light and love.

"Sooo," Kat said slowly after we had calmed down, "if this God of yours exists everywhere and in everything, then he must, even though I highly doubt it," she scoffed playfully, "be in the heart of the spooky Bobby Doucette."

"What's your point, caller?" I quipped back at her.

"My point, oh wise sage of the seashore, is: ask yourself. Why do crows come in threes?"

She looked deeply in my eyes and we kissed. I think it was the closest I had ever felt to her. The image started to fade, and I started to wake up in the backseat of the Buick, waking from a dream inside a vision.

164

I sat up in the first light of the day and I was amazingly hungry. I found some empty plastic tubes, like toothpaste tubes, in a mountain-climbing store years before and always had one or two with me when I went out on patrol that were filled with peanut butter or water. I reached up to my fatigue pocket as I climbed out of the car and found, to my great surprise, that I had two tubes ready for breakfast. I stood there looking around, taking a morning piss and sucking some peanut butter out of a tube, when I sensed I wasn't alone. I made myself laugh at the fact that in this oh-so-serious place of learning, how utterly ridiculous I must look with my dick in my hand and a tube in my mouth. I quickly finished both eating and pissing and wiped my hands off on the dew that had gathered in the grass. Not having any directions to go on, I headed off in a westerly direction, as it seemed to have a certain attraction at that moment. I traveled for what seemed to be an hour because my watch wasn't working. When I looked up ahead of me I saw a slight fluctuation on the horizon. As I got closer I could see there was a person coming toward me and that she seemed to be a female. As she came closer to me, I could start to make out features that were familiar but different somehow. Suddenly in my heart I knew who it was and why she was here. It was my Kat, but she was different, and she had come to tell me that she no longer existed on the Earth plane. I started to cry as an unbearable sadness I'd never felt bubbled forth from inside of me, and I could barely stand. She walked up to me, her eyes transfixed on my anguish-filled face, as I sobbed and tried to deal with the truth of what I knew. My Kat was dead, and she had come to say good-bye.

(PAPA • - - •) " Do not run from the pain. In this modern world we are so averse to pain that it consumes us. A body builds antibodies and becomes stronger after it fights a fever. Most forests won't seed if there isn't

some kind of fire. An airplane can't create lift and get off the ground if it doesn't produce thrust and meet resistance in the form of air pressure. In dreamtime, when we reach something unpleasant, we wake up or we believe the superstition that if we die in our dreams, we die for real, so we wake. You are learning to face your fears, and pain is your training ground. You face it in your dreams because you can't face it in your waking life. Here's a life clue: If you're having weird or upsetting dreams, don't get a useless dream-interpretation book or go to a shrink for eight years; take control. Sit with yourself, meditate on your anxiety, have the courage to face your own mess. Listen, don't talk, and act on the information you are given. This is the difference between a true and a false person. Have courage; there is nothing much worth learning while one is groveling on the floor. Run all you want, as the snipers say, you'll just die tired."

I wanted to quit. I wanted it all to end. I wanted to pop out of this vision and forget all this madness and heartache. I wanted a normal life. I didn't care about psychic phenomena or Indian sweat lodges or Jack fucking Mumford. I didn't care about making the world a better place or how many bad guys there were. There was just pain and an unbearable ache where my heart should have been. As the knowledge I had received hit me full-force, the structure of where I was started to fade. Kat started to fade. Somewhere in my consciousness I knew that if I did not stay with the excruciating pain of the moment, I would not see my Kat again. I choose to stay with it, to become one with the bitter anguish that had consumed me. Not because of some great moral courage, but just simply to be with my woman for as long as I could. As I stood there looking at Kat, dark, angry storm clouds started to gather on the horizon, and I knew there was not much time. I could tell that something else was wrong, but Kat couldn't speak to me. I tried to talk but could not; it was all I could to just breathe right then.

Kat's eyes became very glossy, and then one tear fell out of her right eye onto her strangely unanimated face. Then she cried, and with great effort her face broke into emotion as she spoke.

"Bobby, I'm fine," she said crying openly. "My great-grandma met me, Bobby, everything is going to be OK."

I couldn't speak. I wanted to hold her, to kiss her face just one more time, but for some reason I could not move.

"I have to go now, Bobby. I kind of have to go back to school. Maybe I'll graduate this time." She laughed a little. "Thank you for staying, Bobby, it means we can see each other again."

She paused, and the storm clouds were moving quickly toward us. There was not much time left. It seemed with a great effort that she reached out and touched my face, then said one last thing to me.

"There is only love, Bobby, only love."

Then the storm hit with a vengeance, and she was gone. I stretched my arms out to the sky as the cold, wind-driven rain soaked the prairie. I screamed my pain to the lonely, angry sky as loud as I could and then left that place. The next thing I saw was my body sitting in the sweat kiva where I had left it. I looked around the room as the members of that night's sweat kept drumming and chanting. There were many beings surrounding the people that weren't there when I left. Some of them were chanting and wearing strange clothing. I looked into the face of an old woman. She walked through the body of John Red Truck and stood in front of me. As I looked into her face, I at once felt a great sense of peace enter my being. She reached up and touched my forehead, and with that I left the spirit world and reentered my body.

The coyote had been watching Jack Mumford for about 10 hours, and its body was starting to get hungry. The entity that was in charge of Coyote knew it needed to feed and exercise the body it was now in possession of, and so it crawled out of its position next to Jack Mumford's hide and ran some distance away into a shady draw. The coyote stood motionless except for his breathing and waited. Almost immediately, a small prairie dog appeared and scampered over to where the coyote was standing. The prairie dog's breathing slowed and its eyes closed. A shadow appeared next to both animals and seemed to move a small rodent-shape shadow energetically out of the body of the small rodent. A moment later, the shadow quickly left the scene and there was a momentary opening and glassing of the eyes of the still-breathing body of the prairie dog just before the coyote sunk his teeth fully into its neck.

Jack had been planning to use the meat he accumulated across the country to sustain him and make him stronger until it was time to merge with the energy vortex, but something odd was happening. Jack had carefully packed the body parts in coolers surrounded by dry ice that would preserve the flesh until he was ready. He had done this enough times in the past that he was sure of his methods, even in such a hot and dry place. Something was different this time, and the flesh had started to mortify even though it was frozen solid. Mumford wondered if all the energy he was sending out to do his bidding was somehow feeding back. He had seen this happen before when he was just learning these techniques and suspected intervention this time, but he could not get a lock on where it was coming from. Jack sensed that forces were at work against him, but weren't they always, he wondered? The point for him now was that he needed to get new meat and fast. He decided to use the flesh he had and to go out hunting again. As he was preparing his ritual, he again sensed that someone or something was watching him and decided to investigate. After he cloaked his position with a magical binding and checked the satellite timetable, Jack grabbed a loaded pistol and shotgun and went out to check his perimeter trip flares to make sure everything was in place. Nothing seemed to be out of the ordinary; still, he could tell something was not right. Just then he saw movement near a draw and made out the shape of the scraggly coyote he had seen around. He put the safety back on the pistol in his right hand and followed the coyote as it made its way up the slight escarpment that was behind the storage structure. Mumford's humor about the coyote had vanished as he contemplated getting one of his rifles and shooting the little bastard. Mumford had to work fast, so he went back inside and started his ritual. He would kill the coyote later. Jack worked quickly in the extreme desert heat. What he had planned would take some time, and the flesh he had was starting to go south. Jack Mumford lined up the five human heads that he had stored around him in a circle and got out some of the hearts and livers, putting them on a plastic plate on top of an old crate inside the circle. Jack took off all his clothes and put them outside the circle. Then he took out a piece of old rope and started to tie himself up very tightly. He looped the rope around his genitals through his crotch, around his waist and thighs, then back up around his neck, around and down through his armpits, then around his upper torso, pulling the rope very taught across his breasts. Every wrap Jack made, he pulled the rope tighter and tighter. He had gained some weight over the years, and his once-lean body started to become very Michelin Man-esque, his body fat oozing out from between the rope. When he had the rope tied off the way he wanted it, he began his ceremony. Mumford started rhythmically breathing and chanting his ancient Hawaiian magic. He started to call in his dark spirit helpers. An untrained eye might not have seen anything as he started to eat the livers and rub his genitals, building up the pressure that was necessary to launch his dark desires. If you were allowed close to Mumford's diabolical circle, you might experience things not primarily by sight but by other of your senses, both known and unknown to you. There might be a cooling or heating of the atmosphere proximate to his circle. The hair on your arms or the back of your neck might stand up, and not just due to the fact that you are witnessing one of the tribe eating its own. A rank smell of unseen rotting flesh may invade your nostrils. Dark shapes would move out of the corner of your eyes and may brush against your skin. The entities that tend to be present at these types of affairs are very specialized and have a distinct feel and smell to them. So much so that if someone is just thinking similar thoughts and you are in a hundred-mile radius and sensitive enough, you may have an acute need to go immediately to the nearest bathroom and take a shower or perhaps lose a $15 lunch.

(QUEBEC - - • -) "Pay attention to the information you are given. You can go overboard and start to imagine all kinds of wild shit, and it's your job to learn how to filter out the true from the false, but pay attention! You certainly don't want to end up pushing a grocery cart around town just because you can't pick your thoughts. Even so, you get information all the time, and that very primitive part of your brain gives you its correct response: fight, flight, posture, or submit. Sometimes it is very hard to understand what to do with that kind of ancient knowledge in a modern world. If your boss blows you some smoke, it probably makes no sense to get up and kick him in the teeth and run away. Just remember, the result of not dealing with that honest response will be to take on the anger into your very tissue. Yes, you can learn to meditate so as not to retain the anger and learn how to make your aura strong so that kind of thing doesn't happen to you. You may need to risk everything and leave that job instead of staying

there the three to five years most modern jobs last and getting angina in your heart muscles. If we were more honest and courageous with ourselves, maybe there wouldn't be so many dysfunctional workplaces. We have an onboard guidance system that will always take us safely down the narrowest of paths and keep us free and clear of all danger. However, all bets are off if you just shrug it off as a passing bout of heartburn or goose bumps."

Jack had been at his chanting for over two hours and had built up an incredible pressure in that unholy space. He had eaten one heart, almost two whole livers, and now had next to his face, the head of a woman he'd found near a Wal-Mart, kissing it as he stroked his tightly bound penis, building himself up to the climax he needed to unleash his personal brand of terror. While Mumford stroked himself and chanted, the coyote had returned and was watching him through a dislodged piece of the shed's corrugated steel. As Jack finally climaxed and released his dark spirits to go and do his bidding, there was a momentary halting of time, and some of the guests that Coyote had invited caught the exiting thought forms. They were captured and quickly taken to a place where they could no longer do harm. As the coyote watched the spiritual cleanup squad go to work, he noticed two dark shapes moving rapidly off to the southeast and vanish in a heat wave. The coyote left as he sensed that he was now a target of Jack's hate and went back to where it had left the crow.

Jack packed quickly, making sure that everything except the inside insulation was hidden. He was going back to Las Vegas to find something fresh. Jack was quite aware of the risk he was taking, but he really had no choice; he needed fresh meat. Jack had exposed himself many times to this kind of risk and so had become something of an expert. So much so that it also was, as near as he could tell, the only way he really had fun anymore.

Jack was completely at peace with the fact that he was a hunter and that somehow or another he was fulfilling a certain kind of purpose by weeding out the people who came in contact with him. Jack long ago had done away with the thought of random events, and when he stepped up to his place in the destiny of things he believed he wasn't really killing victims as much as he was thinning the herd. There were things in the human condition that were weak and needed to be taken out for the good of the whole. And when Mumford realized this, he approached his work with a new sense of dedication and purpose. He never felt remorse; it was simply his job to get as strong as possible and take care of any targets that presented themselves to him. If he were to die today or tomorrow mattered little to Mumford; in his mind, he was like a great Japanese Bushido warrior and he was already dead. No matter what anyone thought of him, Jack knew he was doing a necessary job, and he was just lucky enough to be one of those select few who loved their work. It was never an emotional question in Jack's mind, just one of techniques and tactics. So as Jack packed up his stolen truck, he took everything he needed just in case he never made it back. As he pulled out, Mumford again felt he was being watched. It must be that damn coyote, he thought, but the motionless body of the coyote was in a draw a mile away, being watched by a common black crow.

Area 51, near the dry lake bed called Groom Lake on Nellis Air Force Base in Nevada, doesn't really exist. If you ask an Air Force representative why Area 51 seems to have an unlimited black budget, they will just tell you that they have never heard of the place, except for the rumors that have been started by the people who claim to have seen UFOs. In the ancient texts about the Western mystical system of knowledge called the Cabala, there are 10 archetypical energy centers that are taught in an effort to learn how to use them as a link to the spiritual realms. The Sepher Yetzirah is the original four-page document that all Cabalistic study is based on and mentions 10—and only 10—of these so-called centers, or Sephiroth. Yet as you study the mountains of available tomes on the subject, there are veiled references to an 11th Sephiroth called Daath. It is the key to a kind of code that a seeker of Cabalistic study must know intimately if they are to tease out the secrets of the universe and so become able to master their own existence.

The Daath of modern technical society is Area 51. This is why its nickname evokes something existing and yet intangible at the same time. When the hoards of UFO cultists and people who claim to have had encounters with extraterrestrials patrol Nevada Highway 375 next to Groom Lake looking for something to explain the holes in their consciousness, they refer to this bastion of secret government black ops in the same fearfully whispered handle. When the secret military aircraft-seekers who spend night after cold night searching the skies for a tiny glimpse of fantastic craft rumored to be back, engineered from a crashed alien ship near Roswell, New Mexico, in 1947, cannot search the heavens anymore, when they are too tired and have gathered around a desert campfire, they speak of this same mythical place with a dedicated reverence usually reserved for cardinals and popes. They call it by the name that claims it as their own. Dreamland is the nickname of the place where modern technology meets ancient knowing, and all the trappings of both get fed into universal and private cosmologies of the people who inhabit the surrounding high desert. It is a rather grim place, kind of a forgotten American outback next to the contact point of the secrets. Perhaps a Stargate, a time portal to other dimensions and realms, where the existence of life may not be better but at least it's more interesting than a doublewide with a satellite dish. Or maybe the grand conspiracy is true and gray aliens—the ones with the hydrocephalic heads and black almond-shape, pupil-less eyes—are going to lead us all to the second coming through American know-how and might by implanting chips in the backs of our necks. Either way, it is a populist existence where the people are left to find their own way through the madness of rumor and innuendo, eking out a living in the surrounding wasteland. It is a harsh place that is too hot and too cold, with not enough water and not enough money, and if you are to survive out here you must be resourceful or become just another casualty.

This is the area that Markus Chen patrolled in his Nevada State Highway cruiser. A bizarre little bit of the American dream north of Las Vegas called State Route 375 and officially dubbed the Extraterrestrial Highway by the Nevada State Legislature. Chen grew up in the Borough of Queens in New York City and had wanted to be a cop since he was 8. After graduating from the John Jay school with a degree in criminology, he applied for the FBI but was put on a holding list as the Bureau was full of trainees at the time. He decided to put in for the state troopers to wait his turn, and the only force that was hiring at the time, except for NYPD and LAPD, was the state of Nevada. Going into a city department wasn't necessarily the best move a rookie could make if his goal was the FBI. Anything could happen in a city police department, and you might end up looking a little dirty to folks in Washington. There was an even bigger reason for Markus, and he wasn't sure how to handle it and have the career he wanted. Trooper Markus Chen was gay. That wasn't enough by itself to keep you from being left out in the cold by the FBI, but one had to manage the reality of it carefully if he was to succeed. Markus was a good kid, but when he came out in his teens, he did what every young gay man did in New York City and partied like it was 1999. He was never asked during his interview process for the Nevada Troopers if he was gay. They treated it much like the military in a don't ask, don't tell manner. He didn't volunteer any information either and just wanted to have the best record possible and let that speak for him. It wasn't lost on Markus that he was assigned to what the troopers called the "Good Humor Highway"—a reference to all the lost and troubled souls who would migrate to the area near Rachel, Nevada, on the 375 by Nellis Air Force Base that needed to be picked up by ambulances called the good-humor trucks and taken to psych wards down in Las Vegas. There had been a rash of people stopping by Rachel and demanding to have the secret alien/government chips taken out of their necks, and it was becoming something of a tax burden. Markus never complained about his assignment to anyone, and for the most part he was fairly happy that he could be a cop at all. He didn't mind pulling extra shift hours, and his commanders were aware that not all of the hours he logged ended up on his time sheets. By anyone's measure, Markus Chen was a good cop and had a very bright future in any department that would be lucky enough to have him.

Even Trooper Chen could get a belly full, and at the end of his shift when the call came in that one of the lost souls had blown a gasket in his bailiwick, he was a bit miffed. It was early evening and Markus had planned on going down to Vegas that night to have a good meal and some fun. When the description of the man came in, the laughter in the dispatcher's voice was apparent, and

Trooper Chen asked for confirmation just to see if it was a joke. When Chen found the man about 15 miles south of Rachel walking on the shoulder of the road, there was no doubt he was the lunatic that all the motorists' cell phone calls were about.

Clay Schroeder was wearing a red union suit type of long underwear with several pairs of women's panties and gaudy blue-and-gold cowboy boots. To accentuate his provocative ensemble, Clay had fashioned a very large beach towel with scenes of palm trees around his neck for a sort of cape. He topped off the whole shebang with a brightly polished aluminum spaghetti colander worn upside down on his head and tied under his chin for a helmet. As soon as Clay saw the Nevada State Trooper's cruiser start to pull over next to him, he performed the act that the motorists had called in about: He started to walk out into the middle of the two-lane desert highway and do a country and western line dance to an imaginary honky-tonk band.

(ROMEO • - •) "There will be signs and prophets and the truth will come from strange sources. God has a funny bone. Just imagine 2,000 years and some change ago, there's some guy named John dressed like a caveman dunking people in a river and talking about an invisible being. Then just imagine some drifter rolls into town and John freaks out and starts telling you that everything is gonna change and fast, and you'd better get down on your knees and pray to an invisible source of energy. You'd call the good-humor boys, too."

When Clay didn't respond to any of the questions that Trooper Chen posed to him except for telling his name, Markus had no choice but to cuff him and take him in for evaluation at the psych ward in Vegas. He could have called for an ambulance, but his shift was over and he might as well take the cruiser. No drinking, he thought, but a good meal and maybe a show. He had civilian clothes in the trunk and 24 hours off, so he and Clay headed south. They were about 20 minutes into the ride when Clay started his rant.

"You never heard about sink holes before 1981, did ya?" Clay said. "Naw, well maybe in Florida, but shit howdy, they're all over the place now. I mean, think about it," Clay said with authority. "You got sink holes in every state of the Union now."

Markus looked at him in the rearview mirror and winced. He knew that Clay was just getting wound up and this was going to be a painful ride.

"Yep, sink holes. And that ain't all. I mean really, look at any overpass on any highway in the United States and you'll see rebar stickin' out or rust cracks. You know when that rust gets at that rebar it's like a cancer. I mean, you got to cut it out or that bridge is in deep shit. The whole sewer system is old and decrepit, but we just keep going on like sheep and lettin' them big boys spend our money on weapons that's as useless as tits on a fire hydrant. That's why we got the sink holes, Mister …" Clay said with emotion, trying to get through to Trooper Chen. "In the middle of the biggest drought on record, the water is just leaking out of them old pipes and causin' all kinds of hell."

Clay could tell he wasn't getting through, and he looked long and hard in the rearview mirror at the state trooper, trying to figure out how to get his attention.

"You think this is some kind of random event. don't ya?" Clay said, kind of exasperated with himself. "You think that just somehow, out of this whole wide universe, we just ended up in this damn car smellin' each other's stink. Alright, fella," Clay went on, "I'm gonna give ya both barrels, and you better start payin' attention."

Then Clay did something funny and tilted his head and went into some kind of trance, and his voice got a little deeper and his eyelids fluttered as he spoke.

"You're a gay cop, ain't ya?" Clay spoke in a relaxed voice. When Markus heard him he had already started to shut him out of his consciousness, but what Clay said snapped him right back into the moment. He got a sinking feeling in his stomach as he looked hard in the rearview at the man in the back of cruiser.

"That's right, I got your attention now, don't I?" Clay went on. "I just will never understand you people out there, faggatin' around. I mean, dicks is kind of gross. I guess it's alright with a woman, but two men rubbin' them things together is just disgutin'. Hell, I don't even want to think about it no more, it's just too disgustin'. Pokin' them things around like some kind of dog in heat, that's just gross. And a cop, for Christ's sake. They say when you drink the milk with the hormones in it is what does it. Hell, I don't want to think about it any more, its just disgustin'. I'm sorry, but the only reason I said anything is so's you can find him."

Markus wasn't sure what to think, but he was definitely listening and turned his radio down a little. Clay was silent for a while then started in again.

"You're one of them single-bullet-theory guys, ain't ya?" Clay started again, his eyes still fluttering. "Lone gunman and all that shit, right? Nobody on the grassy knoll, just one cheap mail-order rifle that wasn't even sited in. I thought so, too, before they put that fucking chip in my head," Clay said with a sad sigh. "You probably believe that fuckin' Marilyn Monroe wasn't in on it either, don't ya? Why'd you think she got all depressed and weird? It wasn't suicide got her, but she was glad when it come, cause she helped kill the only good president we had since Jefferson. Well, buddy, you better start payin' attention, cause you ain't got much time left to find him."

"Find who?" Markus said on instinct.

"Now you're finally gettin' smart," Clay said, becoming happy again. "I swear, a superhero and a gay cop. Who would have thought that shit would happen, huh, bud?"

"Find who?" Trooper Chen said with more purpose back in his voice. Clay Schroeder got quiet and started to breathe heavier, as if he was gathering up his energy, then he spoke slowly.

"I seen him and he seen me," Clay said with a tone of fear in his voice. "It's that killer they're lookin' for, and you're the lawman that's 'sposed to find him. That's just what they told me. He wanted to get me, shit boy howdy, he wanted a piece of me, but I got my angels watchin' out for me. He was headin' south when he saw me see him when he drove by. Pulled over, too, like he was gonna back up or somethin', but he couldn't and he knew I knew." Clay's words rolled out of him now as if he were reading some kind of cosmic news report about the most important event in the history of the world.

"You ain't gonna find him south, nobody is," Clay said with the certainty of a man who knows truth. "Nobody gonna believe you, either, but you're gonna find him north of Rachel when he gets back. Now don't you be out there faggatin' around, either, cause it's you that's got to get him, boy, and nobody's gonna believe a word of what was said 'tween us tonight. He's got Tennessee plates, boy, and you be careful."

With that Clay came out of his trance.

"Who told you all this?" Trooper Chen asked. "Clay!" he said loudly. "Who were the people who told you this?"

Clay Schroeder's head fell sideways and came to rest on the unpadded backseat of the Nevada State Police interceptor, and he started to snore.

CHAPTER 10

A moment comes in everyone's life where you're stuck with the choices you have made, and you know that to fight the inevitable conclusion of them is to rob yourself of something that you know intrinsically will be scrutinized by someone or something that matters to your future life. It's never clear if that life will be the one you're living now or something beyond the present moment, but you know in your core, deep down in a very secret place, that only you have the key and it matters what your next decision is.

Taxes matter. Corvettes matter. The screwed-up date you had in high school matters. TV matters. If James Dean was gay matters. Did Marilyn help kill JFK matters. What fucked-up shit Jacko did to all those children in his bed matters. How did Kurt Cobain pull the trigger on the goddamn shotgun, or if he did at all, in some fucked-up, tiny little insignificant way matters. It all matters. All the decisions in Congress about your health care made by senators and representatives with free, lifelong, taxpayer-paid-for medical insurance matters. All the treacherous rulings the Supreme Court made based on some religious ideology that destroy the Constitution matter. All the dirty cops in Connecticut matter. Should I put the kids in an advanced academic program matters. Why the guy at the corner bodega charges you one price and his buddies another because you can't understand fucking Spanish matters. But that's not the kind of mattering I'm talking about. That's the kind of mattering that people worry about to occupy their time until it's too late to grab your own soul and shake out everything that is useless, everything that is bad and evil and boring and mundane and gross, and find the one thing in this life that you can do. The one small, little thing that you personally have control over; the one thing that will bring grace to your life, and have the incredible courage to do that thing. Edmund Burke wrote, "All evil needs to exist is for good men to do nothing." That implies that those so-called good men or women need to do something. That is where I was headed. I was going to do something. I was going to do the one thing that I was sure I could do. The one thing in an infinite realm of possible things I could do. The one thing I was good at. The one thing that I didn't hesitate about or worry if it were possible. No, I was going to do the one thing I knew that I could do and do it. I was going to find Jack Mumford and find out what the fuck he thought he was doing.

There is an exercise you can do to find out the difference between believing something and knowing it. When you know the difference, you can start going where you want in life and not just get blown around by some unseen wind and end up with a bunch of choices you don't want.

Get in a comfortable position where you won't be distracted and relax down on your sit bones. Breathe in to the count of four and breath out to a count of four. Now think of something important. God, your future financial goals, the girl or boy you want to marry, and say this: "I believe I am capable of reaching my goal. I believe there is a God, I believe there is a mate for me, I believe in a financial future that is better than earning $7.50 an hour as a barista," and just sit with the feelings that produces inside you. Monitor what is going on in your body and your emotions. What happens? A pressure in your ankle? A thought of movement behind you? A smell of soap? It could be anything, and it will be something unique to you and you alone and where you are and the choices you've made. Now do the same thing but say this: "I know there is a God, I know I won't be a barista until I'm 63, I know I will find a perfect mate." Now monitor those feelings. Can you tell the difference? You see, believing is an opinion, and it doesn't give your subconscious anything to work with. It is an opinion that doesn't allow you to commit to anything. Most of us don't want to commit to anything because then we are not responsible, and we can run around like a bunch of nancy boys wondering why this poor old world is kicking our ass and blaming it on someone else. But if we choose to know something, we're out there on our own. We take control of our life and our choices, and that is the stuff the subconscious needs to get us to our goals. We then become free to start thinking for ourselves and creating our own lives. We free ourselves of our society-think, our political-think, our religious-think, our economic-think, and our family-think of our very genetic makeup. It doesn't mean we're going to join some cult and live in a cave—quite the contrary. It may mean that we finally get that apartment on the Upper East Side facing Central Park. Most people spend their lives trying to fit in and be accepted by people who don't really give a rat's ass about their happiness.

(SIERRA• • •) "*If you don't choose your destiny, it will choose you. Neither choosing nor having it be chosen for you may be pleasant, but change will happen with our without you. You're here to play, not whimper in the corner like a wee baby.*"

I was heading for Vegas, and I didn't like it one damn bit. They have done an amazing job marketing Las Vegas, Nevada, to the world as one of the premier spots that you can go on your precious time off from your life and spend your hard-earned cash building monster resorts for other people. You spend your money and your time becoming more irritated than before and accept the programming like a good little consumer, wondering why your blood pressure is up. Don't kid yourself; the house always wins, and it's just a hot desert there, and most of the beautiful people working there to entice you are just trying to keep the back of their heads from falling off from all the methamphetamine that is running through them as a permanent fixture of their blood type.

There is an exercise the Navy guys talk about called synthetic liberty. After months at sea with no land in sight, you go to the fantail of the ship and throw 300 bucks off. Then go below decks, lick an ashtray, and slam your dick in a drawer and go to sleep. The next morning when you wake up you, think you had a real good time ashore. That's Vegas after you've spent your week there. You go home hurting, thinking you had a real good time.

I had several more visions at Red Truck's camp in New Mexico, and all signs pointed to Nevada. The interesting thing was that I knew I wasn't going to find him in Vegas, but for some reason all my dreams and visions pointed me in that direction. So that is where I was headed. I had a vague notion that he was going to be somewhere north, but I just couldn't get a lock on it. I learned a long time ago that I could do this kind of thing from a distance and save myself a huge travel expense, let alone keep myself safe. For some reason none of that was working this time, and I had decided I would just go with it. Sully was playing devil's advocate at the camp and asked me why I just didn't let it go and let the whole scenario play itself out without me. That was a valid question, and I really didn't have a good answer, at least not in practical terms. I just knew that it was somehow my job, and if I didn't do this one I'd get one much worse later on. What could be worse than going mano a mano with Jack Mumford I didn't know, but I didn't want to find out, either. I didn't know where I was going to stay in Vegas or what I was going to do, so I just pulled into town from the east and felt my way around.

Two minutes off the strip north or south leads you to a kind of consumer backwater hell. They try to make you believe it's as fun as the behemoths, but the truth is you're looking for a bargain and you're already screwed. There are no bargains when you have decided that the most fun thing you could in a capitalistic society is throw your hard-earned bling-bling down the shit chute.

I headed south near the old section and pulled in to get some gas. Immediately a meth-head came over to me while I was at the pump, and I could tell he hadn't made up his mind whether he would try to mug me or beg for some cash. So in his shit soup of a brain when he spoke, the begging sounded very threatening and he started to get too close.

"Yo, yo, listen, listen, you got some money?" the man said, approaching me within 5 feet.

"Naw, naw, serious, serious, I'm not gonna hurt cha. I just need a little ..."

He stopped short when I picked up my T-shirt and he saw the butt of my .45 sticking out of my pants. It was taking too long for his drug-corrupted brain to realize that he was not making the connection he wanted. I stepped away and lined him up with my body and put my hand on the gun, preparing to draw it.

"Shit, you fucking crazy. You know that, bitch?" he said, now backing away quickly.

When he had backed halfway across the parking lot, he started a tirade that was attracting the attention of his local comrades.

It was 2 in the morning, the tank was full, and I was pretty sure the cameras that were trained on me had not seen the gun the way I flashed it. I got inside and started the truck and started chuckling as my new friend ran it down to me as I drove away.

"You crazy bitch, mother fucking white boy. You want some of this, bitch, ugly mother fuck? You got nothin' … you ugly bitch fuck … you want some of this, bitch? …" He faded off into the Vegas night, and so did my desire to stay in this desert rat hole. I found a room in fairly nice motel off Maryland Parkway, grabbed my bug-out bag, and secured the vehicle for the night.

I was tired and the room took a little longer to clear than usual. And after all, this was Vegas, whose motto that's advertised all over the country on 30-second shorts is, "Vegas, whatever happens here stays here." Not exactly family values, this place, but I had some work to do, and I needed to get a lock on Jack and get some sleep. I found a quiet place that wasn't attached to a casino and set about clearing the room for my remote viewing session.

After I got out of the hospital when I was in the service, I was shipped back to my unit's headquarters and put on limited duty while I recouped. I wasn't sure what I was going to do, and it seemed that I might not make it back to operational status. I was pretty much stuck in a training office doing my unit's paperwork and wondering what the hell I was going to do with my life when I received a very strange phone call. Looking back, I realized I never asked for verification from my mysterious caller; I just jumped at his offer, knowing that it was one of those times in life when thinking would only get in the way. It was late on a Friday and I had the weekend off, as my physical therapy was cancelled. The voice on the other end of the line never identified himself, but he knew I didn't have therapy that weekend—and pretty much nothing else going on in my life—and I guess I just assumed he was GI. The thing that intrigued me was the way he set the hook in my mouth like the biggest fish in the pond when he called me by my nickname and asked me if I had stopped any bullets lately. I agreed to meet him at a diner that was about 20 miles from the base on Saturday and hung up the phone. He had instructed me not to tell anyone else, and I didn't think much of it at the time. I guess I was hoping that someone else would realize just exactly what had happened to me and give me something more important to do than to figure out who was qualified to jump out of aircraft or shoot a weapon. I fought the urge to tell someone what I would be doing the next day as a bit of paranoia started to creep in. The thought crossed my mind that there might be elements in the government who just wanted the problem of U.S. Army Sgt. Robert "Scarecrow" Doucette to go away. I dismissed the thoughts and went to the noncom club and got some chow, watched some TV, and hit the rack.

Saturday was a cool, crisp fall day, and I checked out of the base and headed to my mysterious destination. I arrived at the diner at the prescribed time and ordered some food. I wasn't sure what was happening in my life right then, but I had put my .45 under my sweater and wore some baggy pants to hide it just in case. No one showed up, so I ate my lunch and waited. Just about the time I was thinking about leaving, I saw an unmarked car with government plates pull into the parking lot and park by my truck. I got up and paid for my food and went out to see what the skinny was. A man with civilian clothes and sunglasses was sitting in the car, and as I approached he motioned for me to get in his car. I opened the passenger-side door and looked in. Nothing seemed to be out of order. I got in and my life changed.

He was a very surly type, and all I remember is that he asked me if I'd been thinking about what I was going to do as a civilian, because I was probably going to receive a medical discharge sooner rather than later. After some more small talk, he told me he a had a job for me. And when I asked him for some details, he merely pulled out a piece of paper that was my transfer orders to an Army facility in Maryland. The man who would end up being my handler asked me a very strange question: He asked if I had heard of associative remote viewing. I said that I remembered hearing of something the CIA had been doing in the '90s that sounded like that, but that I thought it had been cancelled due to some unpopular politics. He assured me that it hadn't and told me he had to go. He told me to think about his offer, that it would only be made this once, and nothing of our meeting could ever be proved. I was told I would be contacted one more time for my answer and that would be it. I was also instructed not to talk about our meeting with anyone and he started the car. As the little man with the sunglasses drove off, I stood in the parking lot and a cold autumn wind sent a shiver up my spine.

Weeks went by and I occupied my time with therapy. I was starting to do better, so I was given a job as a trainer on the range and for some of the quick-kill courses set up to resemble a Middle East environment. One day when I was alone, coming back to the barracks in an open Humvee, I saw another vehicle approaching on the range road. As the SUV with darkened glass approached and slowed down, I knew who was inside. It was my little friend and two other spooky types. The left rear window rolled down, and it was my friend who spoke first. He asked me what I had decided, and I immediately told him I wanted in. I felt time and space compress as they hurriedly drove off, and I sat there wondering what the hell I was in for now.

My life had been going in slow motion, and I had felt myself getting older before our meeting. Now things started to happen seemingly at the speed of light. I was instructed to start wearing civilian clothing, and orders were cut the next day for my transfer to Maryland. I could tell my comrades were kind of relieved to find out I was leaving. They didn't know what to do with me anymore. It's just not good to have something as strange as me hanging around; it reminded people that the edges are ragged at best. There was no fanfare at all; I simply put my gear into my truck and started driving. As I passed the base gate for the last time, I felt a twinge and I knew my life would never be normal again.

My new unit was involved in a technical remote viewing program for several agencies within the government. Remote viewing is nothing more than government-sponsored clairvoyance. It consists of training to try to get consistent results that can be used for gathering information; it was psychic spying. The primary difference in TRV and grassroots psychics is that the remote viewer always works with a handler, called the interviewer. One person, the remote viewer, gets himself in a meditative trance state, and the interviewer gives him a target and talks the viewer in and out of the target area. One of the difficulties with any trance state is that the one in the trance state has to fight to keep from falling from trance into sleep. This problem is rectified if one person concentrates solely on reporting and remaining in a trance state while another acts as a sort of netherworld guide. Another challenge that beginning remote viewers have is one of scale and direction.

If you are 1,000 feet over the target and not "looking" down, you may miss the secret sub base. A good interviewer guides you into the target, much like a weather-blind airplane is guided by the tower of an airport. In the East, guiding the viewer was not as big a problem as years of study went into training, and one devoted his whole life to being a seer. Technical remote viewing was designed to take someone with a little talent and be able to use the viewer successfully with a minimum amount of time and training. The talent is usually no more than an ability to believe in a split consciousness and use it as one would any tool. So the viewer needs a handler to tell them what to do. Turn right, what do you see? Get bigger, get smaller, is that danger you "feel" or is it just something unknown to you? Maybe you are underwater and your consciousness is telling you that you need to breathe when your mind's split consciousness, in a different space-time unit, doesn't need air at all. These are the questions a good interviewer asks, trying to determine what is sound data and what is just superstition.

Sometimes when we dream, we feel what we perceive as fear when in actuality we are just seeing something or meeting someone we have never experienced before. Some of the most common out-of-body experiences seem horrifying, and much superstition has been built up over the eons. Three common misconceptions are those of being choked, paralysis, or a monstrous-looking thing known as the dweller on the threshold. These are just new steps in a different reality. In the scope of the universe, our human understanding is like that of a newborn baby reacting to common things as if they were monsters.

(TANGO-) *"The monster under the bed may be real. However, you need to realize that to a creature from another space-time continuum, you might look pretty ugly yourself. Don't give up your power and don't give in to fear.*

The universe runs on love, and the closer you are to having that feeling, the safer you will be. There is enough that is really important; don't get scared like some suburban tourist visiting the inner city, wondering why those kids wear such baggy jeans and hoping little Timmy won't start listening to rap. Wherever you go, folks are pretty much the same. Keep your powder dry."

(UNIFORM • • -) "Don't be afraid to challenge what you are seeing. Someone bearing gifts must have a reason. Angels or your grandma may be the ones grifting you, and the big, ugly thing with the glowing red eyes might be your only salvation. It's your life in this world—demand proof. In this world, as the next, the big print giveth and the small print taketh away."

I was lying on the bed and started meditating by bringing energy for my subtle body into my system by way of my hands, feet, and breath. I concentrated for about an hour just on raising my energy and getting deeper and deeper into a trance state. I had both of my forearms elevated into a vertical position of balance right above my elbows. By balancing my arms this way while I meditated, I had an automatic way to keep myself from falling asleep and staying in trance. If I headed toward sleep, my arms would start to fall just a bit, and this would bring my consciousness back just enough to my body so I would not go too far down into my delta brainwave sleep pattern.

The most important thing to think about when you are trying to specifically remote view something is your time-space coordinate. I worked on getting it simple before implanting it in my subconscious. I demanded that I go where Jack Mumford was and be within 15 feet of him without picking a point of consciousness that was in a solid object. Now that I had my parameters of time and space, I decided on size. I was only going to be a single point of consciousness, not a full-blown projection, as Jack would be watching for something and I'm sure he had help. This point of consciousness has been known to shamans and wizards for a very long time as the watcher. There was another problem—one I knew I was going to have to pay for. Jack is a cagey guy, a lot more so than anybody other than me suspected, and he would have dark astral sentinels—thought forms and watchers of his own. The only way a thought form of any kind was going to get to him and find him would be if it came with the same frequency that would allow it to be perceived as helpful to Jack and to the energy entities feeding off his hate.

(VICTOR • • • -) "'As above, so below.' The Bible tells us this many times. It is in the inscription on the Emerald Tablet of Hermes thought to be brought from pre-Egyptian times. We disregard this as we are waiting for a humanlike God to solve our problems for us. It means simply this: You are responsible for yourself, and what goes wrong here usually goes wrong somewhere else. Remember when traveling to the netherworlds the old acronym C.Y.O.A.: Cover Your Own Ass."

I had thought about it for a long time and figured that the best approach in any strategy is always stealth. I would go for the Trojan horse effect by giving them a thought that would get me in and bury its meaning as best I could. You see, as my point of consciousness would pass by where Jack or his minions might be watching for it, if I was not to be found out, then I would have to be seen or felt as being like-minded. There is a karmic price for this one that

I was more than willing to pay. The thought that I came up with was simply this: "I want to help you kill." I believed that if this was given honestly, I would be ushered in as one of their own. This statement must feel like truth to him, and there is only one way to do that, and that is it has to be true. By doing it this way, I will have to recompense for putting that thought form out there and in fact having it help Jack and his lot—helping him because the statement is true.

I started to go down deeper, deeper, all the time concentrating on my own screen of consciousness that was programmed with the space-time coordinates. I felt my arms moving slightly and gently guided my attention back to my view screen in my safe place, and then I was there.

Images and feelings started to flood my consciousness, and I felt like I wanted to vomit. I kept bringing my attention back to my inner screen and started to hear very demonic sounds. An image of a gray wavy world was in front of me, and I was momentarily lost. I realized that this was most likely a problem of spatial orientation, and I did what I was trained to do and spun around slowly getting my bearings. As I did, I realized I had been looking at almost a microscopic viewpoint of the corrugated-steel walls of the shed that Jack Mumford was in now. As I turned around I realized he was there, and I immediately said go up 500 feet. I shot up through the roof and found myself in the hot desert, looking down on the shed and abandoned mobile home where Jack was. I went up another 1,000 feet and tried to get my bearings. I saw a dirt road leading to a main road and some buildings beyond that. In a flash I was there, hovering above a small building. I was starting to fade in and out and knew I didn't have much time, as I expended a lot of energy and would probably fall past my zone and go to sleep. I didn't want to stay too long, either. Jack might begin to feel me and get suspicious. I saw what looked to be a flying saucer being towed by a truck and was trying to deal with that when I saw some words. It's very hard to bring words back for some reason. Words and numbers just don't seem to make it through the mind soup. I was struggling to try to make sense of it when I caught a firm look at the sign. It read "Lit__e Al__n I_n." I got back just those letters, hoping I would remember, then I went out hard and slapped back into my body. I hoped that I had not spent enough time with Jack and his minions for them to notice me coming and going, and that he hadn't suspected anything in my message. I was quite willing to pay the karmic price by sending the hateful thought that got me through the psychic gate, and I just hoped the final word that I camouflaged with a thought form of hate and death didn't get picked up by Jack or his helpers. You see, I had to believe the thought or it would never have passed for real. I wasn't dealing with some sorority girls with a Ouija board; I was dealing with one of the most foul killing machines the world had ever seen. I was hoping that the first part of the message was so thrilling to them that they would just assume it was more of the bad-frequency energy they craved and that they wouldn't see my obscured final thought. If the message got through undetected, I could find him; if not, he could find me. That is the chance I decided to take, and so I sent my Trojan horse to Jack.

"I want to help you kill … yourself …" I sent my message and I received my data and hoped I was safe. I came out of my trance and scribbled down some notes on a yellow legal pad that was next to the bed and turned my tape recorder off. As I double-checked the door lock and made sure my extra magazine was on the night-stand next to my .45, I put a newspaper on top to hide them. I checked that my Walther PPK pistol was in my shaving kit in the bathroom, then I sat down on the edge of my bed. And as I did, I looked into the haunted eyes of a stranger staring back at me in the mirror above the desk. A thought of Kat passed through my mind, and I felt an incredible sense of aloneness. I broke off the stare at myself and got horizontal, pulling the thin blanket and starched sheet around me as tight as I could. Closing my eyes so as not to think about the madness that was gathering around me, I fell into a deep sleep in the city of sin.

CHAPTER 11

Sigmund Freud's most famous pupil was psychologist Carl Gustav Jung, who wrote in his book *Synchronicity: An Acausal Connecting Principle*: "Coincidence is the modern myth. The philosophical principle that underlies our conception of natural law is causality. The connection of events may in certain circumstances be other than casual and require another principle of explanation."

Quantum physicists had to come up with a whole new kind of science to explain why a scientist trying to measure a subatomic particle had to figure in his desire when the particle displayed a tendency to "show up" at the exact place and time the scientist wanted to measure it. This freed science of the bondage of causal thinking when dealing with a nonlocal space-time event. If matter displays tendencies of being made malleable by desire or thought, then the whole program is off. It's kind of like the models of atoms that were made in the 1950s and still to this day reside in science classrooms all over the world. They have nothing to do with a true understanding of the universe and are only there because the scientific propaganda machine is so hard to stop. "Causality," said Jung, "is merely statistical truth and not absolute, it is a sort of

working hypothesis of how events evolve one out of another ..."
Still, Jung's synchronistic events were, in his terms, "acausal." Jung
believed that people could experience but not understand in
casual terms how synchronicities occurred. I think ol' Gustav was
about two sandwiches short of a picnic on this one. There was a
series of events taking place, and in the balance was the difference
of nature seeking not the swing of a pendular universe but trying
to find an equilibrium that kept certain chaotic forces in check. In
this kind of time, the universe used certain entities as one would
use a garden tool. A specific tool for a specific job. A spade for a
hole, and a clawed hoe to make furrows in damp soil. On Earth,
certain people are here (if they choose to understand) so even
though they might not be the center of this or any other universe,
they are the center of all things in their consciousness, and everything in their consciousness is bound by their desires. If you have
certainty that you can affect things and in fact are here to affect
things and show others that insignificance is only a choice of a free
mind, then you will. Certain people drive the bus, certain people
ride—just so you know, there is a bus with your name on it anytime
you want to start taking responsibility for your own trip.

Time was bending. Lives were starting to intersect. A conclusion was in the offing and it was still unformed, translucent, full
of promise and death. This was the quickening that happens, and
to all those souls who have been through it, there is a knowing of
forces at work, of energies far beyond comprehension set loose
upon a situation that is too fragile and small for their awesome
power. Synchronicity is a modern term for an ancient truth, which
had been lost in evolutionary changes that were mandatory in the
grand scheme of things. Magic was lost so that humans could start
the long process of learning to be more than small, sickly children stranded in a wilderness and start to find their own strength

and power. When we became strong enough, then the choice was again offered to us. The choice of remaining in a gross, coarse form or shedding our superstition and limits, so that we would start to understand and learn of our own magnificence. Of course there were errors to be made. It is our way.

(WHISKEY • - -) "Even if you're dealt some cards you don't particularly like, you might as well play out the hand. After all, it was you who decided to play the game, and chances are you decided to play a very, very long time ago. As in any game of chance, there are risks and consequences for failure or success. The trick to it all is realizing that there are risks and consequences for success or failure whether you play or not."

I woke slowly, as if somehow I knew that time had stopped for me and I was in a holding pattern stuck between what was alive and what was dead. It was a bright, lively morning, and light danced around the orange and green curtains in my hotel room. I laid in my bed very still, listening to the start of a day that was as unknown to me as to an explorer seeing a vast wilderness for the first time. I was at the end of a certain kind of time that had literally run out. Events now started to take on a life of their own. Without choosing to do so, I sat up in bed, and again upon seeing my haunted face staring back at me, I was startled by my reflection. It was time to let go of fear, and as I rose from my bed and shuffled to the bathroom, a faint knowing started in the back of my head that this was it. That this was the place where souls were saved or destroyed. I started shaving a three-day-old growth of beard off my face and watched as the tiny hairs became a mass, clumping in the bar of soap from the hotel that I had worked into lather. The soapy whiskers seemed to offer a real resistance before the overwhelming force of the water took away their power and they helplessly ran down my hand and razor, circling the drain and returning to the Earth Mother from where they came. I knew this was the last day of my life that I would live without knowing where Jack Mumford was. I found myself wondering, as I watched the tiny flotsam and jetsam of my face circle the drain and disappear, if I would ever again see them fighting for their existence before being washed away to oblivion. It wasn't overly morbid thinking—just the kind of taking stock one does before moving on from one time zone to another. I was going to find Jack Mumford today, and I had a feeling that in that meeting I would not be alone.

I got out a Nevada gazetteer, with a complete set of topographical maps for the whole state of Nevada, and a straightedge ruler and my pendulum. I was about to perform one of the most useful of all dowsing practices called map dowsing. I sat down at the cigarette-burned table in my quickly overheating motel room and asked my pendulum if it could find Jack Mumford for me today. After some long, slow, lazy gyrations, the pendulum picked up speed as if it were performing a self-check and tuning itself in to the universe. After about two minutes of the strange gyrations, my pendulum settled down into its predictable pattern, signaling that it would comply with my request. Most people assume that using a pendulum is just an exercise in self-feedback, and to some extent that is true. It takes anywhere from one to 10 years of constant daily use and dedication to actually get to a point where any of the data is useful. Just like anything else, there is a learning curve to it, and if it's treated like a parlor trick or an old wives' game, no benefits will be discerned. In almost all modern Psychology

101 texts there is a paragraph of derision about dowsers and their process. It's funny how in these books, the data they point to is only about the documented failures and not the vast amount of documented successes. I guess you can just chalk it up to the fact that almost every human group has its own type of prejudice. A teacher of mine who had worked for the same multibillion-dollar defense contractor for about 30 years and dowsed on a daily basis said he didn't even try to defend the data anymore. He said of his fellow scientists, "They'll never listen. They're too afraid of learning something that would put their own dogma into question."

My pendulum picked out a page, and I placed the straightedge on the bottom of the topo map and asked the bouncing weight to go into its search mode. Immediately the pendulum started tracing a straight swing back and forth. As I carefully moved the straightedge horizontally up the map, my pendulum started to arc slightly off of straight and wobbled a bit. I slowed my progression when I sensed the first coordinate point was near. I very slowly moved the ruler up about another quarter of an inch, and my pendulum broke out into a distinct circular pattern, indicating I had my first coordinate. As I started to push past that point with the straightedge, the pendulum started to be less circular and was wobbling toward a straight swing again. I brought the ruler back down to where the circular motion was the strongest, put the pendulum down, and drew a line across the map with a pencil. I then began the same process along a vertical axis and drew another line. I now had my coordinates, and where the lines intersected was where I was going to find Jack Mumford today.

I quickly packed my things and returned the keys to the lobby, the desert heat melting my air-conditioned demeanor. On the way out of town, I stopped by a coffeehouse that had Internet access and sent a short message to two of Detective Thomas Quinn's e-mail addresses. One went to his cell phone, and I hoped he'd read it soon. I bought some water and got in my truck and headed north out of Las Vegas.

I really hated the shape I was in. I was looking for grace in a place that seemed gray and withered, and I didn't want to give in to the seeming failure of the whole damn planet. It was about 114 degrees, and the air-conditioning just wasn't up to keeping the old truck cooled down. While I was sitting at a stoplight, I rolled down the window. It was hot, but at least I was breathing moving air. As I sat there, I looked over at the sidewalk and saw a small green shoot of some kind of plant pushing itself up through a small crack in the concrete. In a flash it hit me: That is what life is for, and nothing more or less. You can call it courage or DNA programming or the biological imperative of the plant or anything you want to call it, but the truth of it is that the thing that was alive in that small piece of grass was going to live, was going to cling to life and force its way through to the light. There was a force, and it's the same force in all things, and you can't stop it. You could defoliate the whole Earth, you could get rid of all the people—in fact, you could get rid of all the living things on this planet or in this solar system—but you could not stop the thing that was animating that little shoot of grass and making it feel its own sense of life. The animating principle of all things, as it hit me sitting there in that hot, nasty piece of urban desert sprawl, would never be stopped. Life, all life, was the same, and it was eternal. It didn't matter a hoot if I believed in it or could comprehend it or could sense in my tiny insignificant time in the universe if it acknowledged my longings or not. It was going to keep on living, no matter what anyone, anything, or I thought about it. No matter what theology was designed to explain or what atheists denounce, in its all-pervading omniscience it was going to exist. If in my small human comprehension I could not get a picture of its totality and completeness and could only see it as some old man with a bad temper, it didn't matter. Life was going to happen just the way it was supposed to, and there was really nothing I could do to add or detract from it.

I realized the light was going to change, and when it did, I was just as changed as the color red was from green. It didn't matter what happened except that I tried to live, and in that living, not believe in a limited existence with limited resources. I had to fight for what was mine in a place where life happened, and all I had to do was go along for the ride and keep looking for that small shaft of light. That tiny shaft of light that represented my next step, not having to believe that I could make it past the obstacles in my life, but just grow and see where it took me. Not to fight for life, but kind of just get on and ride it like a surfboard out in the breakers. Simply wait for a good-looking wave, then stand up and see what the hell would happen next. If I wanted to have some fun, I could add a little of my own style to the standing and call it grace.

In spite of myself, I smiled as I pressed the accelerator and headed north.

Trooper Chen had left Las Vegas the day before and was back up north dealing with a problem he was not quite sure how to handle—and one that was happening more and more. Dareece Slacker and Janet Muldrow were a couple who had just run out of everything, with nothing left and no place to go. They were an interracial couple who had been abandoned by what little family they had left and were too much on the down side to believe in anything except the love they had for each other. They used the last of their money to get married in Vegas and were heading north to find an uncle who Janet's family considered a black sheep to see if they could stay there. They had badly calculated their finances, and when their 15-year-old Volvo gave up the ghost with a broken water hose, they were stuck. They had managed to limp to where Route 375 began its journey into the wastelands. Heading north out of Vegas on Route 93, the road goes through a series of austere but mournfully beautiful desertscapes, dotted here and there with bird sanctuaries fed by invisible, underground streams. As the road arcs off, you pick up Route 318 toward Hiko. Route 318 again arcs to the right, and as 375 heads left, a triangle is formed in the center of the surrounding two-lane asphalt. At this spot is a small oasis where strange things naturally come to rest, seeking their own entropy. Trooper Chen gave Dareece two of the generic water hoses he kept in the back of his patrol car. Chen had just come back from getting the young couple some more water and some cash from an ATM about 27 miles away, and he was hoping the young hip-hop husband was good enough with his hands that they could drive off under their own power. As Chen stood in the shade while Dareece performed some emergency surgery on the young lovers' wounded beast, a pickup truck caught Trooper Markus Chen's eye as it turned and headed up the Extraterrestrial Highway toward Area 51 and the land of the lost. An unknown chill settled down in the trooper's bones, and a sense of foreboding started to wrap its seducing grip on his heart. As the late-model pickup passed through Trooper Chen's highly trained vision, he saw clearly under the thick desert dust that the plates on the truck were from Tennessee.

Coyote was not responding to Crow at all. He continued to hunt while Crow swooped down at him. It just made Coyote more and more angry. Coyote thought to himself, "I'm hungry, and if Crow won't know that, then he might be the next food!"

Crow had been telling Coyote for three days that it was almost time for Medicine Brother to come, and Coyote was acting just like it was a spring hunt and the Ghost People were herding all the weak ones to him. In fact, it was just the opposite and Coyote knew it. He knew that when it was time to make Earth Mother sacred he was not supposed to eat. Crow sighed to himself. He knew Coyote would never learn; he just hoped Coyote would remember to do what Ghost Brother expected of him.

"Coyote," Crow squawked. "Coyote, listen to me. Ghost Brother wants you to get ready. Empty Man will be here before the sun moves again!"

"When?" is all Coyote said as he lazily sat down in a small piece of shade by a dead scrub pine.

"Coyote, you need to go to where Ghost Brother needs you right now," Crow said as he landed on a branch near the top of the weathered and twisted tree. A hot breeze rolled lazily across the desertscape, picking up momentum and subsiding near where the two small animals sat and tried to figure out what to do. The wind was a horizontal spinning dust worm, making its way over the terrain in a serpentine fashion, the heat of the day not allowing it to climb and become airborne as it eddied and made fits and starts trying to get its wings. In the distance where the now people came from, Crow saw a dust devil give birth to itself and gain momentum as it played and danced its passionate samba across the arroyo. Crow was watching the funnel cloud gain momentum and then start to die when he saw a rooster tail of an incoming vehicle rising, making its way up the sand wash that led to the trailer and outbuilding that had recently been used to satisfy the perverted cravings of a madman.

"Coyote," Crow said slowly, "the Empty Man is here. Go and get ready now."

"Now?" Coyote asked, and a tug went into his bones and he thought about sunsets and moonrises.

"Yes, now, Coyote," Crow said gently to his friend, and he thought about sunsets and moonrises, too.

The small coyote got up and started to lope up the hillock behind the trailer as the obsidian bird flashed its shiny black wings, taking flight and crested the hill in the blink of an eye.

Special Agent John Steger had been driving since he and Lt. Thomas Quinn left Los Angeles for Las Vegas just after 3 a.m., and he was starting to get tired. He had just driven past a full-service exit and was wondering if he should have stopped, as nothing else seemed to be available. His eyes were displaying signs of fatigue, and he decided he would pull off at the next gas station and let Quinn do some driving. Steger could tell his eyes were starting to play tricks on him, and he cracked the window to get some fresh breeze in the government-issued vehicle. Thomas moved and his head flopped to the other side as the pressure differential equalized in the car by the opening of the window, but he did not wake.

John was not very thrilled to be on this task force, and the fact that he was relegated to driving with Thomas to Vegas instead of flying in one of the agency's aircraft didn't help. He was not as upset that they hadn't found Mumford yet as he was by the methodology that seemed to him to be corrupting the investigation. Steger really didn't have a problem with Bobby Doucette or his methods, but he felt it was just one type of intelligence and surely should not be relied on so heavily. At least not with someone as dangerous as Jack Mumford. Somehow the investigation had stalled as the different agencies were trying to figure out how to get their collective heads out of their assess. At least, Steger thought, Bobby Doucette had one thing right. They should not be concentrating so heavily on California. No proof had shown that Jack Mumford even arrived there yet. All they had was some circumstantial events that pointed to nothing more than some bad luck, and not the voodoo, evil-eye mumbo jumbo that people who ought to know better were talking about. Steger had seen this kind of behavior in the past on other cases. He knew that when evidence or intelligence was hard to come by, there was a dangerous tendency to overlook procedure. It wasn't very glamorous to do old-fashioned, dry police work when some whiz-bang theory seemed to offer such an easy solution. It was hard to stay on task while every swinging dick in the agency who was looking for a promotion and a feather in their cap came out of the woodwork, hoping to get noticed. The danger of a case like this is that while people's little egos saw a place for self-advancement, a killer was on the loose hoping the Keystone Cops wouldn't be able to keep their eyes on the ball, let alone find it.

When Thomas came up to him and showed him the e-mail from Doucette that he might have some information and would like to meet in Vegas, Steger jumped at the chance to get out of the circus tent the task force office had become. The tabloids were starting to stake out the task force building, trying to figure out who the players were and what the game was. Luckily, nobody from the press had figured out what the FBI was working on; they just knew it was something big and were out looking for scraps like circling buzzards. Steger didn't mind the press—after all, he knew that freedom, not control, is what keeps a country free—but what really pissed him off was that everyone was trying to figure out how to spin this God-awful tragedy to their benefit. Meanwhile, Jack "The Monster" Mumford was out feeding his pathetically morbid desires.

No one had heard from Bobby Doucette for weeks, and one of the prevailing theories in the task force assumed that he did find Mumford and the outcome was not positive. Bobby had a great track record for finding people or things, but he was a bit of a loose cannon when it involved procedural work. He got himself into trouble, and Steger mused that it was probably because he really didn't believe anyone was going to back him up. Brubaker proved that when he left Bobby swinging in the breeze not once but three times. Steger hadn't quite figured out how guys like Brubaker never got found out and kept working in the system for years, sometimes lifetimes. Politics is a strange art, and perhaps the reality is that you need guys like Brubaker. They are like criminals with a badge, and just like old, spooky Bobby Doucette had some useful talent, the Brubakers of the world serve their purpose as well. Sometimes it takes a person with the ability to have larceny in their heart to be able to catch a thief. "I suppose," Steger thought, his eyes narrowing, "that there are degrees of corruptness, and as long as you kept on one side of some kind of demarcation point, you were useful." As his eyes slowly closed, Agent Steger wondered who it is that gets to set the mark.

Mark Champlain had been driving his Freightliner for a little over a year for American Freight Haulers. He hauled flatbeds for the extra money because, as Mark figured, if he was going to be out here and away from his wife, Gretchen, and their two boys, Kyle and James, for 24 days a month, he might as well get paid the extra 4 cents a mile to haul the unwieldy flatbed loads. When the printing plant in Des Moines, Iowa, where he had been working for 18 years closed down, he needed a job that would pay. The way businesses were closing right and left, about the only thing a guy his age could do could that would guarantee him a living was drive a commercial rig.

Mark didn't even see the car at first. There seems to be rhythm to the road, and if you tune in to it, you can pretty much figure out how to survive out on the highways. You kind of get a feeling about the way traffic starts to behave, and the only real way to get into trouble is to ignore the signs—which Mark would tell Gretchen so she wouldn't worry so much. You kind of get a feeling in the back of your neck that something just isn't right and it's time to slow down or pull into a truck stop to check the rig. A lot of guys talk about driving on borrowed time as they get the signs but choose to ignore them so they can make some crazy delivery schedule.

The section of Route 15 that connected LA to Vegas had been under construction for about two years, and for the past year a good section of it was down to two lanes. It was a nerve-racking ride in the middle of the day, let alone at night. Mark started to get a sign in his neck about three miles back and he slowed down, but there wasn't really anywhere to go. He slowed as much as he dared and was looking all around, so he wasn't completely surprised when he saw the car from the oncoming lane veer straight into him. There was nowhere for Mark to turn, as the Nevada Highway Department had put concrete Jersey barriers on the shoulders that did not really leave enough space for a hazard lane. The only thing he could do was move as far right as possible and try not to jackknife the rig. Mark saw a blue flash and assumed the car went under the truck. There was a slight rumble, but he never felt the car actually hit.

Special Agent John Steger opened his eyes at the last possible second. He thought he had heard a truck horn, and when he opened his eyes all he could see were the two oncoming lights of the semi-rig that was bearing down on him. John was raised Catholic but had not been what he would consider a practicing Christian for most of his adult life. Sometimes when he would get into a sticky situation and he thought about praying to some cold, unknown God, he would stop himself. He figured if he wasn't going to invoke his faith on the good days it would be a sham for him to do it on the bad ones. Tonight was somehow different, for the most significant reason that he was alone. Steger had been in a lot of hairy situations, but most involved a team effort, and there was usually more than just him when he went through a door on a raid. But tonight, with Thomas deeply asleep, when John found himself faced with certain eminent death, he reflexively started to pray. Not the kind of prayer that is practiced on most Sundays by millions upon millions of the faithful, but more like the prayers of soldiers and sailors when every fiber of their being tells them death is actively hunting them.

Time had slowed for John, and in the intensity of the truck's headlamps he looked over and saw Thomas asleep. He remembered looking back at the truck, and then suddenly he was looking at himself looking at the truck. He was outside of his body, looking at his body looking at the truck, and he saw his body start to scream the words "not now" with a force he had never known. In the new place that John's consciousness was inhabiting, he found he had all the time he wanted, and instead of stopping to analyze the place, he instead turned all of his attention to the problem of how not to let his body die. As soon as he did, he found that in this new place he had found a way to control what was happening by picturing the reality he was watching as if he were watching a movie. All of this new knowledge was intuitive, as if he had known it forever, and John simply made the car and its occupants less dense than the truck.

Instantaneously John was back on the road, and skidding back to the right-hand lane there was a break in the Jersey barriers. He pulled the car over hard to the side of the road and brought it to a screeching halt.

Mark braked as smoothly as he could and brought the truck to a complete stop, pulling as far to the right as he could. He reflexively put on his hazards, checked his mirrors, and got out of the truck to see what had happened. By the time Thomas woke up and got a grip on the situation, John had put the blue lights on and was on the roadside in the fits of a reflexive-vomiting seizure. Mark had run back to the car by this time, and traffic was starting to back up, wondering what was going on. Thomas got out of the government sedan with the blue lights flashing and walked over to Mark, who was bent over trying to figure out if John was alright.

"What happened?" Thomas asked the two men. John's vomiting was subsiding, and Mark looked at Thomas' face, and with the most honest Iowan accent anyone has ever heard said, "I think you just drove right through my truck!"

(XRAY - • • -) "Proximity leads to desire, desire leads to belief, belief leads to knowing, knowing leads to faith, faith leads to demonstration. First there is the proximity. When you take a tuning fork in the key of A and strike it, then put it next to another tuning fork of the same pitch, the new tuning fork starts to vibrate also. It's a frequency patch you're looking for. If the frequency you're looking for is A but your own frequency is F, one of two things needs to happen: Change your desire or change your frequency. Things will resonate on their own; just decide what frequency you want to be, that is all you need to do. If your conscious mind says it wants to be one thing but your subconscious wants to be another, the secret desire wins out most of the time.

PS: If your heart hears truth, it will start to resonate to that frequency, and you just may find yourself driving through something very substantial. Don't get dejected if you don't fly the first time. Just remember before they flew at Kitty Hawk, Wilbur and Orville built bicycles most of their lives. Learn to enjoy the mystery."

Jack was not sure what was going on, but he could feel his margin of safety rapidly closing, and he didn't want to stick around to find out if he was going to get put in the hurt locker. He was going as fast as he could down the desert road in his pickup and knew he was leaving a pretty big rooster tail. It was hell time and somebody was going to have to pay for their sins. Jack had more than 500 pounds of iced human flesh in the back of his pickup, so he couldn't go very fast without his coolers jumping up in the air and risking damage to his precious cargo. The cap on the bed kept the coolers from flying out, but it was an old Dodge pickup and there was no way for him to tie down his morbid packages. Everything was speeding up, and no matter how many times he had been through this, Jack was never prepared for the sensation of dread when things started to get out of control. Not a moral sense of dread, but the kind where you might not get to finish what you started. Jack's timetable was a bit off, but it was always this way with a major space-time anomaly. You could get just so close and then you had to wait, and that was usually Jack's problem. When he had to wait, his cravings would get the better of him and he would find himself hunting when there was no need to. His obsessive cravings would lead him to a sort of madness within madness, and the desire for sex, killing, and the taste of flesh would be too much for his genius to contain. Desire is a funny thing when it is indulged and fed the way it wants to be nourished. It will allow you to feed it in a minimal way for a very long time before it rears its ugly head and can no longer be stopped. It is insidious in the way it lets one believe that somehow the object of its focus can be managed as long as a certain threshold is maintained. Most people quite frankly do not have the discipline it takes to find a proper balance for their desires and a place of safety to grow and learn instead of giving in to the impulse to feed their distraction. Internet collectors of NASCAR paraphernalia or little ceramic dolls share more in common than they know with the most devious. After all, how many things with the number 8 on them does one really need before desire turns to insatiable fetish?

(YANKEE - • - -) " *The way of life is the middle way. The way of death is the extremes. It is a false notion to believe that your self-destruction is the way to your most power. Death is death whether you are breathing or not. Do not be fooled by the passion of the edge. The object of the game is to control the ride, not have it control you. I'm not saying the scenery isn't going to get a bit wacky. Just that you have to know how to control the machine of your life. You can't pop a wheelie until you know where your torque curve is, and you learn that by controlling the mayhem and not going full-tilt boogie like some lost tribe of Berserkers or Vandals. Madness doesn't come from seeing how far you can go, but in thinking you're on the only road possible. Down at the crossroads we are all sinners. Just don't believe Mister Scratch when he tells you it's all good. He has been known to sell a car with a bad odometer every now and again.* "

Jack could tell he was being followed, but he didn't know if it was a real-time event or an astral sentinel sent to change his time-table. He was pretty sure that no one knew where he was, and he had 47 minutes until the next satellite flyover, but he was creeped and knew it was time to get out of Dodge. He drove as fast as he could and pulled straight into the shed and opened the hood. He grabbed some aluminum foil and made a tent over the open engine so the heat would appear less dense to a thermal satellite image. After checking on his cargo in the back of the truck, Jack took a shotgun that he had purchased in a pawnshop and used a hacksaw to cut the deer barrel back to about 12 inches. The barrel on the Mossberg 12-gauge pump was now even with the tubular magazine directly underneath the barrel on the gun. He deburred the barrel from the crude cut with a rat-tailed file so it wouldn't crack, then grabbed a Ruger 9mm semiauto pistol and stuck it in his belt. Mumford quickly left the shed and carefully made his way to the trailer to get packed. He still had 28 minutes until the bird flew over, and he was inspecting the dust he had kicked up on the way in. It was all dissipated and the desert was strangely still, but somewhere in Jack's mind he knew there was increasing movement in his direction. The switch tripped on the autopilot in his brain, and all the ghoulies knew it was time to play.

Sound has a very strange quality in the desert. It seems to have more to do with heat and wind than it does with resonance and volume. Things heard in the desert tend to resemble sightings of long-lost ghost ships in a fog out to sea. They become layered and fractured, only to show up again near you, letting you know that a part of your sensing mechanisms let you down. As Jack Mumford started to pack up the supplies and ammunition he had cached, he thought he heard a sound and stopped moving. In the dry Southwestern desert he stood motionless and held his breath, trying to figure out if he had heard anything or not. He took some quiet breaths, keeping still and listening intently for any aural evidence that he should move his timetable extremely forward. After three minutes he was about ready to start packing again when he distinctly heard the roar of an internal-combustion engine propelling a vehicle up the dry, hard pack toward him.

Jack calmly stopped packing, then retrieved some of his ammunition and started placing it around the perimeter of the trailer. He made sure two more of his pistols were loaded, then pumped a 12-gauge double-ought buckshot shell into the chamber of his sawed-off Mossberg. He shoved another shell into the magazine, filling the weapon to capacity. His dry lips started to crack as a smile formed on his sunburned face.

Trooper Markus Chen made sure the two young lovers were as right as they could be and told them he had to move on. Dareece had his arm around Janet, and she was crying as Trooper Chen lied to the young couple, telling them the State Trooper Foundation was where the $100 had come from and they really didn't need to pay him back. Dareece said he had never heard of such a thing, and when Markus told him it was a Republican-held Congress that had voted in the bill, Dareece flashed him a gold-toothed grin and looked the young trooper in the eye. As Chen broke off the gaze, he motioned for the two to get moving; he didn't know how long the old hoses would hold. They drove off, and Chen watched as Janet's eyes never moved from him while she waved good-bye. As he stood there watching them drive into the horizon of their life, he knew he was wasting time, but a feeling like not wanting to go back to work after a long vacation in some tropical paradise made him tarry while the car vanished in the heat waves. Markus walked to his cruiser, removed his hat, and started to get in his car but found that he couldn't. He did not want to do the next thing he knew he had to do, and he had never felt like this before. Something very primitive within him was screaming like a red-hot fire to not do what he knew he had to do. There, in the little oasis of sand and gravel, Markus Chen experienced a fear like he had never known, and it terrified him to his core. His body was revolting—it did not want to die this day and was letting him know that he needed help. He got in the car and tried to call his dispatch.

The repeater towers that allowed Markus to bounce the transmission from his radio back to base were kind of thin out there. They were subject to weather and seasonal anomalies and were not allowed near Nellis Air Force Base directly to the west. He tried several times and then realized he was not going to contact base from his present position. He closed the door to his cruiser and headed up 375 at a high rate of speed. As he approached the town of Rachel, Nevada, population 98, Markus slowed, trying to see if the truck had pulled in for fuel at the service station or food at the Little Alien Inn. He did see a truck, but it wasn't the one from Tennessee, and he kept driving. About 10 miles north he saw a little unpaved gravel side road leading off into the arroyo that he had never noticed before. As he passed it he felt an overwhelming force that wanted him to stop. Trooper Chen did not stop, but he slowed, and as he did he noticed that off in the distance was what looked like a settling cloud of dust. He slowed his police interceptor to a stop, and despite the feeling that had veteran State Trooper Markus Chen almost paralyzed, he turned around. There is something strange in the psyche of people who volunteer to put themselves in harm's way for the rest of us. They have the ability to override their instincts of self-preservation and put themselves between the possibility of destruction and the certainty of safety while standing there with inadequate tools in a defining moment of their and our human-ity. People can confuse someone who is a sociopath and someone who is courageous. A sociopath isn't aware that the path in life they are on is one of their own choosing. A courageous person is the one who is highly aware that the path they are on is one of their own choosing and that it may lead to their own destruction, but they go anyway. Markus Chen was one of these people, and when he turned off Nevada State Highway 375 and headed up the unpaved desert road with no known backup, his fear and his heart jumped into his throat.

Agent John Steger and Detective Thomas Quinn were sitting at a pancake house on the north side of Las Vegas when the message came from Bobby Doucette that he thought he knew where Jack Mumford was. Bobby did not leave the coordinates on the cell phone's e-mail, and the text of the message did not hint that this information was critical. Quinn had been working with Bobby for so long that he thought he knew when Bobby was just keeping him updated and when he was in crisis, so Thomas decided he would finish breakfast before he finding the Vegas field office to retrieve the coordinates that Bobby said he would send to his secured agency address. There was an uneasy silence between the men, almost like the morning after between two strangers whose sexual longings got the better of them in the warmth of the night but realized in the cold light of day that some things are better left unknown. Thomas and John had gone through something that couldn't be explained with the tools given to humans to understand their earthbound existence. As they sat there and the waitress dutifully brought more orange juice and coffee, both men were thinking that, in this paradigm of the mundane, their world had been profoundly altered forever. Later that morning when they retrieved the second e-mail and both men realized Bobby Doucette had duped them into thinking they had more time than they did to launch a full-scale interdiction manhunt, they would concern themselves with the things of the immediate world. For now they continued to eat in a place between the living and the dead, the now and the then, the real and the unreal, and wonder why now that their lives were changed forever.

Coyote was now seeing only with Ghost Brother's eyes, and he was the only living thing left on the arroyo except Empty Man and the other two who were on their way. Even Crow had left, and as Coyote stood on the hillock watching the vehicle approach, he perceived the various entities that had come for the energy. In his second sight he could see the small bowl where the buildings were, and around it, from out of the ether, appeared various energy forms, like strange fans for an impromptu, otherworldly rock concert. As the being that was now inhabiting Coyote's body watched the events develop, a strange wind started to blow. It rose and fell like the inhalation and exhalation of some great giant dog that was trying to get up after a long sleep. Something strange and foreign was forming, and the rules that usually governed this space and time of the universe were changing rapidly. Two thousand years ago one might have explained the events taking place here in this piece of dry wasteland as light and darkness, the players as devils and angels, but in a modern world all of this did not apply. So in this place, on this day, the only ones showing up were coming by a kind of ancient knowing that had nothing to do with maps, coordinates, terrain, volume, or density. The things that were coming were navigating by a second sight just barely hidden behind the reality of human existence. Once, a very long time ago, three men made a great journey over a similar desert, and it was recorded that they were guided by nothing more than what they called a star.

CHAPTER 12

I had been traveling about two hours and something unexpected was starting to happen to me. It would wash over me as if I were a ship trapped on a reef and the coming waves would shove me higher and higher up on a lost shoreline. The feelings started as soon as I left Las Vegas, and I thought it was just the effects of not drinking enough water while I was doing my psychic work. You need extra water to act like a kind of connector or lubricant. The human body tends to become very dehydrated when you are using the higher functions of the mind. When I left Route 318 to start my way up 375, a debilitating feeling of nausea got the best of me, and I pulled off onto a patch of gravel that separated the two roads under some very lonely trees. I had been traveling with an L-shape dowsing rod in my right hand that would twitch and point in the direction I would need to turn at each intersection. I was unsure that the place where I thought I would find Mumford earlier that morning would be where he was now. I put the rod down and steered my truck into some shade and got out. When my feet hit the ground I almost fell down, my legs not wanting to support my weight at first. I caught myself on the armrest of the open driver's door and slumped back against the seat while a sense of dizziness and sickness washed over me. After a minute or two, I felt some strength returning to my legs. I stood up after a short while and walked to a blind spot between my truck and the tree, and I began to unzip my pants so I could relieve myself of the pressure that had built up in my bladder while I was traveling. My hands started shaking, and I found myself unable to get them under control enough to manipulate the zipper of my pants. I stumbled to the front of my truck and caught myself as I started to fall against the hood. As I pushed myself to try to regain my composure, tears started to flow as freely as a spring rain from my eyes and down my cheeks. I knew what was happening, but I didn't want to acknowledge the physiological connection that was debilitating me now with what I had to do today. My body was afraid of its own demise, and unlike most times in my life where I could fool it into thinking that what was happening was for the best, it would not be fooled this time. I had turned my body and my mind into a finely tuned instrument, and the layers that had so valiantly protected me for so many years had been carefully peeled away by the process of my own awakening. In order for me to find truth as it existed in the universe for any given situation, I had to give up my own prejudices and biases, and I was now left without the ability to protect my psyche with false beliefs and superstitions. My mind was naked and my body was afraid, and I didn't have a clue if I had the strength to get back in my truck and continue my journey. Every human, whether an artist who has touched genius through paint, light, and canvas or a mountain climber who has striven to push themselves past the abyss of their own endurance, has a very hard time trying to live in a mundane world once they have found the true grace of existence. The fear of most people is not that the things of darkness will somehow find them but that they will be awakened and will never be able to find their way back to the safety of unknowing. It's better to watch the Super Bowl and drink beer than to dabble in your own awakening and not be able to commit yourself fully to the path that will be revealed to you. You may lose your family. You may lose all the friends you think you have ever made and wind up alone. You may end up like many tortured souls who have felt the grace of God in their life or their art and lose their minds trying to figure out how to get back to that one pure note that, however momentarily experienced, changed them forever. Religion was not invented to free you but to constrain you in a framework lest you get lost in the infinite process of becoming and growing your soul. As Kermit the Frog once said, "It's not easy being Green"—nor is it easy for a human being to find their true path out here in the wasteland.

I managed to get it together and stop shaking enough to relieve myself. As I watched the stream of urine hit the bone-dry dirt and splash on my boots, it occurred to me that this might be the last time I got to piss, and in the realization of the loss of such a mundane function, my sadness became profound. Everything I had taken for granted washed over me and left me without any energy or will to move forward. I should just go back. I should just stop and call in the cavalry. What was I thinking? And what kind of ego must I have to try to do this task alone? I felt like a sham, realizing it must be my ego trying to get me some kind of bizarre props, that I was the only thing here that could do the job of finding this madman. My body was directing my mind, and it was telling me to turn tail and run just as fast as I could in the other direction and let somebody else figure this horrible mess out for me. I stumbled back to the open door of my Land Cruiser and swung myself up into the cab. With great effort, I shut the door and got some water from a Nalgene lab bottle off the seat. My skin started to crawl, and I felt like there were a thousand red fire ants on my back, so I pulled off my shirt and tried in vain to scratch my own skin. After a short while the itching subsided, and my breath and pulse started to stabilize. As soon as I felt my body come back to some sort of equilibrium, I grabbed the gearshift lever and threw it into drive, picking up the L-rod and letting it guide me up 375 toward Rachel.

About 40 minutes later I saw the population sign for the town of Rachel, Nevada, and the anxiety started to creep in, again making me think I should pull over and stop to sort this out. I knew at this late date that if I did, I would probably reason my way out of continuing on my bizarre mission. So as I drove through town, pulling past the Little Alien Inn with its tow truck out front chained to a fake flying saucer, I knew I was leaving behind my last best hope for help. My mind and body felt another wave of fear pass over, and just like an overweight man feeling the first pangs of a heart attack and denying the danger, I told myself it was nothing and kept driving. I was moving along now as fast as my old truck would allow, and I burned up the asphalt. My dowsing rod started to twitch and motion ever so slightly to my right off to the northeast. Instinctively I started to slow, and about a quarter-mile away I could see the outline of where a fire road made its way off to the right and out into the arroyo. I slowed the Land Cruiser, and as I neared the road my L-rod started to swing slightly more to the right. I came to a stop just before the road, and my rod stopped its gyrating and strongly swung in the direction of the road on my right. I could feel the fear starting to well up inside me again and knew it would be debilitating if I let it take over. I threw the rod down on the seat, shoved my old SUV into four-wheel drive, and headed up the wash. I was quickly swallowed up by the desert and surrounded by low scrub as the oversize tires made quick work of the desert hardpack. I looked back and could not see the road or the civilization I left behind; I was out here alone, and as I started to get my old senses back, I pulled to a stop in the middle of the wash. I got out as fast as I could and rolled under my truck, breaking my gun locker loose from its quick-release straps and opening it. Quickly taking out my assault rifle and riot shotgun with extra ammo for my pistols, I put the container in the back of the truck and jumped in, punching the gas before the door was completely shut. I was quite aware that the element of surprise was gone, as anyone could see me coming for 20 miles. The strong wind that seemed to be coming from different directions every few minutes was blowing the dust cloud trailing behind me up to about 200 feet in the air. If anyone was up ahead, they knew something was coming, and I was sure there would be a welcoming committee waiting.

I was barreling down the road, and as I came up a small hillock, I could see the outlines of what looked like an old abandoned construction trailer and another outbuilding next to it. In a flash I knew these were the buildings I had visited remotely the night before and this was where Jack was. I could feel the underlying fear trying to make itself known, but the good-old adrenaline was kicking in and I could feel my old timing starting to regain some ground. I was getting ready to sin again and I didn't care. In fact, as my body and my mind started to remember the tools of violence, a warm, almost comforting feeling started to replace the fear. I knew this. I knew how to wreak my own brand of mayhem out here, and I was remembering all the things I needed to at least make it a fair fight. If I had a plan, it was simple: Arrive fast and start laying down suppressive fire, reloading as quick as I could until I didn't need to anymore.

There was another small knoll in back of the compound, and as the buildings came into view, my plan was to keep the high ground to my right and see if I could get up close to it while I made my way behind the buildings. As I drove past the edge of the road and started bouncing across the arroyo, I saw that there was a state trooper's interceptor near the trailer and what looked like a body lying halfway across the threshold of the door. I circled around to the right and came out of the truck as fast as I could after shutting off the engine and grabbing my weapons. I quickly stashed an extra pistol behind the driver's side front tire and ran crouching low to the back of the larger shed. There was a gap in the corrugated steel, and I looked inside the building I had already visited and saw nothing but an old pickup with Tennessee plates. Detecting no movement, I made my way to the gap between the two buildings, and seeing that there were no windows in back facing the hill, I crossed the space between them, my heart pounding hard in my chest. My next point of cover was the squad car, and without thinking I ran to a position behind the front right tire with the rest of the car between the trailer, and that was when everything changed forever.

As I was lying in a prone position with the cover of the tire shielding me, I looked under the car and could see clearly that the Nevada state trooper lying in the doorway had most of his face blown off from what looked like a shotgun blast. It was a foolish plan but it seemed like my only option: I would lay down two magazines worth of covering fire with the assault rifle, then rush the door with the shotgun and pistol. It was just a matter of getting my breath and going for it, and I would figure this thing out once and for all. My mind was on fire, and the hate and bile that started bubbling up was fueling my desire for some killing in that late-morning desert light. I had a great field of fire, and just as I was about ready to pop up and rock and roll with my M-4, I heard something as clear as anything I had ever heard, and yet was impossible. I eased my finger from its safe position on the trigger guard to the trigger itself, and a voice came from nowhere and everywhere at once.

"Bobby, don't take your guns, don't carry the hate." It was Kat's voice, and I would know it anywhere. My mind reeled, my mouth instantly became as dry as the sand I was lying on, and I thought my heart was going to burst.

"Kat," I almost screamed. "Kat, how?" As my words trailed off, I detected movement to my left rear flank, and I spun around, training my weapon on a black crow as it landed in a small scrub pine, twitching its head toward me and watching as what was left of my reality crashed down around me. I knew at once this was it; this was my test, and I might never get a chance to take it again in this life or any others, and everything mattered now. Nothing that I had trained for or learned could help me with what I had to do next. Everything I was became important and mundane at the same time. I was someone who thought they lived by faith, but in a flash it hit me that I really only lived with a hypothesis that maybe bordered on superstition, and I was faced with the choice of following my instincts or my conscience. It was not lost on me that the possibility of being lost to the spirit that had just spoken to me forever was in the mix, but all I had for reference now was a crow and a madman.

Insanity can strike at any time and put reality into question. I was sitting now with my back to the tire. I flipped around low and covered the house from under the interceptor. As I lay there getting ready to go over the top, I realized I had been presented with a real choice, and just the hope that it might have been my Kat and not some warped part of my brain put me into an incredible conundrum, and as soon as I started thinking about it my timing was off. The fear was back, and my mind reeled again at the possible sources of what I thought I just heard—not the least of which that it might have been Mumford's magic and not my woman at all. As I lay there waiting, trying to decide what to do, I realized the truth of the situation. Maybe it was because I really didn't care about my tomorrow, or maybe it was because that for the first time in a very long time I had clarity about how to live the next few moments of my life. I knew in my heart with a certainty like I had never known that the voice I heard was the woman I loved, and that no matter where or what she was, she was expending a great deal of life force to get the message to me that she just delivered.

(ZULU - - • •) "If you can't run with the big dogs, stay on the porch. In the Hagakure, the book that is the manual for the way of the samurai, it says that a samurai should 'decide on matters of grave importance lightly.' It was said that a samurai made the most important decisions in seven breaths. If you truly understand that whatever path you take you are going to wind up at the same place, you might as well choose to do the thing that seems most true to you. The way of truth is the way of life; you may, however, pay a price for your freedom. They had a saying in New Hampshire once, and most people forget the whole quote: 'Give me liberty or give me death, there are worse things in life than dying.'"

My mind became calm; I put my rifle and shotgun down, and removed my .45 and its holster from my belt and set it down next to me. My life was a sham, and I had been using the tool of violence to prop up my old belief system. A wise person once told me that if the only tool you have is a hammer, then every problem seems like a nail.

I needed to do something and I took one last look at the scene in front of me. I couldn't just sit there any longer. So I stood up and started walking toward the trailer. As soon as I was out in front of the interceptor and I had no more cover or weapons, the fear was back. What seemed like a good decision at the time now seemed like the most foolish, stupid thing I could have imagined. Everything was in a kind of hyper reality, and time was meaningless. I noticed a pop-top from an old soda can, the kind that was removed from the can before drinking, gleaming in the sun and wondered how long it had been there. By the time I had finished that thought, I was almost up to the door, and upon seeing the body up close the fear surged with a vengeance. The trooper's face had been blown off, and blood, meat, and bone were everywhere. His service pistol was about three feet from his hand, and I could tell it had been fired. I tried not to look at the eviscerated head but could not keep my eyes from it, and as I did I became debilitated and could not move.

One of the trooper's eyeballs lay next to his left hand, looking up at me, wondering why I was late. My legs became weak again, and I had to rest against the door jamb to keep from falling. As I leaned into the support of the structure, I heard something moving in another room inside the trailer. Peeling my eyes away from the corpse, I had to fight the feeling of paralysis that threatened to overwhelm me. My body did not want to die, and it was starting to make decisions without me. I turned away and walked toward an open doorway with a door set aside off it hinges, and I entered a dark room.

The butt of a shotgun glanced of my shoulder before it hit my head. I had turned just enough so my shoulder had taken the brunt of the blow, or I might have been dead right then. As it was, I dropped to the dirty floor like a wet rag and passed out. When I came to, my arms were being duct-taped behind me and I was naked. I had made an error in my judgment, and my chest convulsed automatically as a horrible fear caused my thighs to reflexively try to hide my naked genitalia. A booted foot kicked me in my testicles just before the butt of the shotgun slammed into my head again. As the pain made me pass out for the second time, I was slightly aware of the losing of my bowls and defecating on myself.

The flesh is weak. Jesus cried to his Father and wondered why he had forsaken him in his true physical hour of need—the pain was too great to override his spiritual teaching and his human body revolted, mourning its painful demise. We die and we don't like it one bit. For all our beliefs and teachings about the afterlife, death is ultimately a mystery. We cross alone, and even though the sages have told us that our advanced spiritual practice will allow us to pass our physical form or not need it at all, our body doesn't believe it. When the spirit departs, the body immediately starts to break down into its primordial components. The stink starts, the rot begins, the maggots appear, and the body starts to liquefy.

"The worms crawl in, the worms crawl out, the worms keep crawling roundabout …"

There have been societies that have figured out some of the mysteries, and yet still the grim reaper appears and takes his ultimate percentage. We have secondhand accounts and whispers, superstitions, innuendo, and tales, but we are ultimately left with nothing, except maybe a painless exit or a quick end at best. How much terror or pain is in the final seconds no one is sure, but we know this: When life is extinguished, a weight of 5 nickels departs the body and goes somewhere, and we the living can never be sure where that destination is or what those 21 grams represent.

The most advanced spiritual civilizations the planet has ever produced have left us with foggy clues as to the final destination of the dead. The ancient Egyptians, the Christian Gnostics, the Mayans, the Druids, the Tibetan Buddhists, Hawaiian kahunas, Cabalists, American Indian shamans, and even old Atlantis itself got close to the secrets, and when all was said and done died anyway. So there is a grasping for life in the final act, and we the living would trade anything for one more bad day at the office. One more peer review, one more dinner with a lousy waiter. Another night's worth of arguing with a lying lover over their whereabouts the night before. Another hour sorting through past-due bills. For in the end, life is all we really have. It is our reason to be here in the first place, and every second is a precious gift whether we are aware of its gift or not.

When my eyes blinked open the second time, I remembered the trooper's gun lying on the floor next to his body just before my mind registered the tremendous pain I was in. The pistol was a semiautomatic Smith & Wesson 9mm, and assuming it was not empty and still there, it became the focal point of my survival inventory. I had noticed that the breech of the issue firearm had not been blown back, signaling that it wasn't empty, but how many rounds? How many, if any, were left? I was in another room and didn't have a clue as to how long I had been out or if the pistol was still there, but it gave me a point of reference and a way to focus my thoughts on surviving rather than succumbing to this madness.

At the United States Army Academy at West Point, there is a fantastic armory museum with the most amazing relics of warfare and mayhem the world has ever produced, from ancient swords to modern nuclear warheads. Of all the weapons collected there from over the millennia, one in the collection will impress me forever for its cleverness and the psychological understanding of its creators. It is not an impressive Scottish claymore sword requiring a two-fisted skill to wield, or the mock-up of the atomic bomb called "Fat Man" used to destroy Nagasaki, Japan, at the end of World War II. The weapon that impresses me most is a very small piece of metal that almost looks like junk and would be totally overlooked, except for its ingenious deployment just before the Normandy invasion by Allied forces during World War II. It's called a FP-45 Liberator, and it is nothing more than a pressed piece of metal with a spring, a crude firing pin, and a single bullet. Just prior to the Allied invasion, thousands of these simple weapons were parachuted in pods all over occupied France and Holland. With nothing more than operating instructions written in several languages, the logic was simple, cold, and strategically beautiful. No one needed to explain what to do to anyone who had felt the tyranny of fascist rule. The thought that the Liberator was supposed to implant in the minds of the oppressed was as simple as it was lethal: "We are coming and we need help. We know that you are pissed and would like a very nice German Schmeisser machine gun of your own to kill the bastards who killed your loved ones, but we have a problem. If we try to airdrop precious ammunition and firearms to you, they might be used against us. So here is one bullet, and if your will is strong and your aim is true, you can kill one of these fuckers with your Liberator and get a shiny new Schmeisser for yourself." This thought process took about one and a half seconds for the finder of this simple zip gun to figure out how to pull the spring back, stick it up the head of the nearest Nazi, and blow a very small but adequate hole in the back of his neck. No one knows how many underground resistance fighters took advantage of the small trinket, but you can bet that just off some lonely country road in

Holland or France, there is a shallow grave of a Gestapo agent with a Liberator's bullet logged successfully in his skull.

The key to the whole exercise was the belief in one's ability to surmount an overwhelming force. You could not hesitate with your one bullet. You would have to be stealthy, bold, and cunning. You would have to put your humanity and fear on hold and become a hunter. Survival is a skill and must render the participant to the realm of the unequivocal and decisive if one is to acquire its benefits.

A friend once took me to the Museum of Tolerance in Los Angeles. The museum chronicles the descent into madness that pre-Nazi Germany took as a collective act. There is a guided tour that begins with cosmopolitan German Jews dining in fine restaurants and cafes, going to theaters, and living normal lives as members of a society that little by little turned on them. You see them being rounded up, and at some point you realize as a museum participant you are taking the same journey that eventually puts you on a train and walks you through the gates of a formidable-looking concentration camp, while your very persuasive and matronly guide herds you toward your final goal of ending up in a full-scale model of a Nazi death camp gas chamber. The door shuts, and your guide asks you to sit on the concrete benches and be silent. Suddenly the moment of terror dawns on you that must have been lived by those people day after day, hour after hour.

When I was in the museum, I annoyed my friend by refusing to sit down and listen to the lecture. It felt like capitulation, but it was too late; the door had been shut, and if the facilities had been real, my momentary rebellion would have been quelled as soon as the Zyklon-B gas entered my lungs and I stopped breathing. I asked myself many times why they let it happen, why they waited until it was too late. Trusting that somehow they would be delivered from their fate if only they would do what they were told. One's survival isn't determined by the goodwill of others, but upon seizing what little opportunity you might have and honestly understanding your reality quickly enough to act.

My eyes fluttered open again as I heard movement in the other room by the door. Mumford was moving the body of the trooper out of the mobile home. He would be coming for me next, and my only hope was that I was more valuable to him alive right now than dead. My camouflage would be to seem incapable but be ready to seize any and all opportunities. A short time later I heard someone approaching and enter the door. To my chagrin, I then heard the scraping of the gunmetal on the bloody plywood floor as he retrieved the trooper's sidearm.

I moved my head, and the pain almost made me pass out again as I saw Mumford enter the room. He was trussed up in an elabo-rate, self-tied rope bondage array with various pieces of meat and blood stuck to him. A cold fear entered my chest as I looked into his eyes and realized there was nothing left of what we might con-sider a soul. I looked up, and more out of fear than anything else said, "That's not a real good look for you, Jack."

Another boot kicked me in the stomach and caused my face to roll on the dirty, bloody floor, and I was glad as it hid my smile that I'm sure Mumford would have interpreted.

"Shut up, meat," was all that rasped out of Mumford's sun-burned lips.

I had time. I was safe for a very short time, and I hoped that would be enough. He wasn't in too good of shape, and I could tell that moving the trooper's body had worked him. He wanted me to bring myself to my own death, to get up and save him the work of dragging me. I was fairly sure that if I caused too much trouble I was a dead man. Mumford had erred and given me too much information. If I knew him, he had made his power circle in the other building, and after all that work he would want to use my life force there. It was now a game of chance, and I at the very least was in the game. The vision of the gas chamber momentarily passed through my mind soup. I didn't want to get there. I didn't want to get to the endgame, and I had less than 70 feet to figure this out. I needed to let go of my fear and become hazardous material, dangerous cargo. I needed to go over the top right now.

I was tired and bleeding and most of me hurt. Inside, a small voice had started to whisper to me hours ago, it said simply: "Stop, give up, just let go. It will all be over so very, very quickly. You don't need to fight anymore. Why bother? Let go, just let go. It would feel so good to release yourself from this false game of life and come home."

I have smelled death many times, and it is seductive; its answer is profound and wise. It gives us an out, a way to stop the mayhem and bring an end to our anguish, our trial. Death has a wisdom that is built into the very fiber of our makeup. It is as much a part of us as our breath, our sight, our song, our magnificence. We come here, and if we are lucky, we get to feel the life in our bones. We get to feel the pain in our joints, the anguish in our hearts, love in our loins. We look out at the universe experiencing every ripple of awareness we choose. We flex our blood and pump it throughout our unique vehicle and pulse our power through the soles of our shoes. It is our power, and often when the weight of our existence becomes unbearable, we give it up and recede like twilight into an inky black forest. We must rest. We must give up the life force back to where it came from. We must release.

But today was not that day. Today I would not allow the mediocre to take my power. Today was just not a day to allow the devil his due. Fuck his due. Fuck all of them. Today I would not slip quietly any goddamn where. I had life, and whether it was 5 minutes or 500 years, I wanted to take the motherfucking ride. I paid my money, and I wanted to see the credits. I wanted to know how many swings the key grip had for the whole production, including the second unit in Mexico. I wanted the Juice. I wanted the skinny, and I'd be damn skippy if I were going to let some ass monkey dictate my existence.

There was nothing to Mumford or anyone like him. He was a shell; any moron can kill. Any asshole can tear down a barn, but it takes a carpenter to build one. Fuck the bullies, fuck the fascists, and fuck every prick bastard who wants to suck the life force out of anything they're unwilling to put back in. I wasn't going down today with fear in my heart. I wasn't going to cross over and have to answer for the crime of cowardice. I had 70 feet, give or take; I had a secret weapon; and I wasn't going down without giving life the length of a machine gun belt in a World War II fighter aircraft. Mumford was going to get the whole goddamn nine yards, and I wasn't going to let him choose the time of my demise. If all you have left is death, then at the very least make sure you carry in your heart the feeling you want to die with. Don't let the bastards win; go out singing. Let them know by your will that there will be another place, another time, and they will have to answer for their misdeeds. There will be a tribunal, and you show this by your unwillingness to walk into that gas chamber without a fight.

Mumford had duct-taped my arms and legs but allowed enough room so I could shuffle. He had also made one more mistake: I had pissed and shit all over myself, and he had taped over it. I could feel that the tape had not stuck completely to my flesh. As I struggled to get up, he grabbed me and pulled me to my feet. When he did, I noticed that the way he had tied himself up in some kind of elaborate fetish harness prevented mobility in his body. He was stiff and off-center, and his balance was too high for his frame. Achilles had a small spot on the back of his foot that led to his downfall. We all have a weakness, and when we indulge our perversions, we become a prisoner to our desire. We are blinded by the weakness inherent in us. It is death's way of finding a way in.

I stood up and looked into this madman's eyes and I did not flinch. He quickly spun me around by my arms and pistol-whipped me on the side of my head with the trooper's sidearm. I saw light, then blue, then green, then black, and felt the warmth of the blood as my skin burst apart. Jack stuck the pistol back into the rope around his midsection and picked up his shotgun, smashing the butt of it against my chest. He caught me before I fell to the floor and shoved me in the direction of the door. In his eyes I saw nothing. He had checked out, and what was left was a selfish biological machine that had relinquished his right to mercy. He had shown none and deserved none, as life is a reciprocal act.

Tithing is a gross representation with money for a divine truth that the life force is to be acquired, used, and passed on. Energy can neither be created nor destroyed. We are here to do something, to be of some ultimate use, and if we don't, we are just an experiment that failed. We lose our turn and go directly to jail. We are looked down at as misguided children lost in a sea of darkness, waiting to have our gross mass reclaimed by the Earth Mother.

Mumford had not given back. Even a shark's predatory nature is used to select its prey based on a sense of balance that the oceans themselves need to survive. When nature is in balance, her hunters are used to rid the sick and weak so nothing is wasted and the herd is thinned properly. But when something becomes rogue, it shows disrespect for its own existence. It's a bad gear that must be replaced, but if we only think of them as detritus, we become no better than the rogue element. So we must hold compassion in our hearts while we do the work we must. We must thank the Great Spirit for his wisdom and ask for his mercy and pray that our logic is sound and make ourselves worthy. As Abraham Lincoln said, "My concern is not whether God is on our side; my greatest concern is to be on God's side."

I walked, but upon taking one step I allowed myself to fall, trying to turn but smashing my head anyway as my bound arms could not protect me. Another boot kicked my back and Jack shouted, "You fucking walk, meat, or I'll skin you here and now."

"I can't walk, the tape is too tight," I coughed out, and when I did I heard the flick of a knife opening. A terror shot through me as I wondered if my next sensation would be one of my skin being filleted down to my bone. Mumford made a quick slash, and I could feel my slick legs come free from the tape now barely stuck to my body. As I struggled to get up, alarms started going off all around the complex. I realized that whatever the alarms were for, Mumford was now going to have to respond to their warning. His boot kicked me in the ribs and he hissed, "Now get the fuck up and move!"

Mumford grabbed me by my taped arms, wrenching them into an unimaginable angle, and he hauled me to my feet. He shoved me through the door of the mobile home and toward the shed. I immediately realized he had hid both the trooper's interceptor and my Land Cruiser in the shed. He had swept the area of tracks, and the alarms probably meant that some kind of surveillance was inbound. Mumford was out of time, and so was I. If he got me into that shed, I was going to die his way. Terror started to rise again in my chest, and I knew I had reached my endgame. I hesitated, and

Mumford, like the attentive shepherd he had become, shoved the barrel of his shotgun in the small of my back, pushing me toward the shed and my death. I did not want to die in there, in the dark, in the shadows subject to the lunacy of this shit bag and his devious perversions. It was go time, and I didn't have a clue what to do. The fear began to stink in my nostrils, and I felt alone.

I'd like to say that what happened next was because of some kind of wisdom or bravery on my part, but that would be a lie. As I slowed my pace, trying to figure out what to do and waiting for the next blow, a thought popped into my mind. And since it was the only thing there besides fear, I simply chose it as my only option and voted for my humanity.

There is an ancient meditation called the Prayer for the Twin Hearts. You simply imagine your object of derision or consternation as an object in front of you, and project a beam of energy from your heart and one from your head or crown chakra. You can also send energy from the minor chakras in your palms, but I didn't have that option. You can send any kind of energy you want, but if you send anything less than love, you get a kind of slap back and could injure yourself very badly. I imagined a picture of the Jack Mumford behind me, ready to kill and eat me, and I started my silent chant:

"Jack Mumford."

"Jack Mumford."

"Jack Mumford."

"I wish you ..." I hesitated, feeling the anger and bile start to rise in my throat, and then I chose.

"I wish you Peace, Peace, Peace."

What happened next I'm still not sure. Mumford spun me around and said, "Time's up, meat." And he raised his shotgun at me and I saw his trigger finger start to squeeze.

I fought to hold on to feelings of goodwill for him, and in that split second there was some kind of movement to my right, Jack's left. Mumford spun to acquire his new target. In between the two buildings, a scrawny coyote was approaching us with his ears back and his teeth showing. At the same moment, a shiny black crow came out of the sun like a fighter pilot ace and swooped at Mumford's face, his talons glancing off Jack's cheekbone. His point of balance or hara was too high from the rope with the pistol stuck into it, and the spin he did toward the coyote was amplified in the same direction by the crow. Something shifted under Jack's foot, a small pebble or piece of metal, but as he spun Mumford lost his balance and he started to stumble. His hands were still gripping the shotgun with the thought of killing locked in their ganglia, the barrel swinging up to acquire my face as its target.

Instantly I was 15 feet above, looking down on the scene of Jack trying to kill me. I again had left my body; my mind had split, and everything was frozen in time. The crow was not moving. Its wing stopped in the downward-thrust position a foot away from Jack's face, which it had just attacked. The coyote's teeth were bared, and a drop of saliva was suspended three inches in front of his now-silent barking mouth. This was the scene of my intended death, but somehow time had stopped for me in another kind of reality. I knew that at any moment, I would be slammed back into my body, in the reality to which my physical body's death was inexorably linked. I noticed a slight movement in the muscles of the crow's black wing as it started to flap and knew this time that was given to me to use was rapidly coming to an end. Then I saw it. I needed to sweep Jack's leg. It was like a code in the scene. The weak point in an otherwise-lethal still frame of a horrible puzzle. With that thought I was back in my body. I squatted with all my might, and the tape that was soaked with my bodily fluids rode up over my hips. My legs were free. I spun low in a horse stance, pivoting backward hard on my bare foot, ripping it open on the gravel of the arroyo. With an inch to spare, the heel of my foot smashed into Jack's knee as I swept his leg, then I fell to the desert floor.

His right foot lost its grip. Unable to bend at the waist, he fell face-first onto the muzzle of the shotgun as the firing pin hit the primer and a load of a double-ought buckshot eviscerated Jack Mumford's face. Because of the way I was situated, his bloody face and part of his skull blew past me, missing my head by inches and leaving me with splattered blood and flesh. I looked over and saw Jack still alive and clawing at his nonexistent face. His jaw had been blown in half and dangled menacingly, trying to form words. A strange piercing whistle emanated from where his mouth used to be.

He spun helplessly, falling to his hand and knees, and started searching maniacally, crawling fast toward me like some kind of grotesque mechanical insect. Jack came right for me, and as I rolled away from him, he crawled off to my right for five feet more before falling to the ground, the high-pitched whistle ebbing into the nothingness of death. I looked up to where he was headed and saw the mangy coyote standing on the escarpment where a small reddish-brown tornado-like cloud was forming. The crow flew past my head in the direction of the coyote, and my grief, pain, sorrow, happiness, and loneliness all burst up through my chest, and I started to cry convulsively. My chest heaved and my body shook. And with what little strength I had left, I rolled up to my knees and gave the deepest prayer of thanks I had ever expressed next to the dead madman.

I prayed for the dead, I prayed for the living, I prayed that the mayhem would be wrangled for a while. I prayed that a certain kind of terror would be gone from this place for now and would be replaced by the light and the good and the merciful. When I was done giving thanks, I struggled to my feet and rubbed against a piece of torn aluminum siding to cut the duct tape enough to get it off my arms and hips.

The wind was up on the arroyo, and as I looked up to the escarpment, the coyote waited for me to notice the soundless vortex was gaining in size. When I did, he stood up, looked back at me, and entered the vortex.

I was naked, tired, dirty, and bloody. I was reduced. I also knew why I was here and what I was to do next. So I got up what little courage I had left, stumbled my way up the escarpment, and stood before the ancient mystery. I prayed for strength and felt anguish in my chest as a thought of the day's mayhem entered my mind soup. The crow was circling above, signaling it was time for me to choose what my new destiny would be. From my lips escaped my anguish with a gasp, "Kat, I miss you so much."

I walked the last remaining distance under my own steam, and with my own free will I entered the spinning vortex.

EPILOGUE

After spending the rest of the day and night with the FBI and the other law enforcement agencies, I decided I would check into the Little Alien Inn and get some sleep. Steger and Quinn had booked rooms also, and I had spent a good deal of time trying to explain to them not what happened with Mumford, but what happened to them on their drive from LA to Vegas. I slept until late afternoon the next day, and by the time I got up, all the cops, troopers, and agents who had been using the motel as a makeshift field office had gone. I went into the restaurant to get some food and entered a place that made its living off a mixture of myth, legend, truth, and lousy hamburgers. It was filled with the paraphernalia of the great alien and government conspiracies, all fueled by its proximity to the infamous Area 51 and the strange things that have been sighted around that area of the wasteland.

A family came in, and I could tell right away that they were not tourists but were here to find some kind of answer. It was a mother, father, and two teenage daughters who were dressed in the requisite teenage fashions, but you could tell something was different with them. It was a kind of knowing that little girls of that age should not have to know about but often do. It seemed that something had happened to this American family that had traveled from an average neighborhood into the high desert to try to put meaning into the fate that had befallen them. The girls did what all teenagers do on vacation and went looking around the shop at the trinkets and sweatshirts, all proclaiming the existence of otherworldly visitors, but this was not some kitsch visit on a road trip. The girls seemed very protective of their parents, who sat at a table near me and talked very low while the girls tried to be young and carefree but did not believe for an instant that life was what they were taught. Something had happened to the girls' parents, and whatever it was, this family would never be the same. As the younger of the two girls picked up a stuffed doll that resembled the common effigy of a gray alien with the big head and black eyes, the kind with the child's body done up in a skintight spacesuit, she started to laugh until she turned and saw her father's face looking at her in horror. The mother put her arm on him and calmed him down, confirming that they were not here to see the sights but to find others who knew about their story and to help them make sense of a world that would never again be safe.

This place was starting to give me the creeps, so I finished my meal and got up to pay. I was thinking that throughout all of this I felt the most bad for Agent Steger and that he and this family had something very much in common. Everything they thought they knew—their churches, their governments, their schools, and their friends—was a lie. In a normal life, there is no room for the mystery of existence, and any talk of it gets you ostracized from your community quicker than you can say the Spanish Inquisition. I think somehow that these things are being revealed to us a little at a time so we can get used to the fact that we are not alone and someone or something is watching. If people knew of their own power, then we would not have dictators or rogue governments or multinational corporations racing to sell the future of our planet down the drain for the highest dollar. No, we wouldn't let that happen if we knew just how much power each one of us had. We would instead do something magnificent and let our soul shine to its own light and play its own music. I could be wrong. We might just try to blow ourselves up or eat the guy next to us. I'm not sure, but that kind of thing will happen anyway, so we might as well evolve. We will sooner or later, so for my money, I want to see it go down while there is still strange music, dark rum, and an ocean breeze whose smell hints of far-off lands.

If this was some kind of test I just went through, I'm not sure I passed. The bottom line was I swept Mumford's leg and he was killed because of it. I swept the leg, I killed him, and even though I wish it had gone down a different way, I'm glad it was him and not me. There were no winners here, yet it was good to be alive. Another notch in my karmic belt that I would have to deal with later. For now I was still breathing, and the orange ball of the setting sun was making a mad dive for the high desert floor, off to the west near dreamland in Area 51.

I paid my tab and walked outside to my truck, glad to be done with the weirdness for a while. I rolled down the windows and made sure all my gear was packed when an SUV with California plates rolled into the parking lot, full of 20-somethings who looked like they were from central casting for a jeans commercial. I was under the hood, and I could tell they were on a grand adventure to find the aliens and the weirdos who believed in them. I finished checking my oil and was getting in my truck when one of the hipsters got out of the brand-new SUV with a video camera and started walking over to me. I was trying to get out of there, but she beat me to it.

"Oh, hi, were from LA and are filming a documentary on aliens and people who believe in them."

When I did not respond she tried again, while the rest of her crew were getting their courage up and getting out of the SUV.

"Hey," she said as she started to raise the camera toward me, "would you know where the aliens are?"

I formed an image in my mind of her batteries freezing and their power withering away using the new skills I seemed to posses after my encounter with the energy vortex. Something left my eyes as I looked at the camera. Something was projected from me and it was malevolent. As she pushed the button on the expensive-looking camera, I could see her surprise when the camera switch was dead. I shut the door while she tapped gently on the switch and started my truck. I put the truck in gear and looked at her standing there, wondering what to do next.

"No," I said, "I don't know where the aliens are." She looked a little afraid and made a step back while her crew cautiously came up from behind.

"I'll tell ya what I do know," I said, chuckling to myself, my head still bandaged enough to resemble a mummy in an old horror movie.

"What, what do you know?" she said, faking bravado to hide her growing discomfort.

"I know why crows come in threes," I said to her just before her crew finally walked up. I did not wait for any response and gently hit the gas, backing my rig up past the tow truck that was hitched to the fake flying saucer in front of the Little Alien Inn, and dropped the shift lever to drive, slowly making my way out of the parking lot. When I got to Nevada State Highway 375, I looked down the road south from where I had come from and hesitated a moment. I started to breathe, and before I arrived at my fifth breath, I nosed my Land Cruiser to the left and headed north, up the Extraterrestrial Highway.